THE WASTE LAND

HARPER JAMESON

WITH W.A.W. PARKER

The author of this book is solely responsible for the accuracy of all facts and statements contained in the book. This is a work of fiction. Names, characters, places, events, and incidents are either the product of the author's imagination or used in an entirely fictitious manner. Any resemblance to actual persons, living or dead, is entirely coincidental.

This book is printed on acid-free paper.

Published by:
Level 4 Press, Inc.
13518 Jamul Drive
Jamul, CA 91935
www.level4press.com

Library of Congress Control Number: 2019943897

ISBN: 978-1-64630-042-6

Printed in USA

Other books by Harper Jameson

Satchel Paige

Hate Radio

The Last Witch

I Wasn't Really Naked

No Hatred or Bitterness

DEDICATION

For Raul.

1

You can never trust what you see in The Wasteland anymore. An ominous medieval castle looms over the River Thames, or at least it's meant to look like one. Three towers top this scion of society: the Victoria Tower, the tallest square tower in the world when it was completed; a fragile spire sculpted out of more than two thousand shards of glass; and a clock tower, keeping time. Or is it counting it down?

This is the House of Parliament. And Big Ben is the ticking, tocking time bomb that adorns the remains of civilization, wearing the city's sins like a crown of thorns.

Black water. Gray skies. Thirteen tons. Ticking clockwise. A giant bell that gives the clock tower its name is surrounded by a vast, intricate mechanism that keeps the clock accurate within two seconds every week. The minute hand is as tall as the double-decker buses that run on the street below. What do you think would happen if the minute hand plummeted from the sky and drove a spike through one of them? How many would be killed by the blow? How many would stop to see the show? Depends on how crowded the bus is, but most of the time, they're like Piccadilly Circus, heaving with throngs, getting everyone where they belong. People are busy nowadays. And Big Ben keeps them running to time.

Running to time. Running to time. All this clock appears to do is run to time. It has no consciousness. No morality. Just the impending pulse of forward progress. Forward, but to where? We marvel at its machinery and plead to give it a more intimate name, one that's familiar, like an old friend. And good ol' Ben is harmless. He's just running to time. Running to time, keeping us all on track. We all know him. Big Ben is iconic. The only problem is that people kill for icons. It's demonic. Thirty-seven million people died for the icon of civilization in the Great War. Even more died in the flu that followed. It's chronic.

Great. There was nothing great about the Great War. Yes, it was extraordinary, but it only begat pain, not glory. The name the "Great War" itself is an attack on the English language. Poetry lives in the multitudinous interpretations of words. But here, describing this war as "great," by any definition, is tone-deaf. Or at least the only tone it hears is the drone of the clock.

Big Ben is almost as tall as the Victoria Tower. He was born second best, but even his sister is no longer the tallest. Now she's just like all the rest. What once made history now only occupies the annals. No matter. It will all be washed away soon. Because London loves water. Or at least God has decided it does. All it does anymore is rain. The Thames rises in response, threatening to sweep everything into the sea. And it should. That would be the only way to truly cleanse the city.

A Phantom passes beneath Big Ben on Westminster Bridge. Will it haunt these halls? Will we hear its ghastly voice? No, this Phantom is made by Rolls-Royce. And it roars almost as loudly as people say the twenties do, at least in the United States. In London, the twenties limp along like an animal injured in a fight, and rightly so, because it's inured to blight. The Roaring Twenties . . . Americans are so aggressive. Perhaps they wouldn't be if The Wasteland was on their doorstep. The world has already roared. Why does it need to roar anymore? We have already heard its cry.

One such man who couldn't bear the weight of American ignorance, one who joined the woeful throngs in England, is Mr. Thomas Stearns Eliot. He works many cobblestone streets away from Big Ben, but is no less influenced by his pulse. If you don't enjoy walking in the rain, you can take a taxi over to meet him, but beware of the drivers who take their lives into their own hands, and yours along with them, and drive without functioning windshield wipers. London is so wet, always trying to shed its stink. Getting into a taxi with working windshield wipers is as important as getting into a taxi with wheels. Perhaps more so, because windshield wipers make it so you can see where you're going. And we all know the world needs more of that nowadays. You'll find Mr. Eliot if you follow the clicking and clacking feet of well-heeled men on a marble floor as they pass through a revolving door. Well-heeled men always seem to be passing through a revolving door, one after another, a never-ending tide of good intentions, don't they? They're here to visit the Bank of London, where Mr. Eliot works.

"What about this weather we're having?" It's a question one well-heeled man asks another, today and every day. Well-heeled men love to talk about things that are out of their control instead of the things that are.

Tick, tock goes the clock. But the clock in the lobby of the Bank of London is no Big Ben. As ornate and resplendent as it is, it's more of a Baby Ben, a Bijou Ben, or a Bonnie Ben, as the Irish might say. The hands show 5:55. A teller looks up at the clock, his heart beating faster, beckoning the clock to match his rhythm. Please, clock. Please tock faster. Please take stock in the tock of my ticking clock.

Mr. Eliot looks at his pocket watch. 5:56. Almost time to clock out. He wipes his brow, cranks his adding machine, and scribbles in his ledger. Cranks. And scribbles. Crank. Scribble. Crank. Scribble. Tick. 5:57. Tock. 5:58. The day is almost done. Although he's in his thirties, the look on Mr. Eliot's face makes it seem like he doesn't have much time left. His brow is furrowed and his eyes are intense. Tick. Tock. The faint tock of his tiny clock ticks the final tock of the workday.

Mr. Clark, a bank officer, steps up to a large metal triangle with a metal rod in his hand. He looks dapper in his newly pressed tuxedo. Is he going to the opera after this? A fancy dinner with debutantes? No, the sweet, subtle smile on his face says he's wearing this tuxedo precisely to perform his function, which is to summon the ceremonious end of the workday. Clang. Clang. Clang. He whips the metal rod around the triangle as if he were a conductor at La Scala.

Mr. Eliot lets his shoulders slump, his body pooling like the masses of water up on the street. His eyes wander off his work to the men around him, all collections of fluid and flesh, all formerly storming seas that now turn their turgid tension into soothed bones, rubbing their shoulders, necks, and backs, starting the slow process of gearing up their gears for the next work day.

They are all cogs in front of their adding machines, all cogged up in tiny brown suits, crammed into their tiny desks. They are the vast intricate mechanism that controls this clock, keeping the bank running on time. And like the mechanisms in Big Ben, they stay hidden beneath the surface. Mr. Eliot stands up from his desk, hits his head on the ceiling. No, Mr. Eliot is not a teller who works in the grand lobby of the Bank of London. No. He works in the basement, grinding away at an adding machine along with all the other cogs.

When will he remember how low the ceiling is? He rubs the bruise on his head, the one that will never go away until he learns this room was not built for men of his stature. Mr. Eliot is a slight man, but his height at five feet, eleven inches makes him a giant among the men who surround him, none of whom have to watch their heads as they get up from their desks.

But one cog is still cranking away. Crank. Scribble. Crank. Scribble. Mr. Eliot noticed him once before. Actually, he's noticed him quite a few times. He doesn't look like any of the other cogs, his jacket draped casually across the back of his chair, his necktie untied, almost as if the man was already at home. But this man does not seem at home in his work. No, this work is as foreign to him as a duck is to lava. He's not swimming. He's burning up. Sweat pours from his forehead. His body tries to turn the basement into his own personal wading pool.

Perhaps if it did, that would make his flower grow. Unlike all the other desks in this drab, dreary basement, his desk has a hint of horticulture. A lone, solitary lilac standing in defiance of its surroundings. Like the man, the lilac is dying, drowning in the sweat of its owner. Which makes sense. Sweat contains too much salt. And we all know what happens when you salt the earth.

The man jabs his finger at his adding machine, as if he's guessing, not sure which button to press, praying each key is the right one. Damn! No, that last key wasn't it. His adding machine sputters and jams. He looks around in frustration, almost catching Mr. Eliot's eye, but Mr. Eliot is too quick for him. He pretends not to peek, pretends to file out like all the other men.

The man with the lilac is named Jack. Mr. Eliot has heard the other cogs refer to him, but he's never had the gumption to introduce himself.

Finally, Jack looks up, realizes the day is done, a rush of relief washing over his face. How did he not hear the triangle? No matter. He scoops up his jacket, sweeps it in the air, and dons it like a glove, albeit one that doesn't fit quite right.

And how could it fit right with all this rain? Jack uses his jacket as a shield as he exits through the revolving door, out into the downpour with all the other men. His jacket, like all his other clothes, expands and contracts with the moisture, sopping it up in a storm and expelling water when warm. The only thing is all this expanding and contracting causes it to shrink, to tighten until it gets to the point where it's strangling the man it's meant to protect.

Clothes are meant to protect the body from the elements, if not propriety, but how can they perform their function under these conditions? Like London, no amount of washing will ever restore them to their former glory. One simply has to toss them away and buy something new. Nothing ever lasts in The Wasteland.

Mr. Eliot watches Jack as he goes down the street and to the right, out of his eyesight. *But to where?* Mr. Eliot wonders where Jack lives. Does he have more lilacs there? Any other types of flowers?

"Get out of the way!" a well-heeled man yells at him.

Mr. Eliot is in the path of this and all the other well-heeled men making their way out of the bank. Mr. Eliot and the other cogs make way for the well-heeled men who have finished their deposits. Some of these men aren't just visiting the bank, though. They work there as well. Some worked hard for their jobs and others had their fathers do the hard work for them. They inherited a job and a salary, regardless of how much work they do. But that doesn't stop them from depositing their paychecks. Similarly, their wives and girlfriends deposit their husbands and boyfriends into the bank. And like clockwork, they come to collect.

Bright young ladies brave the rain to scoop up their lovers, greeting them with kisses and obligations, focusing their attention before they become tangled up in something, or someone, else.

"Let's go to dinner!"

"I've just heard of the most fabulous cabaret!"

"Dancing. We must go dancing!"

Mr. Eliot would like to dance, but there is no one at the bank to greet him. The couples scatter to the wind as so much in The Wasteland does nowadays, emptying the bank of all its humanity.

A hollow man, standing in front of a hollow bank.

Mr. Eliot collects himself, as if preparing for the long journey home through the rain, and then crosses the street, gazing back at the building where he's deposited so much of his life. He loosens his necktie. Just looking at it makes him suffocate.

Splash! A taxi drives by, drenching him in all the water that was in the street, but now occupies all the crevices of his clothing.

Didn't they see him? Don't they have windshield wipers?

No matter. Mr. Eliot isn't particularly thrown by this turn of events. Things like this happen all the time in his Wasteland. He'll dry off when he gets home, which it turns out, he already is.

Mr. Eliot turns his back on a world that appears to have spat him out. He enters his flat, a building across the street from the bank, a stone's throw away, as they say, and, boy, do they love throwing stones.

2

Mr. Eliot sits at his desk. No, not the one the bank provides for him. This is his real desk, where he does his real work. A blank page sits ready to soak in the ink from his pen. He stares at it, then at the sunset outside the window.

Sunsets. They are the one source of hope in this world. No matter what we have done to our planet, the sun still shines brightly. Perhaps it helps that the sun sits a great distance away. It's safe from us. That's why it's able to give us such a heavenly show every day. Yes, it's on fire, but unlike The Wasteland, it consumes itself with such an intense glory. All who behold it stop in wonder, not in amazement. That's an important difference. Words matter. Mr. Eliot cares about words, but, apparently, he doesn't care for any today, because even the splendor of the setting sun can't inspire him to write any.

He makes his way out of his flat. The outline of the bank across the street is still visible even though much in the now-black night is not. Even if there were no light on the bank, though, Mr. Eliot would still know it was there. It's always there, waiting to welcome him with open arms, more than willing to take more tocks from his clock.

Mr. Eliot walks down the rocks, the cobblestones that make up this and so many streets in London. Light streaks beckon him around a corner. Large banners at the Queen's Theatre announce: "One Night Only! Robert Frost!"

Robert Frost? Could it really be him? The American poet whose work was first recognized and published in England?

Mr. Eliot takes a sharp breath and holds it, because he's a poet. And not just any poet, but an American one who has come to England hoping to be discovered like Mr. Frost has been. Recognized for his genius outside his country of origin in England, where culture and civilization reside, or at least where they used to.

If there's anything that would warm his heart it would be a little Frost.

He runs up to the theater. A limo pulls up and out steps Robert Frost himself.

Flashbulbs light up the night.

"Mr. Frost! Mr. Frost!"

"Can you sign my book?"

"Over here! Can I get an autograph?"

"Would you buy me a drink?" Mr. Eliot asks. "No," he corrects, "can I buy *you* a drink?"

Everyone except Mr. Frost glances at him askance.

Was he too loud? He had corrected himself. Why would Robert Frost buy him a drink? *That was stupid.* He didn't think.

Luckily, Mr. Frost doesn't notice, he's too busy talking to a well-heeled man.

"Say, are you anybody famous?" a reporter asks Mr. Eliot, half out of pity and half out of curiosity, always eager for a scoop. Mr. Eliot's eyes droop.

"No. No, I'm not."

Mr. Eliot steps back. Slinks into the black. Mr. Frost really didn't hear him, did he? Mr. Eliot's cheeks burn from the shame, the redness consuming his face with its radiance.

The reporter pushes forward through the crowd. Mr. Eliot trudges back to the safety of his flat. A family of gargoyles lives on the roof of his building. Their carved stone faces perch high above the street, observing everything. Although they aren't capable of much emotion, tonight they all unite in mocking Mr. Eliot, taunting him: *Why did you say that? Can't you string a set of coherent words together?*

Mr. Eliot escapes their onslaught by climbing the front steps, inside where they can't follow him. Inside where it's safe.

In contrast, the lower floor of Mr. Eliot's building is warm and welcoming. Very comforting. The hallways are wide, well-lit, and luxurious, outfitted in London's finest mid-range metropolitan furnishings.

He passes a partially open door.

"No, stop it!" a woman screams.

"Oh, no. Please don't stop," another woman pleads.

"So many options, ladies, but who to obey?"

The women giggle. It's the trademark high-pitched giggle of women who are with well-heeled men. And Bertrand, the man these women are with, is as well-heeled as they come. Bertrand is wealthy and sophisticated, which means he's also entitled. The two don't always have to add up to one another, but here in The Wasteland they always do. And it doesn't hurt that Bertrand's entitlement comes with a title, Third Earl Russell. He's the type of man who never overtly mentions his position, but always wants you to know he has it.

But Mr. Eliot doesn't admire Bertrand for his title, or his wealth or sophistication. Mr. Eliot admires Bertrand for his confidence. Bertrand has the type of confidence, as we've observed, to have two partially clothed women in his flat and still leave the door open.

"Hey, Tom! Come on in!" Bertrand bellows. "I could use a little help!"

The girls giggle. The red we saw on Mr. Eliot's face makes an appearance, but, no, these girls are not giggling at Mr. Eliot. They're giggling for the well-heeled man.

Even so, even though Mr. Eliot is acquainted with Bertrand, and knows Bertrand's offer was genuine, or at least as genuine as any offer from Bertrand can be, he's conscious of the fact that it's not his place to barge in on such a party.

Mr. Eliot flees up the stairs. The wide, luxurious halls become narrower, more decrepit. Is this the design of the building or the design of Mr. Eliot's mind?

A light flickers. Mr. Eliot halts his escape. Flicker. Flicker. The lightbulb flicks. And ticks. This piece of machinery has its own rhythm. Flick. An electrical pulse, but one that is being disrupted. Short-circuited. Flick.

Tick. Mr. Eliot puts his hand to his heart. It's beating fast. Tick. Tock. Tick. Tock.

He takes in a deep breath. He takes stock of his ticking clock, and exhales, letting his breath take flight into the night with the might of a thousand kites.

Mr. Eliot tightens the flickering bulb. He waits. There's no flick. No tick. His heart is at rest. If only his mind were.

Monks have calm minds and the way he lives, you'd suppose Mr. Eliot was one. His flat is sparse. It's the type of one-room affair for which the term "bachelor flat" was coined. Only a single man would live in such a spartan space. It's small and sparely furnished. The bed, or bedroom portion of the flat, straight ahead. The open-plan kitchenette to the left.

His only real furnishings are all the books he's burnishing. Some are scattered on the floor. Some are on his desk. Some are on the shelves. Some are on the stove. What a strange little cove. The place looks like a bookseller was robbed.

But what robber would steal photos of Mr. Eliot's family? The truth is, there were none to be hanged, and therefore, none to be stolen.

Tick. Tock. Tick. Tock. No, Mr. Eliot's heart isn't racing. That's just the sound of his clock, or rather, his clocks. There's one on the mantle, one on the wall, and another, standing tall, the grandfather of them all, his grandfather clock.

Mr. Eliot sits down in his chair. He has only one chair. Why would he need another? He turns a dial on his radio. Bang. Clash. The cymbals smash in Rossini's "William Tell Overture."

Mr. Eliot puts the volume on low, not wanting to put on a show for his neighbors. He sets the table with good china. A single setting. He makes dinner. No, he makes a sandwich. Dinner is something you eat with those you love. It's a meal, a shared experience. Mr. Eliot eats a sandwich. It's baloney, like so much in The Wasteland. There are no trimmings. No lettuce. No tomato. No matter. Nothing grows now that the earth has been salted.

The sandwich has no salt. No pepper. No mustard. No mayonnaise. There are no side dishes. This sandwich is not a meal, it's a punishment. But for what?

Mr. Eliot lights a candle on the table. It's nice. The warmth from the flame is calming. This fire does not burn. It's just bright and warm. Nothing to be afraid of.

"This just in," the radio announcer interrupts Mr. Eliot's first bite and Rossini's finale fireworks. "Over thirty-thousand of Benito Mussolini's Blackshirts have descended on Rome, demanding his election as Leader for Life. This March on Rome has great implications for Europe after the Great War."

Mr. Eliot twitches. That word. Yes, that one. Great. And used twice in the same sentence. He knows the news is breaking, but so is his heart. Surely, the announcer must have said more about this stain upon civil society, but by the time his ears perk up again, the voice is already on to something else, something to rejoice.

"Ladies and gentlemen, the BBC is proud to announce that the Nobel Prize in Literature was awarded to our very own William Butler Yeats. Hip-hip-hooray!"

The radio announcer must have an audience in the studio with him, because a crowd of companions clamors to chant, "Hip-hip-hooray! Hip-hip-hooray! Hip-hip-hooray!"

Yes. Hooray. For him, the man of the day.

"We return you now to our regular broadcast," the announcer drones.

"Clair de Lune." Claude Debussy. Relaxation. Baloney.

Mr. Eliot looks at his still uneaten sandwich. He's no longer hungry. He tosses it in the trash, vigorously washes a dish that had only a few crumbs on it. He dries it, puts it in a china hutch. He needed to wash the dish because he has only one. And he has only one fork. One knife. One spoon. Only one.

He winds his clocks, giving attention to grandfather first. Then the one on the wall, and finally, the one on the mantle. He watches the tick, tock of the clock. 7:44. The minute hand spins in a circle, always spinning. It approaches the moment of tension. It's almost time. 58, 59 . . . chime. All the clocks chime at the same time.

Mr. Eliot takes a breath but doesn't allow this one to escape. He stands, opens a folio on his desk, full of inky pages. Apparently, other sunsets have been more inspiring.

He selects one, inspects it.

"Would you like to go for a walk?" Mr. Eliot asks the piece of paper.

But the poem cannot respond, there is no speech to parse with this parchment. Even so, a hint of a smile crosses Mr. Eliot's face. Then he puts on his hat and takes his scroll for a stroll.

3

Mr. Eliot stands outside a compact, casually crumbling coffeehouse called George's. Mr. Eliot has never heard of a man named George in this establishment, but then again, there are many Georges missing.

A sign announces, "Poetry reading tonight at 8 p.m.," but it's not as resplendent as the signs at the Queen's Theatre. No, this sign is dreary, sad, and unfinished. It looks like whoever made it quit about halfway through, like most poets do.

Mr. Eliot will not be one of those poets tonight, not part of the half that quits. He saunters into the cafe with the strut of a well-heeled man, even though this cafe caters to a clientele that is anything but. Caffeine and bohemia waft through the air.

A barista barks at Mr. Eliot, "Your usual?"

But it's not the bark of a dog about to bite. Rather, it's the bark of a woman who must make her voice heard above the din. The voice of this barista belongs to Vivienne, a vivacious, captivating woman. It's a madhouse around her, but somehow, she's keeping her sanity.

And it's no wonder she has to raise her voice. How anyone could calm this chattering crowd is anyone's guess.

"Yes, please," Mr. Eliot replies, perhaps a bit too softly.

"What?"

"Yes, please," he repeats.

"Here for the reading?" she asks, preparing his tea.

Mr. Eliot fingers his poem, then puts it away in his pocket.

"No, just for the tea."

"Well, it might be a little loud when the Bright Young Things arrive. Sometimes they get a little zozzled." Vivienne hands over the tea. "Well, here it is."

Mr. Eliot clutches the cup, but for some reason, Vivienne doesn't let go.

"Is there anything else I can get you?" Her eyes probe deep into Mr. Eliot's soul, searching for a sign of life.

"No. No, thank you," Mr. Eliot responds, flustered. Not sure what to make of the ordeal.

In the corner, several vacant chairs form a loose circle. That must be where the reading will be. Mr. Eliot makes his way toward it.

Outside, a jalopy arrives, disgorging a crew of half-drunk and half-hearted hipsters. These three trite young men and one woman are part of the Bright Young Things, whose clothes scream flamboyant counter-culture almost as loudly as they scream, well, anything that comes to their mind.

"Does this coffeehouse have booze?" one of them shrieks.

"Ooh, I want absinthe!" another squeaks, this one even louder.

"If they don't have it, I do!" This last one doesn't scream his response, but, rather, punctuates it with the penetrating pull of a hand between breasts. His breasts. Or rather, the breasts he's made for himself, pushed up with a bra and suspended by the strength of a corset from Dorset.

He takes a swig from his tit flask and screams, "*Vive la révolution!*" But then his heel crumbles. He stumbles and tumbles to the ground.

Yes, this mess of a man in a dress is Auden. He's a homosexual man who's fond of dressing like a woman when it's time to have a night on the town. For Auden, though, a night on the town can happen any time of the day or night. The stuffing and tassels on his tarted-up tits belie the stuffiness of his prep school upbringing.

Another Bright Young Thing named Joe helps Auden to his feet. Joe only recently came out to himself, but that won't stop him from climbing the nearest rooftop and shouting it to anyone within earshot.

The last two Bright Young Things are John and Mary, hopelessly in love with one another, and hopelessly under-prepared for the maturity needed in the marriage they have recently entered. They love and fight with equal passion. Which one will win? John or Mary, desire or fire, is anyone's guess.

The Bright Young Things descend upon George's like the four horsemen of the apocalypse, galloping in stride, hastening its destruction.

Shortly thereafter, Bertrand drives up in his Phantom. No, sorry, he doesn't drive a Phantom, but his driver does. He choreographs two women out of the car and into his arms, one on each side, in a smooth motion that would make Casanova take note.

Vivienne greets them all, and hands each Bright Young Thing their beverage of choice. Auden sprinkles absinthe from his tit flask indiscriminately into all their drinks.

"*Vive la révolution!*" Auden shouts.

"*Vive le café!*" Joe crows.

"*Vive la poésie!*" Mary caws.

They all toast their spiked drinks and giggle. Down the hatch. Mary downs hers first, a real champ, and goes back for another. Vivienne, always ready for action, has Mary's second round ready before she asks.

Auden comes up from his draught. "O, true apothecary! Thy drugs are quick!"

John finishes the refrain, "Thus with a kiss I die," and then grabs Mary, stabs her with his lips, planting a huge peck on her mouth in the most overly dramatic of fashions.

"You'll die of shame if you don't keep up," Mary says, sending her second drink down the hatch.

Vivienne pours Mary another and turns her attention to Bertrand. "So, what'll you have today, Bertie? Half the time it's tea and half the time it's java. You can't seem to make up your mind."

Bertrand picks up Vivienne's hand and stares into her eyes, probing for the opportunity to probe even deeper.

"With so many lovely things in the world . . . why choose just one?"

He kisses her hand, his gentle lips grazing the surface of her skin. But then he's tugged backward by the eager arms of his eager companions. "Especially when they choose you."

"And why stop at one?" Auden asks, shaking his empty glass at Vivienne.

Mary jokes, "Better make him two so he can keep up."

John clutches Vivienne's hand and kisses it, then the other one, laying kisses on both before he lays it on thick. "Why choose one, when two blushing pilgrims ready stand, to smooth that rough touch with a tender kiss."

He glances toward Mary. "Two can be twice as delightful."

"Good pilgrim, you do wrong my hands too much," Vivienne snaps back at him.

"Coffee!" Bertrand bellows across the din, apparently too busy frolicking with his friends to come to the counter himself. "It's going to be a long night!"

Vivienne leaps at the opportunity. "I'll bring it to you!"

She clings to a cup, wades through a turbulent sea of youth waiting for the world to hear their words. Many have come to sip and share at this poetry reading. Many are assembled over by the chairs in a circle, but since order and decorum aren't one of his strongest suits, John jumps on the nearest chair and starts spouting.

"They say that marriage is forever!" His tone is overdramatic and affected. But it does have the effect of silencing the room, which waits for his next words with bated breath.

"They say true love will never die!" He looks at Mary, and her heart melts a little.

"They say true love's to be forgiven."

A smile creeps across his chin. "The things they say are all a lie!"

A riot of laughter ricochets across the room. The crowd whistles, claps, laughs, and shouts.

Mary pushes John off the chair, takes center stage. "Should I forgive him?"

"No!"

"Never!"

"Yes!"

Mary echoes their answers, positing them as questions. "No? Never?"

She goads the audience into her good graces, and then tamps down their energy with her hands, motioning for calm. They need to pay attention to what is about to be unleashed upon them.

She clears her throat, looks at her husband. "Livin', lovin', lyin', losin'."

The laughter that travels across the room is now hers, and she turns her attention toward it.

"Life's miseries and miscreants. Bottles, pills, screamin', boozin'."

Hoots and hollers. She knows this crowd and what they love.

"Try to leave him." The room goes silent, serene.

"Somehow can't."

Mary kisses John as everyone laughs, stamps feet, and applauds.

Joe takes Mary's applause and rides it to the top of his chair. He's now the third Bright Young Thing to stand up on a chair and proclaim his importance, not waiting for the official poetry reading to begin, but making the world bend to his will.

And while Joe has the room's attention, he turns toward Auden, making him an audience of one.

"There was a young man born in York; Who said, 'I must soon pop my cork!'; He thought of a hen, but a rooster came in. Avoiding a scene with the stork!"

Joe punctuates the last line of his limerick by leaping into the air and landing in Auden's outstretched arms.

"Bravo! Bravo!" Auden screams.

The audience chortles, but barely joins in Auden's enthusiasm.

Now it's his turn, and Auden takes the stage like a bullfighter about to put on a show. Poetry can be a messy business. There are a lot of barbs and bull.

But Auden seems to have weathered all these storms before and come out a trusted captain. The room becomes quiet, not in anticipation of his final words, but in anticipation of his first. They respect Auden as a serious poet.

He recites:

> My thoughts wander
>
> from sex to verse to God without periods. Without differentiation.
>
> If I do evil . . .
>
> No, *when* I do evil, My God, my victims and I are equally bewildered.
>
> And I know, that bones ascribed to saints who never existed
>
> are more holy than statues of generals that did.

Auden's thoughts are not mere flights of fancy; they are the formed words of a poet. They are not words, but poetry incarnate and must be encountered as such. Additionally, they must be encountered with enthusiastic applause, and the audience obliges him greatly.

"All right, I suppose now that the poetry reading has officially begun," Vivienne announces to the room, standing next to the circle of chairs by Bertrand. "I . . . I didn't really want to go right after Auden, but someone has to!"

Hoots and hollers join in the sentiment, increasing her confidence. The mood of the audience is respectful, tender. Vivienne is well liked, and not only because she's the woman who supplies their drinks.

She intones, "Roses are red, violets are blue. Only work lies ahead, and bills—overdue. A cold, lonely bed that's waiting for you."

Whistles. The waggle of skin against skin. It's the polite clap of a polite audience. She looks around the room seeking the one set of eyes she's been searching for, not just now, but as long as he's been coming to her cafe. She searches for Mr. Eliot's eyes, hoping that his meet hers, and that he will finally see her, not for who she is or what she does in this cafe, but for what she could be to him.

But her eyes don't find his, only an empty table where nothing remains but an empty teacup. Had he really gone without saying goodbye? Had he really gone without hearing her poem? Or worse, had he left *after* hearing it? She doesn't need him to say he liked it, but running off afterward without saying anything . . . it would be an embarrassment too frightful to bear. But who is she kidding? She does need him to say he liked it.

Luckily for Vivienne, even though Mr. Eliot abandoned her, the Bright Young Things have not. They greet her with open arms.

"You were wonderful."

"Positively delightful!"

"I shall always remember tonight," John says.

"I won't," Mary responds, downing her latest beverage.

Joe asks, "How many is that?"

"The historical record is fuzzy," Mary responds.

The Bright Young Things light up with laughter. This is one of many nights of fun and frolicking for them. Vivienne basks in their glow. Then it happens, the brief pause where the world shifts and Vivienne must go back to tending the counter, now no longer just their friend.

"Can you get us another drink?"

4

Mr. Eliot waits in the park for the sun to rise. Or at least he's waiting for something. Perhaps a person?

He's in a park with paths that stretch out in all directions, but he's only focused on one. His eyes have adjusted to the light, or rather, the lack of it, but they strain to see. On this lovely eve, he's not the only one in the park. Other men stroll about, enjoying its many curves, its many corners. There are patches of trees just off the path. Mr. Eliot sits on a bench in the park, but the other men are much more adventurous in the dark. They explore the trees with glee, hopping off the path that has been laid out for others to tread, creating their own path instead. But Mr. Eliot doesn't join them. He doesn't even walk on the path. He just sits. And waits. With dread.

How Mr. Eliot longs to be one of the men who visits the trees. How he longs to be one of these arborists of the night. They appear to be so free. They float from tree to tree like birds. Mr. Eliot has often visited the trees during the day, studying the landscape should he venture into it after the sun has set. But the trees are different then. There are no men admiring them. Mr. Eliot has heard that the men who visit the trees during the night often visit the spa around the corner during the day. That makes sense. After so much vigorous nocturnal activity, these men must need to soothe and pamper their bodies. What type of treatments do they get at the spa? Do they get massages? Maybe a back rub? Mr. Eliot would like to have the strong hands of a masseuse upon his shoulders.

Do they talk? Mr. Eliot would like to talk. He can't imagine getting truly comfortable with someone without talking to them first. Or do they just sit in the warm water of the spa and relax, commiserating as a brotherhood of men?

"How are you?"

Mr. Eliot freezes in terror. Who said that? He scans the night, finds the friendly face of Jack staring back at him.

"Enjoying the park?" Jack asks.

"Yes, thank you."

Jack sits next to Mr. Eliot on the bench.

"We work together, don't we?" Jack asks.

"Yes, for five months, two weeks now." Mr. Eliot blushes. Jack hadn't asked how long they've worked together, but for mere confirmation of the fact.

"I see." Jack smiles. "And how long have you worked there?"

"I live in that flat right over there," Mr. Eliot says, pointing across the park. He immediately damns his response, which again, was not an answer to the question at hand. Why must he be so stupid? *Stay calm. Stay calm.*

"I've lived there for the past year. When I started working for the bank," Mr. Eliot recovers.

"Makes it easy to get home from work," Jack says.

Mr. Eliot smiles. When was the last time he smiled?

"Where do you live?" Mr. Eliot asks, but then immediately regrets it. "I'm sorry, that's much too personal a question. I'm a stranger."

"No, it's all right," Jack responds, "I know you."

Mr. Eliot's eyes search Jack's for answers. What did he mean by that?

"We're coworkers, remember?" Jack reminds him.

Mr. Eliot lets out a breath. "Yes, of course, we're coworkers, not strangers." He bobs his head a little as if it were a life preserver on a body of water. If only it were. Mr. Eliot needs a life preserver. "Yes, we're coworkers, and I must be going to bed. We have a long day of work before us tomorrow. I hope you have a good evening."

And before Jack can respond, Mr. Eliot has extended his hand, shaken Jack's vigorously, and darted off into the distance, off toward his flat.

But even though it was Jack's hand that was vigorously shaken, it's Mr. Eliot's core that's been shaken more.

Tick. Tock. Tick. Tock. Mr. Eliot's clocks welcome him back to his flat with their incessant counting. Always counting. Always counting. All they ever do is count. All he ever does is count. How long will he work at the bank? He will never be a man who goes into the trees with the other men. Did Jack want to go into the trees with him? *No, surely not.* Jack is a coworker, a man he works with, and nothing more. *Oh, my God.* That means he'll see Jack at work tomorrow, won't he? Hopefully, Jack won't mention their meeting. What would everyone think if they found out two cogs were grinding away in the park, and not in the basement of the bank where they belong?

Mr. Eliot lies in bed, his eyes closed. He wishes this night would end. He wishes this fright would end. He tries to avoid the thoughts that keep him awake. He tries to avoid the thoughts that make him quake.

He keeps his eyes held tight.

But then . . . crank. He hears a noise, opens his eyes, and, suddenly, he's in the bank.

Where has the morning gone? The long night has stretched into a long day. He goes back and forth, back and forth between the bank and his flat. Sometimes he forgets what happened between. And how could anything happen between? He lives across from the bank precisely because he doesn't want anything to happen. It would be horrible if something happened between the two. Just awful and horrible.

Mr. Eliot gazes longingly at Jack's desk. The desk is there, but not Jack. Where is he? He's been late before. No, he's been late often, but not this late. Jack's lilac sits on his desk, wilted, needing Jack's attention. Mr. Eliot empathizes with the lilac. Should he tend to it? Maybe

Jack is out sick. He would hate for Jack's lilac to wither and die. Should he check on him? Find out where he lives and bring him something to feel better? Jack didn't answer him in the park last night. *Or did he say where he lived?* Mr. Eliot can ask Mr. Clark, the bank officer. Mr. Clark will know where Jack lives. And then he can bring him soup. Mr. Eliot's mother used to bring him chicken soup and give him a kiss on the forehead when he was sick. That used to make him feel better. Maybe he could do the same for Jack, but just the soup. *Just the soup.*

There's Mr. Clark now. Mr. Eliot spots him leading another cog down the aisle.

Mr. Eliot raises his arm to catch his attention. "Sir!"

"Yes, Mr. Eliot," Mr. Clark says. "I'd like you to meet Mr. Addington."

Mr. Clark extends his arm to a brand-new cog, a newly minted man in his tiny brown suit.

"I'm Mr. Addington," Mr. Addington says, shaking Mr. Eliot's hand.

"Mr. Eliot," Mr. Eliot responds.

"I'm so delighted you popped up to say hello to Mr. Addington," Mr. Clark says. "Mr. Eliot is one of our finest men. You should do well to take his example. I'd say you should scrutinize his every move, study it, and replicate it. Of course, I'd like to say that, but if you do, you wouldn't have your eyes on your own work, now would you?"

Mr. Clark leads Mr. Addington over to Jack's desk.

"This is your desk, Mr. Addington. Settle in and I shall return with your first stack."

But, no, that's not Mr. Addington's desk. That's Jack's desk. Why would he put Mr. Addington at Jack's desk, unless . . . perhaps Jack was promoted? But, no, Mr. Eliot knows no one like Jack would ever be promoted. Jack has been sacked.

Mr. Eliot gazes longingly at Mr. Addington, or at least at the space he now occupies. Perhaps Mr. Addington will take care of Jack's lilac? No, Mr. Addington discards it in the trash with a look of disgust. This man is no nature lover. *I bet you'd never find him amongst the trees.*

Mr. Eliot is stunned. It's odd what we do with trash nowadays. We throw so much away that could be cared for, tended, and reclaimed as something beautiful. What is dying could be made to grow again, but, no, we throw it in the trash because it's not convenient. Not wanted. Who wants to take the time to grow something when you can pretend that it never existed, that it never happened?

Mr. Eliot discreetly pulls out a crucifix suspended around his neck. It's a bit odd to hang a crucifix around your neck, isn't it? Or perhaps it's just ironic? But Mr. Eliot isn't concerned with such questions. He wrinkles his brow, his mind in sharp focus. He's focused on something, but that something is no longer Jack or his desk or the lilac. His focus is on something much farther away, somewhere he can find the things that need to be found, and hide the things that need to be hidden.

5

Mr. Eliot stands in the Garden of Eden. This is where it all began. So many artists have tried to capture its beauty, or at least their estimation of it, but none have come close to depicting its true grandeur. No artist can mix paint for colors they have not seen. No poet can write words for emotions they haven't felt. And even if they could, words should not exist for this splendor.

The Garden of Eden, according to Mr. Eliot's imagination, looks a lot like the left panel in Hieronymus Bosch's triptych *The Garden of Earthly Delights*. The oil that fed the machinery of war has also been used to create some of its best paints, and many of them are on display here. The grass is a deeply saturated hue that could only be called green. The water is so blue it seems to stretch all the way to the sky.

Naked nymphs cavort in the distance. Mr. Eliot stares at them. Although they are far away, their fleshy forms enchant him. They dance in circles, then pair up, twirling around one another, and then switch partners. It's hard to tell from so far away, but the male nymphs dance with the females. When they switch partners, though, some of the male nymphs dance with each other. Mr. Eliot runs toward them, but the ground stretches somehow, sending their frolicking forms even farther away. He picks up the pace. He runs. It's a race. But the faster he runs the farther they disappear into the distance.

Everything is made of oil paint, everything except Mr. Eliot. Mr.

Eliot stands apart in this arena, a grim toehold of realism in this fantastical world.

Crank. Scribble. Crank. Scribble. Mr. Eliot can hear the adding machines in the basement of the bank, but the babbling brook next to him drowns out those sounds to little more than a dribble.

Mr. Eliot splashes his face in the brook, the cool water, and the cool-blue oil paint it's made of, refreshing him.

"Welcome back, Mr. Eliot. It's always nice to see you."

Mr. Eliot turns to Mr. J. Alfred Prufrock, an older, oil-painted, and proper English butler wearing a top hat and tails, sporting a cane with a carved wooden handle in the shape of a parrot's head.

"Thank you, Mr. Prufrock," Mr. Eliot responds.

"Shall we work on your poem?" Mr. Prufrock asks.

"Yes, please. I . . . no. No, not today. I won't be needing you."

Mr. Prufrock nods. "Very well, sir." He turns to leave, but then Mr. Eliot stops him.

"Mr. Prufrock?"

"Yes, sir?"

"I'm not sure I can do it anymore."

"Do what, sir?"

Mr. Eliot has a pinch in his throat. "It. Everything. Anything."

Mr. Prufrock squints, the whites of his eyes mixing with his peachy flesh tones. "Everything, sir?"

"Yes, everything."

The brook stops. The water is at a standstill.

The pulse of adding machines from the basement of the bank vibrates through the air, counting to time like the ticking of a clock.

Mr. Eliot paces to and fro. His feet pace at the pace of the counting, to the tock of the clock.

"I get up and go to work at the bank. I go home and go to sleep. I get up and go to work. I go home and go to sleep. I get up and go to work. I go home and go to sleep. I get up and go to work. I go home and go to sleep. I get up and go to work . . ."

Mr. Eliot stops speaking, but his mind repeats the pattern.

Mr. Prufrock posits, "Wavering between the profit and the loss, your work and home, the twilight between birth and dying."

Mr. Eliot peeks at Mr. Prufrock, his eyes glazed over.

"What did you say?" Mr. Eliot asks.

Bang. Before Mr. Prufrock can answer, a ruler slaps across Mr. Eliot's desk, although it might as well have been slapped across his face.

Mr. Eliot is a shaken man. First Jack, and now, this new attack. Not the one on his desk, but the one against the inner workings of his mind, the place that he keeps sacred, safe from others.

Mr. Clark glares at him. "Mr. Eliot, I assumed you'd be setting a better example for Mr. Addington on his first day." Then Mr. Clark turns to the new cog. "Mr. Addington, I hope Mr. Eliot's disruption did not distract, disturb, or disorganize you in any manner."

Mr. Eliot tries to disappear into his desk, but, no, everyone can still see him, their eyes digging into his skin like a thousand pinpricks. Here in the basement, there is no babbling brook to drown out the sound of adding machines. Adding machines add. Gears crank. Cogs perform their function. And Mr. Eliot gets back to work.

Crank. Scribble. Crank. Scribble. Tick. Tock. Tick. Tock. Clang. Clang. Clang.

Mr. Clark rings the metal triangle with the metal rod. The day is done and Mr. Clark is glad to greet it with the sweet tweet of metal upon metal. The ladies are happy to greet their well-heeled men, too. They gasp with giddy delight when the well-heeled men exit, as if they were witnessing Christ emerge from his tomb.

Mr. Eliot feels like death, like he's living in a waking nightmare. And now the only solace is he gets to go home and go to sleep where he can have nightmares of the dreaming kind.

Without his poetry, he is nothing. Without his poetry, he feels nothing. Without his poetry, he's like so many in The Wasteland. Devoid of meaning. Devoid of humanity. Devoid of self.

Mr. Eliot stands in front of his flat, the gargoyles circling overhead, waiting for their chance to turn into vultures and find sustenance in his remains. Mr. Eliot looks around. The street is empty. Everyone else is long gone. Night has descended. How long has he been standing there?

"I get up and go to work at the bank. I go home and go to sleep," Mr. Eliot says to himself.

"Not today." The words surprise Mr. Eliot, even though they are his.

He wants to go somewhere. Somewhere new. Somewhere exciting. *But where?* Although his mind doesn't know where he's going, his feet guide him down the street toward his destiny. It's just around the corner, down a cobblestone street he's traversed many times.

There it is, the gleaming neon sign, "Madame Sosostris Knows All," its phosphorescence lighting up the night sky, penetrating the air with its unnatural glow. This is the place he must go. It's the place he's wanted to go. It's a place others have found answers when they were lost. Unlike the throngs who usually frequent this establishment, though, Mr. Eliot is a thinking man. Surely, there are no answers for him in such a place.

In the window, a gypsy made of wax beckons Mr. Eliot into the shop with its stoic pose. It stays there, forever greeting, forever entreating wandering souls to come inside and wander no more. The faint hint of music and incense wafts over Mr. Eliot. But the sound isn't coming from inside. *Where is it coming from?* Some far-off land? Or somewhere much closer at hand?

Mr. Eliot's feet have brought him here, but his mind holds him back, barring his entrance.

"What say you," Mr. Eliot asks the wax gypsy in the window. "Shall I come inside?"

But the gypsy does not answer.

"Well, then. I should be on my way." But before Mr. Eliot leaves, he catches the gypsy blink. No, surely that did not happen. *No, it didn't.* But his feet opine otherwise, and lead him inside, overpowering his mind.

Wind chimes announce Mr. Eliot's arrival. There's a new customer.

New clay to be molded. Mr. Eliot fingers the crucifix under his shirt, as if doing so could ward off unwanted spirits. Mr. Eliot doesn't know what to make of the place, but that makes sense since this place doesn't know what to make of itself either. Elements of the British Empire cohabitate nicely, or as nicely as any imperial elements can, with colonial ones. Big paintings with sailing ships dominate the walls. A plunder of pineapple shades adorns the lamps. Madame Sosostris's parlor has the uncanny ability of seeming simultaneously both quite lived in and under construction. Or is it just disrepair?

A heaviness descends on the room. *Or is it smoke?* Whatever it is, Mr. Eliot can feel it weighing down on him. He rubs his neck. No, there's no yoke, but something is amiss. Is he having a stroke? Something has shifted. Is Mr. Eliot in Madame Sosostris's parlor or is he in an oil painting? The colors of his imagination are usually so bright, so vivid, but now they're dark, muted, impenetrably slick.

"Is Madame Sosostris here?" Mr. Eliot asks, to no one in particular, but directed at a pack of young gypsies lounging in a corner. Their bodies lie upon the couch, their eyes gazing up toward the heavens. Mr. Eliot has heard of such people, those who occupy opium dens and lie on cots, staring up toward the sky. *Are these those people?* The people who gaze toward heaven while trying to escape hell?

But no one answers him. No matter, Mr. Eliot shall try again. "Is Madame Sosostris here?"

But still no answer. Sometimes it doesn't pay to be persistent.

Mr. Eliot turns to leave, but then a flash of smoke and flame blocks his exit.

"Are you looking for me?" Madame Sosostris asks, having appeared out of thin air.

Mr. Eliot's mouth falls open. "Yes, how did you know?"

"My name is on the sign above the door," Madame Sosostris responds matter-of-factly.

She moves over to a table, lights a candle, and pours two cups of tea. "Join me for some tea?" she asks, gesturing for Mr. Eliot to sit.

"How do you know I like tea?"

"Americans don't move to England if they don't like tea."

"How did you know I was an American?" Mr. Eliot asks, perhaps a bit too quickly.

"Because I heard you speak."

Mr. Eliot frowns. *Yes, of course. That was a stupid question.* But before he can get lost in thought, Madame Sosostris says, "I have saved this afternoon for you, Thomas."

Mr. Eliot perks up. "How did you know my name?"

"Will you sit down or are you going to ask me stupid questions all day?"

Mr. Eliot sits. Madame Sosostris looks into her tea, sips it. Mr. Eliot's nerves fill the air with anxiety. "This place isn't right. It's only half-finished."

"Of course, it is," Madame Sosostris replies. "Are you surprised?" She shakes her head. "You shouldn't be."

The words hang in the air. Mr. Eliot remembers what it was like to be slapped on the wrist as a child. The sting.

"Why have you come to me?" she asks.

"I need your help," Mr. Eliot answers, trying to gulp the words down into his throat.

"Of course, you do. That's why you created me."

Mr. Eliot fidgets in his seat, he looks around the room, unsure where to look, but trying not to meet Madame Sosostris's gaze. He's uncomfortable. He looks left, then right, then . . . *no, that wasn't there before, was it?* The wax gypsy from the window stares back at him, now standing in the corner next to the lounging gypsies in purgatory. The wax from the gypsy's face drips, mixing with the decrepit wall behind it. Wink. The wax gypsy winks. Mr. Eliot turns away and finds his eyes locked with those of Madame Sosostris. For some reason, he can't pull his eyes away from her.

"Tell me your problem," she demands.

"I don't . . . I'm not really . . ." Mr. Eliot stammers.

Madame Sosostris leans in, eyes wide. "Open your mind."

Mr. Eliot becomes transfixed by her eyes. They're speckled with the light of a thousand galaxies, dots shining and spinning around the black hole of her pupil. Mr. Eliot leans forward, then forward a little more, and forward again until he's sucked into her eye. His body contorts into the smallest of shapes as it soars past stars and nebulas, floating in the zero-gravity of space.

A comet zooms past! Mr. Eliot smiles. His face glimmers in the shimmer of the comet, the wonder filling up his soul. But the wonder is not filling up his lungs. Mr. Eliot heaves, chokes. He's a man in a desert looking for an oasis. There is no air in space or in Mr. Eliot's chest.

He gasps, coughs, comes to life back in Madame Sosostris's parlor. And although he's escaped one peril, Madame Sosostris is busy laying out another for him. She places her tarot cards face down on the table with precision.

"Let the cards see your deepest thoughts."

The room spins. The faster it revolves, the brighter it gets. It gives off heat, as if its dark, oil-painted facade were set ablaze.

Madame Sosostris's voice brings order to the chaos. "Let the cards see your deepest thoughts so they can advise you."

Stillness. Everything stops moving.

"Here is your card."

Madame Sosostris turns it over and intones, "The drowned Phoenician sailor." She elongates the syllables for emphasis, a hint of whimsy in her voice.

The sailor lies face down on the sand, having run out of air and life. Did he drown, though? Ten swords stick out of his back. This man may have drowned, but someone wanted to make sure he stayed dead.

"You will meet a tall dark stranger," she continues, then laughs. "Yes, he will be tall, but he will be dark in a way that you do not yet know. You will develop a relationship with this man, but it will not work out well."

Mr. Eliot is enraptured, but perplexed. "Are you sure it will be with a man?"

Madame Sosostris studies him. "I never said what type of relationship you'll have with him."

Mr. Eliot blushes. Had he been over-eager? Had he shown his hand?

Madame Sosostris turns over another card. This one is . . .

"Belladonna," Madame Sosostris notes, slipping into an Italian accent, or at least her interpretation of one.

A beautifully seductive woman wearing the costume of death stands in front of a hellish background ripped from the right panel in Bosch's triptych.

"The Lady of the Rocks, the Lady of Situations, the Lady of Death," Madame Sosostris says. "She's a lady of many names."

Tick. Tock. Tick. Tock. Mr. Eliot's heart beats faster. He waits for Madame Sosostris to continue, but she doesn't. She pauses, her face almost as still as the wax gypsy when it's not winking.

"What does she have to do with me?" Mr. Eliot asks.

Madame Sosostris spasms, as if her soul just returned from a long trip in the cosmos.

"You will marry, but that will not work out so well either."

Mr. Eliot sighs, somehow resigned to the fate even though he's not sure whether any of this is to be believed. But then again, where have beliefs gotten everyone, anyway?

Madame Sosostris turns over the third card . . .

"The Wheel of Torture."

A man is lashed to a medieval wheel of fortune, a whip on one side of him, inviting you to take part in the torture and lash out at him yourself. But not everything seems bad for the man. On the other side lies gold and jewels. *Is it treasure? A reward?* It might be, but for what?

"The Wheel of Torture. The Wheel of . . . Fortune," Madame Sosostris says, enchanting Mr. Eliot into her spell. "Torture, success, torture, success. An endless cycle."

She leans back in her chair. "We both see what the fates decree for you."

"What have they said?" Mr. Eliot implores.

Madame Sosostris smiles. She turns over the fourth card. But . . . the card is blank. It's a plain white card, no image, no meaning, no direction.

"What does it mean? Am I going to die?"

Madame Sosostris looks at the card, surprised to spot one that offers hope. "The card is blank. It's something I'm forbidden to see."

"But what does a blank card mean?"

"Thomas," she scolds. "You have a blank card! It can be anything."

Mr. Eliot deflates in his chair. He came here for answers. He came here for direction, and now he has none.

"But—" Madame Sosostris starts.

"But what?" Mr. Eliot asks, jumping at the chance to find another way forward.

Madame Sosostris settles in for what she's about to say. "There are many paths open to you, Thomas. But most lead to disaster. Some paths are slower, some paths are faster. Lilacs without water wilt, and all that's left is guilt."

"Mr. Prufrock said 'wavering' between the—" Mr. Eliot starts, but Madame Sosostris cuts him off.

"Alfred? That old fool. Don't listen to him, Thomas."

Mr. Eliot gulps. "How do you know him?"

"I thought we were done asking stupid questions," Madame Sosostris replies, venom in her voice.

She seems to have venom in spades, because Madame Sosostris suddenly morphs into a giant snake. She slithers around the room, her shiny scales dappling light across the parlor like a gleaming pendant.

"You need to ssshow your hand, Mr. Eliot," she says, her Ss slurring across her mouth in a hiss.

"Ssshow your hand, Thomasss. Ssshow your hand!"

She coils around Mr. Eliot, crushing him. "You let life flow. Sssay, 'I don't know' and act asss though your sssoul is dead."

Madame Sosostris gives him one last big squeeze and releases him. "But it'sss really up to you. You can live the life you choossse. You can live the life that'sss in your heart, ssso . . ."

The glazed gypsies who were lazing on the couch suddenly come to life and take part in Madame Sosostris's demand, "Ssshow your hand!"

They dance around Madame Sosostris's snake like witches at a séance. "Take a chanccce. Take a ssstand! Choossse romanccce to have the love that you dessserve. All it takesss isss a little bit of nerve!"

Madame Sosostris hisses in Mr. Eliot's ear, "To live life like you want, to give love like you want, to live life like thisss isss posssssible."

"But you're afraid," the gypsies note. "Though you've prayed, you're betrayed."

"By fear of sssin," Madame Sosostris says, and joins them, "though it'sss really up to you. God won't watch your rendezvous. You can live the life that'sss in your heart."

The gypsies dance around Madame Sosostris, chanting. "Ssso ssshow your hand! Take a chanccce! Take a ssstand! Choossse romanccce!"

The gypsies twirl in the air and then disappear, flaming out in a whirl of smoke.

Madame Sosostris sits in front of Mr. Eliot, still slurring her Ss even though she's no longer a snake. "Though it'sss really up to you."

Mr. Eliot wants, more than anything, to make that choice, but he knows it's impossible.

"You decccide, Thomasss," Madame Sosostris says. "The card is blank. It can be anything you desssire."

Mr. Eliot nods his head, shuts his eyes.

"Oh, you think you can get away from us, do you?!"

Eyes open. Mind awake. Time for the spell to break.

Mr. Eliot scans the parlor. He heard a man shouting, but there's no other man in the room. And there are no gypsies either, only naked Rubenesque portraits hanging above the parlor couches.

Thump. Oof. "Yeah, you like that!"

The shouts are coming from outside. Outside the parlor. Out in the squalor.

What's going on out there? Mr. Eliot is concerned and confused, not only by the beating outside, but for how the world ever got this way. And more specifically, *What happened here?* The dark, muted, slick oil paint that permeated the parlor is gone. The room is now as real as the photographs that well-heeled men like to take with their girlfriends. No, the room is now even realer than that. He looks at Madame Sosostris. She's not the Madame he's come to know. She's not part of an oil painting, but a flesh-and-blood woman sitting across from him. And she's staring, cross at him.

"That'll be two pounds," she says, no longer slurring her Ss but still spouting plenty of venom.

Thump. Thump. Ah! Oof. The beat of the beating continues outside. Mr. Eliot gives Madame Sosostris a curt nod, lays down his payment, and dashes out the door.

6

Mr. Eliot rounds the corner into an alley, interrupting the altercation, interrupting the thumping, a street lamp casting sharp shadows onto three men whose ideology is as Fascist as their behavior. They circle a man on the ground, raining down on him with all the hate they can muster. The shadows on the alley walls frame the fight, making it look like a boxing match, but there is no boxing going on. The Fascists kick the man on the ground, pounding his poor body into the pavement. Their kicks are swift as lightning, matching the insignia on their arms. A bolt of white lightning is centered on a red armband, the symbol of the British Union of Fascists.

If only this were a boxing match, maybe this poor man would put up more of a fight. But he's not a fighter. He lies there, curled up in a ball, trying to protect everything dear to him, or at least trying to maintain some sense of dignity.

That poor man, Mr. Eliot empathizes. He's receiving the punishment Mr. Eliot deserves.

Thump. Thump. Ah! Oof. It's like the ticking of a clock, a clock that will not stop until—

"Jack?" A look of recognition crosses Mr. Eliot's face. He races over, fists clenched, and shoves his way between Jack and the Fascists.

"Leave him alone. You've done quite enough!"

"What's it to you?" one of the Fascists asks.

"Maybe he's one of them," another posits, a gleam in his eye.

But Mr. Eliot will not be their victim. Not today. He jabs a finger in their face, his only jab that wouldn't end in disgrace.

"I, sir, am Mr. Thomas Stearns Eliot," he says in a steady, low-pitched voice. "And I would advise you and these other 'gentlemen' to leave before the police arrive."

"Yeah, you called the police, did ya, ya little punk?" the third Fascist says. He's even bigger and more menacing than the other two. He must be their leader. Mr. Eliot can tell this man is not to be lied to. And he can tell what he had for lunch. It was onions. Lots and lots of onions. The man smacks his lips as if he's about to have Mr. Eliot for dinner. Perhaps it's the smell of the onions, but Mr. Eliot holds back tears.

"Yes, I called them before I came out here," Mr. Eliot says as calmly as he can, as calm as any buoy on top of a storming sea could be.

Smack. The man hits Mr. Eliot squarely across his jaw, sending him sprawling to the ground right beside Jack.

"That'll teach you to call the coppers," the leader says before walking off. The other two hesitate for a moment and then saunter off as well.

Mr. Eliot maneuvers to his side. He nudges Jack, who startles from his stillness with a jolt, a quick look of terror on his face. Jack rolls over on his side, scrutinizes Mr. Eliot, still scared but grateful.

"Thank you, Tom," Jack says.

"You know my name?" Mr. Eliot asks, perking up.

"Do you always ask stupid questions?"

Mr. Eliot squints his eyes, furrows his brow. *Jack's choice of words is . . . curious.*

Jack catches Mr. Eliot's consternation, rolls his eyes. "I asked. At the bank."

Mr. Eliot nods his head. *That makes sense.* Then he looks at Jack, who gazes back at him expectantly. Panic. Sheer and utter panic takes over Mr. Eliot's mind. What is he supposed to say? Then he realizes.

"I'm sorry. I never . . ."

"Asked my name?" Jack finishes, smiling, not realizing Mr. Eliot has known his name for quite a while. "Jack. My name is Jack."

Mr. Eliot sweats. This is more anxiety-inducing than facing off against a few Fascists.

Milk crates. Mr. Eliot spots milk crates off to the side of the alley, hops up to collect them. He places a couple next to Jack and offers him a hand, but Jack is still assessing his injuries. He's not ready to move yet.

"Are you hurt badly?" Mr. Eliot asks.

"No, nothing serious at all," Jack lies, before affecting the air of a pompous British gentleman. "A minor scuffle," he continues, "really not much more than a bit of vigorous exercise."

Mr. Eliot chuckles. The corners of Jack's mouth curl up into a smile.

"But those men . . ." Mr. Eliot tries to ask, but the memory of what they did, or could have done, stops him.

Jack reaches out his hand. Mr. Eliot helps him up on one of the milk crates.

"Boys will be boys," Jack says haughtily, still in character. Mr. Eliot's eyes linger on Jack as he examines the damage. Jack's jacket is torn in half. His shirt is ripped and covered in grime.

Jack tries to wipe it off but succeeds only in getting the grime all over his hands. He shrugs but then winces, his body reminding him of the beating it's taken.

"You're a mess," Mr. Eliot says.

"Thanks," Jack rejoins.

Mr. Eliot's eyes go wide. "No, I didn't mean—"

"It's all right. I was joking."

Mr. Eliot takes in a quick, nervous breath. "You can get cleaned up at my place if you like. I live across the park."

Jack squints at Mr. Eliot. *What's the extent of the invitation?* "I'm across the park, too, but on the other side from you."

"How do you know where I live?"

"You pointed it out when I saw you the other night," Jack states matter-of-factly.

Mr. Eliot blinks, inhales. "I'm sorry. I can be somewhat . . . private."

"No, I get it, I do," Jack says, flashing his eyes at Mr. Eliot. "And I'll be fine, really. I just want to go home and get cleaned up."

"Well, take this at least," Mr. Eliot says as he removes his jacket and hands it to Jack.

"Get your hands off him!" A man wearing a large cravat screams as he runs into the alley, another man hot on his trail.

"It's all right. The war is over, Frederick," Jack says.

"Oh, good," Frederick replies. "Are you all right? You look like a mess."

"We heard the noise and noticed those bastards coming out of the alley," the other man says.

"And it sounds like you came running right away," Jack jokes, "not taking any time to tuck your tail . . . or anything else, between your legs."

The man scoffs in a high-pitched voice, "Bitch."

Mr. Eliot notices Frederick wears a cravat so large it's almost a blouse. The other man is dressed much more simply, more simply in that he has skipped the cravat and gone straight for the blouse. No, not straight. Nothing this man does is straight. He's gone gaily forward toward the blouse. He's eager and introduces himself to Mr. Eliot.

"I'm Daniel. *Enchanté*," he says as he extends the top part of his hand like a duchess. "Who are you?"

"This is the gallant knight who came to my rescue," Jack says.

"And here we are," Frederick says, taking center stage, "the queens, to take you back to your kingdom."

"More like trolls in a dungeon," Jack remarks.

"Bitch," Frederick squeaks in an even higher-pitched voice than Daniel.

Mr. Eliot steps back. He's uncomfortable. He's never witnessed men act like this, even the men who visit the trees at night. *Is this one of the things they do back there?* Somehow, he could confront the Fascist men in the alley, but these men seem much more menacing.

Jack, Frederick, and Daniel notice Mr. Eliot's panicked face. They give each other knowing side glances.

Frederick half-smiles. "Well, time to go home then."

Frederick and Daniel help Jack off the milk crate, supporting him on each side. Jack winces.

"Are you sure you can walk?" Mr. Eliot asks.

"Yes," Jack says, "they'll take care of me."

They walk down the alley, Jack wincing every step of the way, but less and less with each one. After a few paces, Jack stops. "Wait," he says, turning to Mr. Eliot, who stares back at Jack with the naive urgency of a runt trying to be picked from a litter.

"Tom, your jacket," Jack says as he starts taking it off.

"Keep it," Mr. Eliot responds confidently. "Are you sure you're okay?"

Jack gives Mr. Eliot a quick look, but then darts his eyes to the ground. Is he in pain? No, he's disappointed, and he doesn't know what to say.

Frederick fills the air, assuring Mr. Eliot, "We'll take care of him."

"Thanks for helping," Daniel adds, before punctuating his exit with an, "Au revoir!"

Mr. Eliot stands somewhat awkwardly as they exit the alley. His hands are down at his side. *No, that's not where they should go.* He searches for something else for his hands to do, somewhere else for his hands to be. He smooths down his shirt. *Yes, that looks nice, even with no jacket.* Mr. Eliot doesn't need his jacket. He doesn't need any jacket. *What's a jacket for, anyway?* For looking nice and respectable? For protecting yourself from the elements? To keep you warm? Mr. Eliot doesn't need warmth. He's used to the cold. But he's glad that Jack has his jacket. He hopes it keeps him warm, because London can be a cold city. And The Wasteland is getting colder by the day.

Mr. Eliot puts his arms around his shoulders, his body instinctively reaching out for the warmth he's denied himself. But, no, Mr. Eliot puts his hands down, back at his side, overriding his instincts. He doesn't need warmth. He doesn't need it. He doesn't.

If only Mr. Eliot were referencing his jacket and not its current occupant. Mr. Eliot sighs, hangs his head, and walks home.

7

Crank. Scribble. Crank. Scribble. Tick. Tock. Tick. Tock. Clang. Clang. Clang.

Mr. Clark rings the metal triangle with the metal rod. The day is done and Mr. Clark is glad to greet it with the sweet tweet of metal upon metal. It's six o'clock and six o'clock feels like six o'clock every day. Every day the same. It's the same cycle of déjà vu, the same cycle of Samsara. Mr. Eliot can sense the cycle of Samsara sucking away at his soul. He wonders if he's wandering. Wandering. It's one of the multitudinous definitions of Samsara. It's the karmic cycle of reincarnation, but it's also a cycle of wandering, drifting from one thing to another with no aim, no sense of meaning. It's an existence that lacks excitement, an existence that lacks life.

Mr. Eliot feels trapped in it. And he should know. He studied Sanskrit at Harvard. Yes, that Harvard. He hates bringing it up with people until he's well acquainted with them. People always act prissy around the privileged. Lord knows he does. So, when Mr. Eliot notes that today the well-heeled men emerge from the bank and their women gasp with giddy delight in the same manner that they always gasp with giddy delight, rest assured that he's an expert in the field. Mr. Eliot knows a well-heeled man when he sees one. It's funny that you can always spot your own kind, especially if you hate what you see.

But Mr. Eliot is not like other well-heeled men. There is no warmth waiting for him when he exits the bank. Still no girlfriend waiting to scurry him off to the comfort of home. No warm honey to have tea with. Mr. Eliot slogs across the street, alone. He looks up at the gargoyles. Their greeting is gleeful but not giddy. No, their glee springs from a more hellish well.

Not today, Mr. Eliot concludes. He can't keep getting sucked into the cycle. Work. Home. Work. Home. No, today he'll go for a walk. *But aren't walks part of the cycle, too?* He sighs, resigns himself to another day of Samsara, another day in the cycle.

He walks down the street, past a pub.

Jack sits at a window table. When Mr. Eliot passes, Jack lights up, giddy, and then taps on the window. Tap. Tap. Tap. "Hey there, hold up."

Mr. Eliot can barely hear him through the glass, Jack's muffled sentence coming across as something closer to, "O the . . . hope." And indeed, sighting Jack has given Mr. Eliot more hope. He stiffens his posture, blinks rapidly. "Hello there. Hello!"

Jack exits the pub. "I've been waiting for you."

Mr. Eliot blushes. It's probably best the sky is gray because in direct sunlight the bright red in his cheeks could have blotted out the sun. Jack hands Mr. Eliot's jacket back to him.

"I wanted to return this to you."

Is that it? The bright red of his cheeks pales to a faint rose color.

"Thank you," Mr. Eliot replies.

"And I wanted to thank you," Jack says.

"It was nothing, really."

"No, it wasn't nothing," Jack says. He steps toward Mr. Eliot for emphasis, but then takes a small step back, averts his eyes. "At least let me buy you a beer."

Did the sun come out? Or is it just the brightness returning to Mr. Eliot's cheeks?

"Well, I suppose," Mr. Eliot says, trying to act coy. He starts toward the door, but Jack steps forward again.

"Not here," Jack interjects. "I know a better place."

"Where is it?"

"Close," Jack says, smiling. "You'll like it. Come on."

Mr. Eliot follows as they walk down the cobblestone street together, in the opposite direction of the well-heeled men and their girlfriends.

They walk in silence until Mr. Eliot asks, "Why aren't you at work anymore?" But he immediately regrets broaching the subject.

"Oh," Jack responds with a twinkle in his eye. "We had a disagreement about math."

"Math?"

"Yes, I said they owned me for nine hours a day, but they were very adamant that they owned me for all twenty-four."

Mr. Eliot laughs, but doubts Jack's account of the matter. "I see."

They enter a narrow alley.

The patter of a pulsating piano permeates the air.

Mr. Eliot stops. "Where is that music coming from?"

Jack grips his arm. "It's coming from where we're going." He pulls Mr. Eliot down the alley and out onto a new street, one that Mr. Eliot has never been on before, the rhythm of the music pumping, until the source of the music is in full view. A red brick vaudeville theater is decked out with carnival-style posters with risqué phrases such as, "Masculine Women! Feminine Men! Which is the rooster? Which is the hen?"

A sign above the door reads, "The Pansy Club," and the marquee proudly announces, "Gladys Bentley — Live Performances Every Night!"

An eclectic crowd of patrons mills out front, including Frederick and Daniel. Mr. Eliot looks wary. "Why did you bring me here?"

"I thought you might want to go inside. We can have that beer. See what it looks like for yourself."

Mr. Eliot huffs. "What gave you the idea that . . ."

Now it's Jack's turn to be embarrassed.

"Lots of artists, poets, and musicians . . ." Jack interjects. "I found a poem in your jacket. You're talented."

He read my poem? Mr. Eliot looks back toward the alley, searching for an escape.

"It's a great crowd," Jack reassures him, touching his arm.

Mr. Eliot pivots clockwise, finds Jack's pleading eyes. "Only for a minute," Jack offers. "Just to look around."

But Mr. Eliot shakes Jack off. "I'm not a homosexual!"

Frederick and Daniel notice the outburst, but keep their distance.

"Listen," Jack says, "I'm not saying you are or you aren't. All I'm saying is that I'm going inside. If you want to come in and join me . . . for a beer . . . that would be great. If you're not ready, that's okay, too."

Jack tries to step into Mr. Eliot's eyeline, but Mr. Eliot turns away.

Dejected, Jack shuffles over to the club, into the waiting arms of Frederick and Daniel, who greet him warmly.

"Jack, darling!"

"Absolutely, positively, delightfully lovely to see you!"

Frederick's eyes flash toward Mr. Eliot. "But Jack, darling, it's time to call a spade a spade."

"That man is trade," Daniel declares.

"Afraid I'll end up like you, an old maid?" Jack laughs. It's good to laugh about this. It's always good to laugh about the pain.

Mr. Eliot peeks over his shoulder as they enter the club, brothers in arms. But why hasn't Mr. Eliot already left? He is not a homosexual. This is not the place for him. Dare he go inside? *Is it a trap?* Jack seems so free. *How can this be?* He's a flirt. But why does he care? *Do I care?* Jack seems genuine. *Should I go inside?* What's he got to hide?

They could have that beer, maybe share a dance, a little romance. *No.* He must stay out here. *Refrain, restrain, abstain.*

Yes. That's what he must do. *Or I could take a chance.* Take this opportunity to advance.

A couple of curious looky-loos stare at the more colorful patrons outside the club.

Let them stare! Mr. Eliot dares. *I don't care! I must not despair. Because I want passion. I need passion!* Jack's in there, waiting for him. Mr. Eliot sets his jaw. He knows what he needs to do, but he's still afraid.

Mr. Eliot takes a step toward the club. His chest heaves like he's already summited Mt. Everest, but then he regrets the trek, fears the freezing, and takes off down the street.

He turns a corner, passes a pub, its patrons overflowing. He only slows down when the crowd thins out.

Mr. Eliot wheezes, due to the running and the anxiety that caused it. He leans against a stone wall, on the edge of crying from frustration, his lips pinching, his head shaking. He finds the crucifix lodged into his chest, fingers it.

A hiss of a snake fills the air. Mr. Eliot looks around for the source, afraid of what this serpent brings. But all he notices is the wall he was leaning up against is no longer there. He's confronted with a massive door with the initials "PC" written on it in the most elaborate cursive.

A small grill on the door opens, and a set of eyeballs attached to a bouncer poke out.

Although his eyes are kind, his voice is gruff. "What do you want?"

"No. Nothing. I didn't mean to . . . I'm sorry."

"You here for the Pansy Club?"

"I . . . uh . . ." Mr. Eliot stammers.

The bouncer becomes impatient. "Are you coming in or not?"

"No, I couldn't," Mr. Eliot answers, but then immediately reconsiders, albeit tentatively. "I mean yes. Yes, I'd like to come in."

But the bouncer shuts the grill on the door, and Mr. Eliot is left standing in the alley, all alone.

Mr. Eliot grits his teeth, stamps his feet, and shouts, "Yes! I want to come in!"

The door opens. "Yes, of course. Come right in. There's no need to shout about it," the bouncer says.

Mr. Eliot takes a step forward, then another, then another, until he's about to enter the club. Then he takes another step forward. It's like he's floating across the threshold. *This must be what a bride feels like on her wedding night*, he imagines. A giant weight is lifted off his shoulders.

8

Whatever he was expecting. It was not this. *Where are the men drinking? Where are the men dancing?* Mr. Eliot had imagined places like this before. Yes, he had imagined them many times. But he had always pictured these establishments with more . . . men.

There is no one else in the room. No patrons. No bartenders. No waiters. A giant golden globe on a golden stand gleams golden light, dappling the room in intricate dots, much in the same way that Madame Sosostris's scales had. It lights up the room's corners and crevices, all the places that Mr. Eliot would have liked to explore with the bar's clientele, but there is no need to explore at the moment. Mr. Eliot can roam the room with his eyes. He can see the grand piano in the center, waiting for someone to tickle its ivories. He can see the stage, waiting for a crooner to croon, a dancer to dance, or a comedian to make him laugh. He can see the round tables set out with silverware, waiting for the well-heeled men to wine and dine. And he can make out the red booths in the back, the booths in the dark for the less well-inclined.

A zeppelin zooms overhead, high above, highlighting the second story, up where you can see everything happening below, especially in the red booths. If only anything was going on anywhere in the club. On the walls, two large faces do what they do well, and face each other. One has pink eyes and the other blue, and together, they make two.

Two faces. Mr. Eliot turns to each face in equal measure, inspecting them. Beneath each of the faces, there are two bars, one on each side of the room. Which bar should he approach to get a drink? Will he be happier at one bar over the other? Does it matter so long as he chooses one? Does it matter if there's no bartender to tend to his desire?

A golden ceiling bounces golden light off golden candelabra. But, no, the golden light isn't bouncing, it's dripping. Drip. Drop. A drop of liquid gold falls from the ceiling, plops onto Mr. Eliot's forehead. He rubs it off. It's soft, smooth . . . oily. It's not gold at all, but paint. Oil paint.

The entire room is composed of oil paint, not paint that's been set, but rather, paint that's just been applied and is still wet. The whole room is damp, and we all know what happens to oil paint in a damp room. We're all aware of what happened to Leonardo da Vinci and his *Battle of Anghiari*. He had just finished the painting, the largest wall painting in the world, when an unseasonably rainy Florentine spring decided the city did not need to celebrate that particular victory. The air was damp. The paint was wet. And with no dryness in the air, the entire painting melted off the wall onto the floor. Leonardo lit fires to stop the melting, but he couldn't dry the paint in time. So, instead of championing Florence's victory at the Battle of Anghiari, Leonardo sat before a pool of his ambitions, defeated.

Mr. Eliot embodies that devastation. He finally allowed himself to enter this establishment, and here he is now, defeated by an unfathomable force.

"Good evening, Mr. Eliot. Do you have a reservation?" Mr. Eliot turns to find Mr. J. Alfred Prufrock, his butler from his Garden of Eden. *Where did he come from?* How had Mr. Eliot missed him?

"What are you doing in this place?" Mr. Eliot asks.

"A reservation?" Mr. Prufrock responds impertinently.

Mr. Eliot is flustered. "I'm sorry, I wasn't aware I needed one."

"So, you don't have a reservation?"

"No," Mr. Eliot answers, his head hanging. "No. No, I don't."

"Then I'm afraid I can't let you in," Mr. Prufrock intones with no rise or pitch in his voice, and no compassion or empathy either. "Shall I escort you to the door?"

Mr. Eliot looks around. "It's lovely here, but where is everyone?"

"Really . . . this is not the place for you, Mr. Eliot. Shall I arrange a nice park bench? Perhaps a nice garden?"

"Yes, I suppose so," Mr. Eliot answers.

Mr. Prufrock leads him toward the door. "You are confused. So, I am here to guide you. There are some things you must not do, some thoughts you must not have, some places you must not be."

Mr. Eliot nods, agreeing with him. He scans the club. It's not what he thought it would be, but he wants to linger nonetheless.

"It's time to go, Mr. Eliot."

He looks at Mr. Prufrock, the man who has always been so helpful, the man who has always kept him safe. "Thank you. I . . ."

But then something shifts behind Mr. Prufrock. Mr. Eliot tries to sidestep him, catch sight of what it was, but Mr. Prufrock matches his move. *What is he trying to hide?* There it is again.

Mr. Eliot clocks it. Mr. Prufrock blocks it.

"What are you doing, Mr. Eliot?"

"I just want to see what it is," Mr. Eliot answers.

"Thomas! Is that you, Thomas?" a man's voice beckons.

"Thomas? It's you!" a woman's voice bellows.

Mr. Eliot gives Mr. Prufrock a stern look, sidesteps him to spot whom the voices belong to. But he doesn't see anyone, only a wall of paintings. There's one of two men in a garden standing next to a secret door. There's another of a man who looks like he's taken H.G. Wells's time machine into the future, or at least to another planet. And there's another with a king and queen on their thrones being entertained by a court jester.

"We thought you'd never come!" the queen screams.

Mr. Eliot swallows. *Can it be true?* Is the queen in the painting talking to him?

"Welcome, my boy. It's so good to see you," the king says, answering Mr. Eliot's internal question.

"It's good to see you, too," Mr. Eliot stammers nervously. Why did he say that? He's never met these people. No, not people. Royals. He's never met royalty. *How does one act around royalty?* But this king and queen are no regular royals. No, they are King and Queen Bolo. They are not constrained by your typical royal robes. King Bolo doesn't even wear a shirt under his metal jacket. His crown is, to put it nicely, unconventional. It blares out in all directions, a fanciful mix of everything you'd find at an estate sale for a mad king. And, boy, is this king mad. The top of his crown is adorned with a miniature grandfather clock locked away in a glass case. Two horns stick out of the sides. In true King Bolo fashion, if you could call this fashion, one horn looks like the receiver on a telephone and the other looks like a horn on a record player. But this crown doesn't need a horn to amplify its message. No, that's coming in loud and clear: King Bolo is quite queer.

Queen Bolo, not to be topped by her husband, occupies a grand Victorian gown. Perhaps she ate a peacock for dinner and it didn't agree with her, though, because it looks like she vomited a rainbow of color upon her dress. Brightly colored specks and stripes streak out in all directions. It's a mess of a dress, but one that couldn't be worn by anyone less. Only a woman who answers to no man could wear it. Queen Bolo is confident, her head held high. Her hair is even higher, looking like bits of pink cotton candy (or are they clouds?) wafting into the air.

Both of their faces are painted, but not with the oil paint that everything else is. No, these monarchs are painted black and white and all the colors of the night. Their faces look more like skeletons than royal ones. Their clothing has so much life, but their faces contain only death. They have teeth painted upon their lips. The bones of their cheeks are painted on their cheekbones. Mr. Eliot scrutinizes Queen Bolo's face. *Where is her nose?* No one knows.

The Bolos leap from their canvas into the club, their feet landing with a thud.

"Come in. See the place for yourself!" King Bolo says welcomingly.

"You've outdone yourself this time, Thomas," Queen Bolo compliments.

Mr. Eliot squints at them. *It can't be.* "King Bolo? Queen Bolo?"

"At your service!" King Bolo states.

"At your service!" Queen Bolo reiterates.

"The Bolos are bozos," Mr. Prufrock intimates. "They are beneath you. You should burn them and pretend they never existed."

Yes, that's what you do with things that are inconvenient in The Wasteland. Burn them and hope they never come back.

"Oh, hush, you old fart!" Queen Bolo says, launching an attack.

"Are you talking to me? You old tart!" Mr. Prufrock attacks back.

"Don't start!" King Bolo shouts, having had enough of this bout.

"Don't mind him. Alfred doesn't know how to act around royalty," Queen Bolo says, holding out her hand regally. But Mr. Eliot doesn't know how to act around them either. What should he do? Does she expect him to shake her hand? *Or kiss it?* Mr. Eliot decides on kissing it, and takes her fingers in his, placing his lips oh-so-nervously upon her glove.

"Oh, now it's my turn, love," King Bolo says, extending his own hand.

At first, Mr. Eliot can't tell if he's serious, but then he looks in King Bolo's eyes. He's mysterious, delirious, and, yes, very serious. Mr. Eliot gives his glove a peck.

"Okay, now one on the neck," King Bolo demands.

"No, no. Let's not get out of hand," Queen Bolo reprimands.

King Bolo looks around, confused. There's something he wants to know. "Where's Columbo?"

"Columbo's here, too?" Mr. Eliot asks.

"I thought he was right behind us," Queen Bolo says, her eyes avoiding any close inspection.

"I'm here, my King!" Columbo shouts. And, yes, there he is, the court jester from the painting, or rather, still inside it.

"I'm stuck. Please help me," Columbo pleads, his foot lodged in the painting's frame.

"Thomas, will you help me pluck him?" King Bolo asks.

"Yes, your majesty," Mr. Eliot answers enthusiastically.

They grasp Columbo's arms and pull, but Columbo is wiry and hard to hold.

"I'm usually quite agile," Columbo says apologetically.

"I can attest to that," King Bolo states.

"The current situation might suggest otherwise," Queen Bolo berates.

"Will you help me, my Queen?" King Bolo asks.

"I'll leave you two to this task," she answers. "Plucking Columbo is not my forte."

"Touché!" the king responds. Then he turns to Mr. Eliot. "Let's give him one good thrust, shall we?"

Mr. Eliot nods as they wind up to wrench him free.

"One, two, three!" King Bolo shouts before they yank on Columbo with all their might.

"It hurts! It hurts! It hurts!" Columbo bawls, but then he's pulled clean from the wall and they all fall in a pile on the floor. The three men's faces are close to one another, or as close as they can be with the horns on King Bolo's crown and the spikes on Columbo's jester hat.

"Well, that's enough of that," Queen Bolo says.

"Show some compassion, my Queen."

Queen Bolo perks up. "Oh, Columbo, are you all right? Did that hurt?"

"Yes, it did, your majesty," Columbo says.

Queen Bolo bares her teeth, and not the ones painted on her lips. "Good, perhaps that'll teach you to be so agile."

"Mr. Eliot," Mr. Prufrock tries to interject.

But it doesn't connect. Mr. Eliot didn't hear him. "Did it hurt?" he asks.

"Not a bit. Easy as pie," Columbo answers.

King Bolo smiles. "It only hurts for a moment, but then it gives you the most wonderful sensation!" King Bolo and Columbo giggle.

Mr. Prufrock puffs out his chest. "Mr. Eliot!"

But he still doesn't hear. He's too entranced by King Bolo and Columbo. Their relationship might not be what he had guessed.

Mr. Eliot looks at the king, the queen, and this man, the one in between. "I can't believe that all three of you are here!"

Mr. Prufrock can't take any more of being ignored, that much is clear. "Mr. Eliot!"

Mr. Eliot's whole body clenches. "What? What is it, Mr. Prufrock?"

Mr. Prufrock grips him by his shoulder, leads him a few paces away. "I understand that it's good to blow off steam every now and again. Sow those wild oats, as they say. Exhaust those perverted passions." Mr. Prufrock straightens his jacket, stands stiffly. "I'm pleased you got that out of your system. I'm pleased you can tell right from wrong, good from evil, grace from sin." He opens the door to the club for Mr. Eliot. "But you need to leave. Now."

He needs to leave? Now that he's met King and Queen Bolo, and Columbo, how can he?

"Did he sssay sssin?" Queen Bolo asks, slurring her Ss like Madame Sosostris's snake.

"Why that's nothing to worry about!" Columbo begins. "Sin's the best part of life."

"My boy," King Bolo says, as coy as a child looking at a new toy. "There's no reason to be worried! Look at me. I'm a sinner."

"He'sss a sssinner," Queen Bolo slurs.

"A real winner," Columbo concurs.

"And here I am," King Bolo continues, "with Queen Bolo, my beautiful wife. Columbo, my trusted . . . advisor. And . . ." King Bolo grasps Mr. Eliot's hand, steers him back to the middle of the club to reveal, "all of my loyal followers!"

Mr. Eliot is stunned. The club is now full of the clientele he imagined, full of all shapes and sizes. Some of the men are round, their corpulence and joie de vivre on full display. Some of the men are square, like Mr. Eliot. And some of the men are lithe, but all writhe to the pulsating piano. *Where did the music come from?* Mr. Eliot wonders.

But he doesn't take too much time to contemplate the question. A dirty dozen denizens dance with abandon to the beat of the music, in the heart of the club. It's overwhelming. He needs a drink.

He tries to make his way to the bar, but King Bolo dips him dramatically in the middle of the dance floor.

The revelers shout in delight. "Ooh!"

"Ah!"

"I wish my man did that!"

A spotlight sears down on them from the second story. Tick. Tock. Tick. Tock. Mr. Eliot can hear his heart beating, but it's not to the beat of the music. He doesn't like the spotlight.

"My boy, I say," King Bolo croons, taking center stage and temporarily easing Mr. Eliot's nerves. "To live a pious life is boring, and life is too short to waste. So, why should we waste our life hiding from who we are? From what we are?" King Bolo smiles, sits with his legs splayed on the stage. "So, let's stop this foolish whining, and embrace the glory of sin!"

The revelers congregate around King Bolo, caressing him, and then lift him in the air, his legs still splayed in a split.

"You could pray every day. Meditate. Flagellate. Be a good little boy."

The revelers join in. "Be a good little boy!"

King Bolo winks at Mr. Eliot. "Or else you could"—and then the revelers finish the thought—"have a little fun and live a life of sin!"

The revelers release King Bolo. He makes his way over to Mr. Eliot, circling him. "Try a new prescription. Drink it. Take it in. Why not enjoy the friction?" He points Mr. Eliot's head at all the sexy revelers. "Have one, have them all. The more we have, the more we want to have."

Columbo bats his eyes at Mr. Eliot. "It's really not our fault."

King Bolo grasps Mr. Eliot's hands, leads him in a tango, the other revelers quickly following suit. "Better to give in. Why have a life that's filled with dreary monotone? There is a rainbow out there waiting for you." King Bolo spins Mr. Eliot into the spotlight. "To debut."

Mr. Eliot smiles, a glorious possibility shining out of him that almost blots the spotlight. He bears the heat from that bright light above. It's warm. But then, like a frog in a pot, it gets hot. Mr. Eliot shakes and quakes with terror.

Luckily, Queen Bolo swoops in on a zeppelin to steal the spotlight. "If you live a life of sssin you'll find your life sssoaring. Ssso lovely and debasssed."

Columbo takes over. "If you're not debased, life's a waste." He bends his backside toward King Bolo, who playfully thrusts his crotch at him. "See the lovely slope of sin, gliding in. Love who we are. Love what we are."

King Bolo slaps Columbo's ass before making his way back over to Mr. Eliot. "Live life like ol' Pandora. She wants you to open her box. Have fun like in ol' Gomorrah." He thrusts into Mr. Eliot's backside. "Have one. Have 'em all. Have a ball." The revelers reach out for Mr. Eliot, their hands and eyes pleading with him to join in. In one final dramatic thrust, King Bolo pushes Mr. Eliot toward them. "Don't stall." The revelers engulf him in their sweaty mass.

The trio of King Bolo, Queen Bolo, and Columbo arrange themselves in a triangle and chant, "Savor the time you're given. Drink it. Take it in. Love like there's no tomorrow. Life's a game to win."

Columbo shouts to the revelers, "Whoever sins the most will win the prize!"

King Bolo nods, "Seek the prize that lasts eternal."

Queen Bolo prods, "So what if it's infernal?"

Columbo shouts to the gods, "So, whenever you're nocturnal!"

Then all three of them, together, against the odds, "Live a life of sin!"

Mr. Prufrock dives into the wet mass of men surrounding Mr. Eliot. He yanks on Mr. Eliot's lapels, wrenching him out of the wretches, and pins him against a wall.

"You . . . don't . . . belong . . . here!"

9

Mr. Eliot leans with his head and palms pressed against a stone wall. He's back on the street. Outside. All alone. The backdoor to the Pansy Club has disappeared. *Where did it go?* Was it ever there? *I don't care.* He doesn't. He doesn't care. Mr. Eliot becomes self-conscious, self-aware. He collects himself and what's left of his dignity, stands straight, and strides down the street.

He knows where he must go. He must pray. St. Paul's isn't much of an uphill climb, but it is the highest point in London. Mr. Eliot can always find it, like a liturgical north star.

He kneels under the dome, but maybe he should have chosen a better spot. Some of the more scantily clad souls on St. Paul's ceiling dance above him, filling his imagination with the thoughts he came here to pray away. Next time he'll go to St. Stephen's, where there are no heathens.

He prays aloud, "Lord Jesus, for too long I've kept you out of my life. I know that I am a sinner and that I cannot save myself. No longer will I close the door when I hear you knocking. No longer will I enter doors I should not when I hear them calling."

His hands clasp tightly together. "By faith, I gratefully receive your gift of salvation. I am ready to trust you as my Lord and Savior. Your mercy flows to me in spite of my faults and failures. I understand that even though I am scared, my emotions don't have to control my actions. Father, may your sweet words saturate my mind and direct my thoughts. Help me release the hurt and begin to love as Jesus loves. Thank you, Lord Jesus, for coming to earth. I believe you are the Son of God who died on the cross for my sins and rose from the dead on the third day."

He takes out his crucifix, fingers it, and then cranes his neck at the life-size crucifix hanging before him, Jesus dangling limply on the cross. His face turns ashen, white, pallid. He wants his next words to be true but doesn't know if they are. "Thank you for bearing my sins and giving me the gift of eternal life. I believe your words are true." His hand clenches his crucifix. "I believe my words are true . . . please come into my heart, Lord Jesus, and be my Savior. Amen."

Mr. Eliot leaps to his feet, ready to be finished with the prayer and the emotions it stirs up, but his legs are wobbly and his knees buckle. Has he always been this heavy? He stumbles back a step, but then recovers. Yes, he will recover from this. Mr. Eliot gazes at the large crucifix before him, his mind in a haze, and then trudges out of the church.

London is a maze, especially when your mind is in a daze. *Is this a phase?*

So much turmoil. So many gargoyles. Mr. Eliot summits the steps back to his flat. Bertrand's door is shut. *Good.* Now is not the time to be summoned inside. But then Bertrand's door opens abruptly. A woman wearing a blouse slips out, and the door clicks shut behind her. *It is a woman, isn't it?* Her hair is rather short. Mr. Eliot's mind is ablaze. Usually, when Bertrand is entertaining women, he keeps the door open, but perhaps some visitors are best kept behind closed doors.

No, of course it was a woman. Bertrand's visitor was bloused. Mr. Eliot must be soused.

Mr. Eliot plops down at his desk. Some poets write better when they're drunk. Yes, he'll try to capture this moment, even though he hasn't had a drop.

He just needs to put his head down for a second on his desktop. Then he'll start writing. Nothing will make him stop.

Inspiration. All he needs is a little inspiration. If only there were a sunset. Sunsets are inspiring. Or at least they used to be. But now there's only darkness outside. Only dark, where anything can hide.

Mr. Eliot looks like he's about to weep, but then he shuts his eyes and goes to sleep.

Beep. Beep. He wakes up to the sound of a taxi.

Mr. Eliot peers out the window. Even though the sky is gray, he can tell it's now well into the day. He let the night slip away.

No matter. Every day is a new day. He can start writing now. He *will* start writing now. Mr. Eliot steadies himself. He readies his pen. Readies his paper. Everything is ready but the man to connect the two. Because Mr. Eliot is blue, and the sky is gray. No, there will be no writing today.

And how could Mr. Eliot write with what's going on in the park across the way? But, no, it's not dark. There are no men frolicking in the trees. These men frolic in the open, their bare chests on full display. *Is this another dream?* An extremely fit Japanese man instructs Jack and a group of other extremely fit men in the art of judo. Their muscles are rippling, but to Mr. Eliot, it's a tsunami.

Tap. Tap. Tap. Bertrand raps at the door, but then enters immediately.

Mr. Eliot jumps at the sound and says, "Come in," after Bertrand already has.

"It was open," Bertrand explains.

"Unlocked," Mr. Eliot corrects.

"Yes, that's what I meant." Bertrand smiles, then sees something out the window. "What are you looking at?"

Mr. Eliot's chin quivers. "Can I get you a cup of tea?"

Bertrand's eyes go wide. "Ooh, now you must tell." Then he makes his way to the window, spots Jack and the other men. "A few sporting lads."

"I wasn't looking at them."

"All the more for me," Bertrand says. "And, yes. Tea, please."

Bertrand loves tea, especially if it comes with a little honey. He bats his eyes. "I spied you coming home rather late last night."

"I . . . uh . . . took a walk. Said my prayers at St. Paul's." Mr. Eliot smiles through a clenched jaw. It's not a lie, but he'd rather change the subject before he's caught in one. "Tea it is," he says tersely.

Mr. Eliot clomps over to the kitchenette, puts on a kettle. Meanwhile, Bertrand starts to meddle. He flips over Mr. Eliot's blank sheet to find a treat underneath. Words. So many words. When did Mr. Eliot write all these words?

"What are you writing?" Bertrand asks.

"Ah!"

But Mr. Eliot didn't burn himself on the kettle, nor is he reacting to Bertrand's meddle. A man's scream came from outside. Out in the park.

Mr. Eliot dashes over to the window. "Is he hurt?" But, no, Jack isn't hurt, he's smiling. The instructor helps him off the ground and judo throws him to the ground again with an, "Ah!" The instructor helps him up again, shows Jack how it's done. You grind your buttocks into their crotch and hope for the best, or something like that.

Mr. Eliot is relieved, a slow smile creeping across his face. He wipes a tear from his eye. Is he weeping? No. It was one tear, far from a flood. But if Mr. Eliot wasn't crying, what he's about to see might make him.

He turns around to find Bertrand reading his poetry. Was Bertrand reading it when Mr. Eliot went to the window? He didn't notice Bertrand reading it. *Why is he reading it?* It's personal. Much too personal for anyone to read, especially Bertrand, but that isn't stopping him. A breath catches in Mr. Eliot's mouth. He's not breathing. *Is there any air in the room?* Has he been transported to space?

Mr. Eliot asks as calmly as he can, "What . . . are . . . you . . . doing?"

Bertrand barely looks up at Mr. Eliot before reading, "'And I will show you something different from either your shadow at morning, striding behind you, or your shadow at evening, rising to meet you; I will show you fear in a handful of dust. White bodies naked on the low damp ground; Burning, burning, burning, burning. O' Lord Thou pluckest me out burning.'"

Bertrand's hands fall to his side. "My God, you're talented."

"It's nothing, really," Mr. Eliot says sheepishly, mortified. Sometimes it's easier to hide.

"Can I borrow this?" Bertrand asks, but doesn't wait for an answer. "I'd like to show it to someone. My friend Ezra. He knows more about poetry than I do, more than anyone I know really, and I bet he'll be impressed."

"No, I—"

"Ah!" A man's scream cuts off Mr. Eliot's protestation and takes his attention back to the park. *Is Jack okay?* He's smiling. He's fine. *Jack is fine.*

Mr. Eliot is anything but. He can't think of what to say to Bertrand. How can he explain he's not ready for his poetry to be out in the world? Mr. Eliot groans, turns back to Bertrand. "No, I . . ." to find that he's already left.

Panic. Sheer and utter panic. Mr. Eliot sweats. He looks around the room, spots his clocks. There's the grandfather, the one on the wall, the one on the mantle. Each and every one . . . the tocks of his clocks stop. Silence.

Tick. Tock. Tick. Tock. But there's still a beating. Mr. Eliot holds his chest, then his ears. The tock of his clock is deafening.

He runs out of the flat, eager to stop Bertrand. Eager to stop the tock. Eager to stop the clock. Yes, this clock is counting. Keeping time, keeping time. Counting down to doomsday. Mr. Eliot knew this day would come. Everyone knows this day will come in The Wasteland. But he didn't know it would come at the hand of Bertrand.

Mr. Eliot leaps down the stairs, descending rapidly. He flies through the first floor, flushed. Normally the first floor calms his nerves, its wide, well-lit halls welcoming him with their warm embrace. But not today. He charges out into the street.

"Ah!" But this scream doesn't come from Jack or the judo instructor. It comes from Mr. Eliot himself.

Jack is standing there, outside Mr. Eliot's flat, waiting for him.

"Well, hello there," Jack says. "Are you all right?"

Mr. Eliot is not all right, but he holds himself together long enough to reply, "Yes, thank you."

Jack shifts his stance, nods toward the judo. "I wasn't sure I'd see you again. So I thought I'd make sure you saw me."

And, boy, did Mr. Eliot see Jack. But he tries to play it cool. "Oh, is there something going on in the park today?"

"Ah!" the instructor screams.

"Ah!" So does Mr. Eliot.

He peeks at the men in the park. The instructor has thrown another man to the ground, and two others are grappling. Yes, Mr. Eliot is well informed of what it's like to grapple with something. But these men aren't grappling with their hands, or their minds, they hold each other closely and grapple with their feet, trying to trip and throw each other.

"Are they allowed to use their feet like that?" Mr. Eliot asks.

Jack turns, stands next to him.

"I think so. It's a style of no-holds-barred fighting, capitalizing on something new called judo. It's Japanese."

"I see," Mr. Eliot responds, his attention not on the judo, but Jack standing next to him. He swallows hard. "And he's a good instructor?"

"Oh, yes. And he's famous, too." Jack grins. "Mitsuyo Maeda. Known as a terror in the ring."

Mr. Eliot inspects the instructor. He would like to be like that man. "He seems fearless."

"What else would you expect from someone who goes by the name Count Combat!"

Jack smiles. Mr. Eliot giggles.

Now it's time for Jack to swallow hard. He turns his torso away from Mr. Eliot ever so slightly. "Meet me at Pierre's for dinner tonight and please don't say no."

"No, I . . ." Mr. Eliot stammers, but then catches himself. "Okay."

"Okay?" Jack asks.

"Okay," Mr. Eliot answers. "I'll see you there."

10

Lilacs. He needs lilacs. Jack likes lilacs. *Doesn't he?* But where will he get them? *Think. Think.* Mr. Eliot's heart races. Tick. Tock. Tick. Tock. His clock tocks, speeding itself toward his meeting with Jack. *No*, his clock needs to slow down. Mr. Eliot needs more time. He needs to find lilacs. Where has he seen lilacs?

Mr. Eliot roams the cobblestone streets. *Where is it? Where is it?* There. A flash of red, and then yellow, white, pink, and finally . . . purple. It's the most fantastic bouquet of lilacs he's ever seen. A purple cloud sits on top of a white ribbon handle. Mr. Eliot ambles up to the flower shop he's passed a million times. *It's still there.* It wasn't a vision. He must have it. For Jack.

"How much is the bouquet of lilacs?" Mr. Eliot asks.

The florist sizes him up. "Ten shillings."

"Isn't that a bit much?" Mr. Eliot asks, but then immediately retracts it. "No, sorry. I'll take it. Can I have them now?"

"As soon as I get my ten shillings."

Mr. Eliot gladly pays the man. He smiles. He has lilacs. For Jack. He races over to Pierre's Cafe, but when he gets there he has the most painful realization. *What time had they set dinner for?* Mr. Eliot checks his pocket watch. It's 5:00 p.m. Much too early for dinner, even in London. But what time had they made plans for? *Had they set a time?* Was he in too much of a panic to ask? To get clarification? It's silly, setting plans for dinner with someone but not setting a time. You might as well plan to meet in the middle of the English Channel. But no matter. Pierre's is across the street from the park. Mr. Eliot can sit on a bench and wait for Jack. Mr. Eliot is good at sitting on benches. *This is not a problem*. Only, Mr. Eliot doesn't seem capable of sitting. He paces around the bench. No, he races around it. Mr. Eliot can't stand still. His body is moving as fast as his mind. *What time will Jack show up? Seven? Eight?* Eight is when most Parisians eat. Pierre's is a Parisian-style cafe, or at least an Englishman's idea of one, so maybe that's when Jack will arrive. He just needs to be patient until then. But Mr. Eliot is not patient. He checks his pocket watch again. *Has it stopped? Has time stopped?* He could have sworn he checked it five minutes ago, but the minute hand has not budged. It still says the same time. 5:00 p.m. But the second hand ticks around, still circles the clock. Mr. Eliot nods. *Good, it's working.* Then he goes back to circling the bench.

Mr. Eliot's hand tightens around the bouquet. *Soon*. He will see Jack soon. And then he can give Jack the lilacs. Okay, but after the lilacs, what will he say? *What will we talk about?* Mr. Eliot sweats. He hadn't thought about that, but now, it's all he can. Thousands of scenarios run through his mind. Will Jack ask him about his childhood? Mr. Eliot had been born in St. Louis, Missouri. Schooling? Mr. Eliot was a Harvard man, but it's too soon to breach that subject. What are his thoughts on love? Mr. Eliot has many thoughts on that subject, but one in particular. He wants to feel it. Should he talk about The Wasteland? No, that's much too sore a subject, even over dinner. He wants to bring gaiety to the proceedings, not grief.

"Tom! Hello there!"

Mr. Eliot breaks out of his trance, looks around, sees Jack crossing the street. *Is it eight already? Where has the time gone?* He glances at his pocket watch. It's not eight, but 6:00 p.m.

"I'm sorry, we didn't set a time for dinner," Jack starts, "so I decided to get here early and wait for you, but I see you beat me to it."

Indeed, Mr. Eliot had been waiting. It had been a grating wait. But at least he wasn't late.

"Oh, don't worry," Mr. Eliot says, trying to play down his eagerness. "I thought I'd sit for a while in the park." But Mr. Eliot isn't sitting. No, he never did sit down on the bench.

"And how is that going for you?" Jack chuckles.

Mr. Eliot's eyes edge over to the bench. He gets Jack's point, but there's no time to be embarrassed. *Deflect. Deflect.*

"But then I thought I'd go for a walk instead. Parisians usually eat at eight, so I thought I might be waiting for a while."

"And so, you were going to try and find a place to plant those flowers?"

Mr. Eliot looks down at his lilacs. *No, Jack's lilacs.* Or at least they used to be lilacs. Mr. Eliot has killed them. Strangled them. He loosens his death grip around the bouquet's handle. His hand is so stiff. What did he do? In his anxious trance, he must have held on to the bouquet so tightly that he broke the stems. The lilacs hang limply out of the handle, wilted from Mr. Eliot's worry. This is what happens to beautiful things in The Wasteland.

Mr. Eliot can't give them to Jack now. He can't make Jack think this is what he thinks of him. "Oh, I almost forgot," Mr. Eliot lies. "I picked these up . . . on a whim, but I don't have anyone to give them to. Silly of me. I suppose you can have them if you like."

He hands the lilacs to Jack, who looks at them skeptically.

"I expect you got a good deal on them."

Mr. Eliot rocks slightly back and forth. No, he can't let Jack think he bought him cheap flowers. But what will he do?

He must expose his con.

"Oh, I, uh—they looked much better when I bought them," Mr. Eliot stammers, looks to the ground. "But I've been carrying them around for some time."

Jack leans back, takes in the admission. Smiles.

"Thank you very much. They're beautiful," Jack compliments.

Mr. Eliot pulls his eyes off the ground. "You're welcome."

"I'm glad you came. I wasn't sure I'd see you again. I thought maybe you'd stand me up."

"I'd never stand you up," Mr. Eliot says, perhaps a bit too seriously. "Why would you assume I might stand you up?"

"You kind of stood me up at the club the other day," Jack says, playfully shrugging his shoulders.

"Oh, I, uh—I'm sorry about that," Mr. Eliot apologizes.

"Completely understandable," Jack forgives.

"I, uh . . ."

"No need to explain," Jack interjects. "Shall we?"

Mr. Eliot looks across the street at Pierre's. He looks across the street into his future. At each table, a loving couple is sharing dinner. But they're sharing much more than a meal. They're sharing their lives.

"Yes. Let's." Mr. Eliot smiles. He looks over his shoulder as they cross the street. Over the tops of the trees, the sun sets, splashing the sky with pinks, oranges, and lavenders. It's inspiring. If only he had paper and pen.

"Bienvenue to Pierre's," a portly English host greets them. "How many will it be?"

"Deux," Jack responds, holding up two fingers.

"What? I asked how many—Is it just going to be you two lads?"

"Yeah, two," Jack smirks.

"Then why didn't you say that?" The host grimaces as he leads them to their table. The restaurant is ornate and gaudy, what an Englishman assumes a cafe in Paris looks like, but it's still quite nice. They walk underneath a large trellis toward a mural of the Eiffel Tower.

"I'll give you our best table, right by the tower," the host says. "Don't know why the frogs don't like it."

"Oh, so you're not French?" Jack asks cheekily.

"No. I'm from Bristol."

"Oh. I'm curious then," Jack says. "Why did you name this restaurant Pierre's?"

"You know, because Paris is . . . fancy."

Jack's face freezes. "Thank you for illuminating me," he says stoically.

"Of course. Enjoy your meal," the host responds over his shoulder as he walks away.

As soon as he's out of earshot, Jack's face falls. "Psst! Did you hear that?" Jack laughs. He's so alive.

Mr. Eliot chuckles. He wants to be that alive.

"I'm sorry," Jack says, "I thought this restaurant was . . . fancy." Jack devolves into another fit of laughter. When he comes up for air, he says, "I just wanted it to be nice."

"It is nice," Mr. Eliot says earnestly.

Now it's Jack's turn for his eyes to find the ground. He's not used to men being so . . . sweet. Most of the men he's acquainted with are somewhat more . . . let's say worldly. They've seen some of the world's secrets and have the cynicism to prove it.

"So, you're a Yank. What are you doing in London, anyway?" Jack asks.

"Is it that obvious?"

"It's the accent."

"I thought I had got rid of my Missouri accent when I was in Cambridge, but I guess some of Boston must have rubbed off on me."

"I'm sure it did," Jack says coquettishly, "but I don't mean your American accent. I mean your fake British one."

"Oh, I thought I was blending in pretty well."

"You weren't blending. You were smearing, darling." But then Jack smiles. And so does Mr. Eliot. Jack could say anything to Mr. Eliot as long as he did it with a smile.

"Don't worry about it," Jack says. "It's kind of cute."

Mr. Eliot melts. No, it's not cute. Jack is cute. Jack is the cutest thing he's ever seen. He's so . . . dreamy. This dinner is a dream. *Is it a dream?* Mr. Eliot has a hard time concentrating on their conversation. All he can focus on is how cute Jack is. And that's when he notices the pile of dishes sitting in front of them. *Did we eat all this food? Or does the restaurant need to bus the table before our meal comes?* Mr. Eliot can't remember all these dishes being there when they were seated. He checks his pocket watch. 10:00 p.m. They've been sitting there for four hours. And, yes, Mr. Eliot is full. He hopes they've had a good conversation, and from the look on Jack's face, they have. Mr. Eliot probably told him all about his childhood. He probably wasted all his good anecdotes in the first hour. He didn't tell him about Harvard, did he? No, he wouldn't. Not yet. But he probably told Jack about how he came to London to be a poet and took a job at the Bank of London even though he didn't want to work there. Jack could probably relate. It wasn't his dream job either.

But Mr. Eliot can't remember telling Jack any of that. All he remembers is Jack sitting there, beaming back at him, and he'll remember that for the rest of his life.

The moon shines down on the cobblestones as Jack drops Mr. Eliot off outside his flat, making them look like ripples in a calm sea.

"I've had a really wonderful time," Jack says.

"I . . . yes," Mr. Eliot stammers. "It's been one of the most marvelous experiences of my life."

"Can I kiss you?" Jack asks.

Mr. Eliot doesn't answer, but his eyes say yes.

Jack grips Mr. Eliot's arm, guides him into a shadow on the stoop, and kisses him.

Mr. Eliot jerks away as if hit by a jolt of lightning, but then he kisses Jack back, seeking another dose of electricity.

"Would you like to come up for a cup of tea?" Mr. Eliot asks.

"Tea? Hmm. Are you trying to keep me up all night?"

Mr. Eliot smiles. "I might."

Jack looks him over. Is he weighing his options? "Yes, I would like to come up for tea, but not yet. Not tonight. Not until you do something for me."

"Oh, yeah, and what would that be?"

"Come to George's tomorrow night, for the poetry reading. Read that poem I found in your pocket."

"What?" Mr. Eliot shakes his head. He was not expecting this. "Why would I—what are you trying to do?"

"You can't keep hiding."

Mr. Eliot steps back, crosses his arms. "I'm not hiding. I'm not ready."

"You're talented."

"How would you know?" Mr. Eliot shoots back.

"I know what I like," Jack says, disarming him. Jack always has kind eyes, but right now they seem even kinder.

"Think about it?" Jack pleads.

Mr. Eliot nods.

"Good night," Jack says before placing a kiss on Mr. Eliot's cheek. "And I really do hope to see you there tomorrow."

"Good night, Jack."

Mr. Eliot purses his lips. He has feelings for Jack, but at the moment, he doesn't feel an urge to puts his lips on him.

Jack swims away on the sea of cobblestones. No, Jack is not swimming. He's walking on water. He's Mr. Eliot's savior, but currently, Mr. Eliot can only focus on persecuting him. Mr. Eliot's not ready. Why would Jack try to push him like that? *Tomorrow? It's too soon.*

Mr. Eliot notices the gargoyles leering down at him, judging him. They spied what he did in the shadow with Jack. There's no shadow too dark for them to see. Mr. Eliot needs to shield himself from their view. But going into his flat will not do. Because even if he goes in there, there's always someone else looking down on him from above.

11

Wood. Mr. Eliot is surrounded by wood. He's boxed in. Is he in a coffin? Has he died? Mr. Eliot could die. He senses God's hands around his neck, strangling him. He's going to hell. It's bad enough that Mr. Eliot has these thoughts, but he acted on them. He sinned. *I'm a sinner.* And he cannot get away with merely praying for this sin. No, he must confess it. Mr. Eliot sits in a wooden confessional waiting for a priest to arrive.

He says a small prayer. It's one he's said before. It's one he's said many times. "Lord Jesus, for too long I've kept you out of my life. I know that I am a sinner and that I cannot save myself . . ."

Where is that priest? Mr. Eliot needs to confess his crime. He needs God to hear how sorry he is. He wants to repent. He wants to be absolved. *Where is that priest?* Mr. Eliot can't wait any longer. He does his best impression of Christ and bursts out of his wooden tomb.

"Where is the bloody priest!" he shouts into the nave. The question echoes into the heavens, multiplies, and bounces back, each shock wave digging itself into his ears like a nail. Mr. Eliot is shocked. He shouted. In His church. Mr. Eliot assumed he was familiar with shame. *Yes, shame.* He knew it well. But he did not know it like this. Mr. Eliot looks around and exhales a sigh of relief. *No one is there.* No one heard him blaspheme in His church.

"He's gone home for the evening, but he'll be back tomorrow," a young novitiate says, popping his head around a pedestal, a broom in his hand.

Mr. Eliot develops stigmata in his cheeks, or at least they look like stigmata. They're beet red. Mr. Eliot can't bring himself to say thank you to the novitiate. All he can do is slither out of His church like the snake he is. *Stigmata. Ha.* God would never impress His divine favor upon someone like him.

God doesn't dole out His favor to those who don't deserve it. *Please, God,* Mr. Eliot thinks. *Please shine your favor on me.* Mr. Eliot wants to be a writer, not a banker.

But then again, most people don't want to be what they are. Vivienne doesn't want to be a barista. She wants to be one of the couples that come into her cafe. She wants to be carefree. She wants to be in love. But how will she ever be in love as long as she stays behind that counter? There's nothing wrong with the counter, per se. It does what it's designed to do. It separates her from everyone else.

Mr. Eliot enters.

"What will it be?" she asks.

"Coffee, please." There are dark circles around Mr. Eliot's bloodshot eyes.

Vivienne notices, places her hand on his shoulder. "Are you all right?"

Mr. Eliot shakes his head. He's far from all right. "I didn't sleep last night."

"Tom!"

Mr. Eliot shudders at the sound of his name, or at least how boisterously it's been shouted. Bertrand enters in the manner he normally does, with much fanfare and noise.

"Tom! Tom! Tom! So glad to see you here!" He slams his hand on the counter. "One carafe!" Then he turns to Mr. Eliot with a look of manufactured surprise and delight on his face.

"Tom! Tom! Let's sit! Let me introduce you to Ezra."

He pulls a couple of chairs around a small table, motions for them to be seated.

"Tom, Ezra. Ezra, Tom. There, now you're acquainted and we can get down to business."

"Ezra? Ezra Pound?" Mr. Eliot asks.

Bertrand slaps Ezra across his shoulder. "It seems we've found one of your fans."

Yes, indeed they have. Mr. Eliot has heard of Ezra Pound, an ex-pat poet like him, but truthfully, he didn't imagine he looked like this. Perhaps it's his mustache, or perhaps it's his hair. It looks like a bird's nest. It's wiry, like a man's chest. No, not a bird's nest, more like a hat made of his own hair, standing straight up in the air. Should Mr. Eliot ask about it? No, he wouldn't dare. But does he comb it that way? No, Ezra's styling seems more laissez-faire.

"Bertrand was right to bring you to my attention. Your work has a lot of potential," Ezra extols. "It might even be better than Auden's."

"I was sure I detected something," Bertrand says with the surety of a man who gets to be sure about most things in his life.

Mr. Eliot can hardly believe his ears. And he can hardly believe his eyes either. He rubs them vigorously, which only causes them to get redder.

"Great potential," Ezra continues. "Some of the best I've seen . . . even if it's somewhat unpolished and rough . . . I'm sorry, what's wrong with your eyes?"

"Exactly what I thought!" Vivienne interrupts, plopping down three cups of coffee on the table.

"I thought I asked for a carafe," Bertrand berates.

"Since when have you *asked* for anything? You order," Vivienne says, irate. "I'll start you on a cup and work up to a carafe. How about that?" Her anger deflates and she turns to Ezra. "And that's exactly what I thought about Tom. It's the peepers. Gives it away every time."

"The peepers?" Ezra asks.

"His eyes," Vivienne explains. "Those deep, dark, mysterious eyes. He's a poet, no question about it."

Mr. Eliot's bloodshot eyes thank her for the courtesy she's done him.

"Thanks, Viv," Bertrand says curtly, releasing her, informing her she's no longer needed.

Vivienne nods, returns to the counter, back where she's wanted.

"How far might he go?" Bertrand asks.

"That's impossible to say," Ezra expounds. "Talent is only part of the equation. Great art requires dedication, courage, sacrifice."

"But if I did those things?" Mr. Eliot asks, suddenly part of the conversation they've been having about him.

Ezra gazes at Mr. Eliot, sizing him up. Mr. Eliot has seen men size up things in this manner before, but he hasn't seen it happen to this extent since a state fair in Missouri when he observed a rancher evaluate a prized heifer.

"Maybe," Ezra says, squinting his eyes. "I'd like to work with you."

Mr. Eliot's heart skips a beat, but then stops when Ezra asks, "How are you in front of a crowd?"

"Oh, I don't—"

"Perfect!" Bertrand bellows. "They're doing a poetry reading here tonight! That'll be a good start!" Bertrand looks at Mr. Eliot, but he's not looking for an answer. No, men like Bertrand don't look to men like Mr. Eliot for answers. He turns his attention to Ezra. "Do I have time to go get Hemingway?" But he doesn't wait for a response from Ezra either. "I'll go get him," he says as he bolts out of the cafe.

"I couldn't," Mr. Eliot says to Ezra, wrinkling his brow and rubbing his eyes.

"You can. You're ready," Ezra consoles.

"Ready or not, here we come!"

The Bright Young Things descend upon the cafe.

"Absinthe! Absinthe all around!" Auden hollers.

Vivienne grimaces. "We have coffee and tea."

“Glad I brought my own then!” Auden says as he drinks from his tit flask. He’s drunk. “Have the readings begun yet?” he asks.

Joe nabs Auden’s flask, takes a swig. “They have now that we’re here.”

Auden stands up on a chair. The room goes quiet.

He recites:

> My thoughts wander
>
> from sex to verse to God without periods. Without differentiation.

But wait, isn’t that the same poem he read before? The audience grows wary, confused by the déjà vu.

> If I do evil . . .

“You do evil if you repeat the same poem!” Mary points out.

“From verse to verse with nothing new to say!” John rejoins.

“Boo!” Mary and John shout, cupping their hands to their mouths and pumping their fists, riling up the crowd.

“‘My God, I am bewildered,’” Auden says innocently.

“That’s another line from his poem. Boo!” Mary says with conviction.

“Boo!” The audience joins in, sentencing him to his fate.

Auden’s irate, steps down from the chair.

“Who’s next up on the gallows?” Mary jokes.

“Perhaps Hemingway would like a go!” Bertrand bawls as he enters the cafe, Ernest Hemingway in tow.

“I think Tom should go!” Ezra announces.

Mr. Eliot fingers the paper with his poem. “I can’t.”

Ezra is surer than Mr. Eliot has ever been. “You’re ready. You must.”

Mr. Eliot stands up to leave. Hemingway pats him on the back. "Way to take the bull by the horns!"

Mr. Eliot shakes his head. "I'm sorry. I thought I could." He starts toward the door, but Vivienne stops him.

"I'll go!" she says to the room but then leans in to whisper to Mr. Eliot, "I need your help. Please."

Mr. Eliot swallows. Should he help her? But it looks like he doesn't have time to decide. Vivienne is already leading him to a small platform in front of the audience.

"About time someone used the stage," Vivienne says, glaring at the Bright Young Things.

She glances down at Mr. Eliot's poem in his hands. "May I?"

Mr. Eliot nods. Vivienne gently takes his poem from him.

She scans it, turns to the crowd.

"So, this is a repeat-after-me poem. First everyone . . ."

She reads:

> Madame Sosostris, famous clairvoyante

Vivienne coaxes the audience with her hands to repeat, "Madame Sosostris, famous clairvoyante."

She turns to Mr. Eliot. "Now, your turn. Repeat after me . . ."

She reads:

> Is known to be the wisest woman in Europe.

Mr. Eliot hesitates, but states, "Is known to be the wisest woman in Europe."

Vivienne sidles up next to him, whispers, "And now, together with me."

They read:

> With a wicked pack of cards.

Then Vivienne hands the poem to Mr. Eliot, steps off the stage, and takes a seat in the front row, ready to take in the show.

There's no spotlight, but Mr. Eliot feels trapped in one, or at least he would feel that way, but Vivienne's eyes. They're so . . . lovely, so gay.

Mr. Eliot reads:

> Here, said she, is your card.
> The drowned Phoenician Sailor,
> Those are pearls that were his eyes. Look!
> Here is Belladonna, the Lady of the Rocks,
> The lady of situations.
> Here is the man with three staves,
> and here the Wheel,
> And here is the one-eyed merchant, and this card,
> Which is blank, is something he carries on his back,
> Which I am forbidden to see.
> I do not find The Hanged Man.
> Fear death by water.
> I see crowds of people, walking around in a ring.

Mr. Eliot looks up at the audience. Applause. Wild and thunderous applause. Mr. Eliot's body relaxes, like he's just paid his taxes. Relief. Pure and utter relief. Mr. Eliot's modesty can't contain the smile on his face. If only Jack had seen him. Wait, if Jack didn't see him, does that mean he has to go again when Jack arrives? He can't go again. Once was enough. But all Mr. Eliot's thoughts are all for naught.

"Woo!" Jack screams from the audience. "Encore. Encore!"

Mr. Eliot laughs, relieved. "I'm afraid there's no more." He steps off the stage. Vivienne tries to congratulate him, but the tide is pulling Mr. Eliot to another shore. He walks up to Jack expectantly. "So, now what's in store?"

Jack grins. "Don't look at me that way. I'm not your whore."

"I read the poem. You said you'd come over. You swore," Mr. Eliot says with newfound confidence, channeling Bertrand.

Jack squints, not sure what to make of this shift. "Come to the club tonight at ten. Or be a bore."

Jack turns and leaves. Vivienne is pulled away by a customer, off to another chore.

Mr. Eliot stands there, his eyes on the door.

12

Red. *Why does the door have to be red?* Red is such a cliché color, especially for this type of establishment. Mr. Eliot sits on a bench across the street from the Pansy Club. He watches the pansies enter their club, dressed to the nines with their cravats and blouses. Mr. Eliot could never dress like that. But is that a new pocket square in his jacket? Yes, it is. A red one. Mr. Eliot hasn't dressed to the nines, he's dressed to the ten. 10 o'clock, that is. The time when Jack said Mr. Eliot should meet him. He's dressed up for the occasion, however slightly.

Tick. Tock. Tick. Tock. Mr. Eliot's heart races to the beat of the clock. He hears the minute hand ticking away in the clock at the top of the church next to the club. The Pansy Club is adjacent to Hammond's Church, a gray, stone Renaissance-style church with a large, white window in the shape of a wheel. Redemption is so close to this haven for heathens who will never get into heaven.

Mr. Eliot waits for the minute hand to turn to ten. 9:59. It's almost time. Almost time to chime. Mr. Eliot fingers his crucifix. Tick. Tock. Tick. Tock. The clock makes an unnaturally loud tock as the minute hand advances.

Gears rumble. Bells play. The street transforms. Crumbles like clay. Then walls rise around him. It's time to put on a play.

Mr. Eliot surveys the wreckage. He's seated in the center of a cathedral. It must have been spectacular once, but now it's in ruins. Moonlight streams through holes in the roof. There are no pews, only piles of kindling. Defilers have beheaded a statue of a pope, but they seem to have taken pity on him and placed his head in his outstretched hands. Purple robes pool on the floor like water. No, they pool like paint. The oily blacks of the night mix with oily purples in this painting come to life.

"Sinner!" a man booms at Mr. Eliot, startling him.

Mr. Eliot whips around to find Reverend Hammond, a pompous preacher, flanked by a horde of gospel singers, all ready to whip him.

Mr. Eliot looks around, then points to himself. "Me?"

"Yes! I'm talking to you!" Reverend Hammond says loud enough for heaven to hear him.

Reverend Hammond struts in front of his singers, marches toward Mr. Eliot. "Oh, woe! Oh, woe and damnation!"

Mr. Eliot shakes his head. "Go away! You're not real. This isn't where I'm supposed to be."

Reverend Hammond squeezes Mr. Eliot's arm. It feels real.

"It's not about where you are," Reverend Hammond says. "It's about where you're going."

"Praise be!"

"Let Him into your heart!"

"He's knocking!"

The gospel singers back up the reverend's message. He leans toward Mr. Eliot, whispers in his ear, "Hear me, your pastor. Hear the choir!"

"Hear us!"

"All you got to do is listen!"

"Take a knee and hear it!"

Mr. Eliot tries to back away, but Reverend Hammond brings him in close. "Forget your objections."

"Say bye-bye!"

"Too-da-loo!"

"Au revoir!"

Reverend Hammond holds Mr. Eliot's head in his hands, looks at him lovingly. "It's a sin. Don't begin on the road to damnation."

Mr. Eliot wriggles out of Reverend Hammond's grasp. He runs to the back of the church, finds a locked door. He turns around, cornered by the purple parade of parishioners.

"You don't understand!" Mr. Eliot says. "I'm not hurting anyone. No one even knows."

Reverend Hammond shakes his head. "Think!"

"You better think!"

"Open up that noggin!"

"You know He knows!"

"Think of your Father," Reverend Hammond pleads. "Upset by confessions of your sin!"

Mr. Eliot pushes his way past them. He's sweating, gasping for air. He scans the church for an exit and finds, "Mr. Prufrock!"

Mr. J. Alfred Prufrock hovers overhead in a dilapidated choir loft.

"What are you doing here?" Mr. Eliot asks.

"We needed a little help to get you on the right track, Mr. Eliot."

"But this man, he's a maniac!"

Mr. Prufrock crosses his arms. "You didn't listen to me so I had to try another tack."

"No one needs to know," Mr. Eliot pleads. "I'll be careful. I have needs."

"There are needs you need, and needs that bleed, Mr. Eliot."

"I don't need a screed. And besides, He'd still love me if He found out."

Mr. Prufrock doesn't respond, but Mr. Eliot knows what he would say if he did. He lowers his chin to his chest, and then points it toward Mr. Prufrock, hoping to God the answer to his question is yes. "He'd still love me, wouldn't He?"

Reverend Hammond spins Mr. Eliot around. "Cry for your mother. Her lonely depression! She sees your sin as you walk to damnation!"

"Oh, God, don't tell her!" Mr. Eliot begs.

"Don't take His name in vain in my church! What would your neighbors think?"

"Oh, God. Please don't tell them."

Reverend Hammond and the gospel singers back Mr. Eliot into a corner.

"Ridin' the road? Fly from the road!" Reverend Hammond demands. "And you can forget about that poetry career, boy. They don't let sinners like you out in front of decent folk."

Mr. Eliot covers his head with his hands.

"No!"

Red. Reverend Hammond saw red. And now, again, so does Mr. Eliot.

The red door of the Pansy Club stares back at him, and so do some of its parishioners.

Parishioners . . . ha, the men entering the Pansy Club only get on their knees for one thing, and that's not to pray.

Mr. Eliot removes his hands from his head. He looks disturbed, guilty. Mr. Eliot swallows hard, leaps up, and marches down the street, leaving the red door behind.

"Hey! Where are you going?" Jack shouts.

Mr. Eliot turns around, sees a bouquet of lilacs in Jack's hand. They're fresh. He hasn't manhandled them like Mr. Eliot did.

Jack hunches, sits down.

Mr. Eliot eyes the lilacs. He doesn't want to go back, but he's unwilling to leave.

One step, then another. Then a few more. Mr. Eliot's feet graze the cobblestones as he plods back to the bench.

"I thought tonight it was you standing me up," Mr. Eliot says.

"Stand you up? The clock tower just rang ten. I can almost hear the bells ringing in my ears."

The bells. Mr. Eliot can still hear them ringing. The church. Mr. Eliot can still feel the stinging.

"These are for you," Jack says, indicating the bouquet. "I thought you'd like to see how beautiful they can be if you don't strangle them to death."

"Well, they've already been cut, so they're still dead," Mr. Eliot says, perhaps a bit too curtly. "I'm sorry. I shouldn't have said that."

"No. It's okay."

"They're dying much more slowly, though."

"No, really. It's okay," Jack says. "We're all dying slowly, Tom. Still, it's nice when someone appreciates us."

"Beautiful," Mr. Eliot says, the word bursting out of his mouth. "The flowers are beautiful . . . and so . . . was that."

"You're beautiful," Jack compliments.

"You're . . . I like you." Mr. Eliot bobs his head as if he's realizing this for the first time.

"It's time to go inside," Jack purrs. He stands. But Mr. Eliot doesn't. Mr. Eliot sits there, frozen in fear. Jack's face sags. His eyes, usually so full of light, become duller. He places the bouquet of lilacs on Mr. Eliot's lap.

"Come in when you're ready," Jack says consolingly, although it's not clear whether he's consoling Mr. Eliot or himself.

Mr. Eliot watches as Jack enters the club. He sits and watches. Sit and watch. Sit and watch. All Mr. Eliot does is sit and watch. He sits at the window, and watches. He watches and tries to write. He tries to write, but he can't, because he hasn't lived, and therefore, there's no life in his words. If not for his own sake, perhaps he should go into the club for the sake of his writing. *That's a good idea.* He's not doing this because it's what he needs. It's what his writing needs.

Mr. Eliot stares at the red door. Jack has taken him this far, but now it's up to him. He must take a stand. Mr. Eliot leans forward, places his weight on the two feet in front of him, and then pushes off the ground. All he's done is stand, but it was a Herculean task.

He crosses the street. It's now or never. He's ready.

"Ready or not, here we come!"

Mr. Eliot looks down the street expecting to see the Bright Young

Things, but what he sees is much more sinister. There's a storm brewing. There's lightning. White bolts streak across the red armbands of a red mob of Fascists who join ranks around the Pansy Club.

They shout and sing:

Comrades, the voices of the dead battalions
Of those who fell that Britain might be Great
Join in our song, for they still march in spirit with us
And urge us on to gain the Fascist state!

We're of their blood, and spirit of their spirit,
Sprung from that soil for whose dear sake they bled
Against vested powers, Red Front, and massed ranks of reaction
We lead the fight for freedom and for bread

The streets are still, the final struggle's ended;
Flushed with the fight we proudly hail the dawn!
See, over all the streets the Fascist banners waving
Triumphant standards of our race reborn!

Poetry. The lyrics are almost poetic. Perhaps Mr. Eliot might enjoy it if he didn't recognize their true purpose.

Mr. Eliot wants to vomit. And in this, unlike so many things in Mr. Eliot's life, he's successful in getting what he wants. The insides of Mr. Eliot's stomach make a grand entrance on the street before him. He announces it with the most awful wrenching noise, giving the Fascists the reception they deserve.

A crowd of curious club-goers are drawn out by their singing, drawn out by their shouts. One man who comes out is Jack. He came out to hear more, but he's driven inside when the Fascists begin their encore. They throw rocks, bottles, and bricks. Windows break.

"Run, faggots!"

"How'd you like a little sip out of this bottle!"

"Want to see what a real man looks like?"

A Fascist yanks Mr. Eliot by the collar, but he jabs the lilacs in his face, making him holler. People scream and flee. So does Mr. Eliot, leaving the Fascists and the lilacs behind. He runs down the street. Around a corner. Running fast so his mom doesn't become a mourner. His breaths are quick and shallow. He passes an alley, and finds an ally.

"Tom!"

Mr. Eliot sees Jack and a few other men spew out a back door.

"Thank God I found you," Jack exhales.

"Are you—?"

"I'm fine. There were too many to fight, so we ran out the back."

"Where do you think you're going?"

Thump. Thump. Ah! Oof.

Mr. Eliot can't see inside the club, but he's heard the beat of that beating before. Tick. Tock. Tick. Tock. Mr. Eliot's clock tocks fast.

Jack starts down the alley. "Follow me!"

"Where are we going?"

Jack shakes his head. "Does it matter?"

Thump. Thump. Ah! Oof.

Mr. Eliot takes after Jack. They run. Down the street. Around a different corner. Mr. Eliot runs with Jack, no longer a loner.

Clack. Clack. Their feet slap against the cobblestones. Quick. Quick. They're running so fast. Mr. Eliot will be sick. He wants to vomit again, but he has nothing left to give this street.

Jack slows down to a stride. He looks over his shoulder, eager to find a place to hide.

"Where are we?" Mr. Eliot asks.

"We're almost there," Jack answers absentmindedly.

"And where is there?"

Jack doubles over, the stress of the evening's events causing his torso to collapse.

"Are you okay?" Mr. Eliot asks.

"We're fine . . . I'm fine."

Mr. Eliot furrows his brow. "I should have fought back. I should have helped."

"You'd have a lot to show for it . . . beaten up for no reason."

"They can't just . . . do whatever they want to whoever they want."

"Oh, can't they?" Jack says, cocking his head to the side. "Seems like they just did."

"Still," Mr. Eliot says, more in recognition than agreement.

Jack caresses Mr. Eliot's arm. "If you make a sacrifice, make sure it means something. Make it important."

"It would have been important. It would have been to save you."

Jack shakes his head. "Something more important. Achieve something. Fighting the Fascists wouldn't have achieved anything."

Mr. Eliot spots a trickle of blood on Jack's forehead.

"You're bleeding!"

Jack touches the wound, looks at his finger. "So I am," he simpers. "I didn't notice. Must have been the glass."

Mr. Eliot squints his eyes. Jack is oddly nonchalant about his injury.

"Let's get you to a hospital."

"It's nothing," Jack responds.

"We need to get you some help. Get you bandaged up."

Jack nods toward the building beside them. "I have alcohol and bandages at my place."

"This is . . . your place?" Mr. Eliot asks.

"Sure is."

"And do you have everything you need? I could go get something."

Jack shakes his head, takes a step forward toward Mr. Eliot. "No. As I said, I have everything I need. Bandages for my forehead. Alcohol for us." Jack smiles, but then his face sours. He's mulling something.

"Would you like to come up?"

Mr. Eliot nods the tiniest of nods. *Oh, God.* What has Mr. Eliot agreed to? What level of hell will he proceed to?

"Are you sure?" Jack asks. He's been burned by Mr. Eliot before, but Jack is a moth, and Mr. Eliot is his flame.

"Let's go."

13

A nude man greets Mr. Eliot. He lies there, sprawled out before him, teasing him, taunting him, wanting him. The man occupies a frame on Jack's wall. Jack has many such men in his flat, several abstract paintings of nude men. How brash. How careless. How . . . Jack. It's a bachelor flat much the same as Mr. Eliot's, but here there are paintings, a vase with fresh flowers on a table, and a few lamps with cravats strewn over them. It's a very masculine flat, but in the most artistic and feminine way possible.

"I could use a drink. Scotch okay?" Jack asks and then pours.

Mr. Eliot looks at Jack's bookcase. You can tell a lot about a man by looking at his library, and Mr. Eliot wants to know all about Jack. Most of the books are leather-bound. *That's a good sign.* And there are hundreds of them. *An even better one.*

Jack has *Ulysses* by James Joyce; *In Search of Lost Time* by Marcel Proust; *Don Quixote* by Miguel de Cervantes; *Moby Dick* by Herman Melville. There are a few plays by Shakespeare, *Antony and Cleopatra*, *Hamlet*, *Coriolanus,* and *The Tempest*. There's *The Odyssey* by Homer; Dante's *Divine Comedy*; a book of poems by William Blake; *Crome Yellow* by Aldous Huxley; a libretto for Wagner's *Tristan und Isolde*; John Webster's play *The White Devil*; two plays by Thomas Middleton, *A Game at Chess* and *Women Beware Women*; Milton's *Paradise Lost*; Oliver Goldsmith's *The Vicar of Wakefield*; *A Glimpse Into*

Chaos by Herman Hesse; Ovid's *Metamorphoses*; *Great British Poets*; and the Bible. But that's not all Jack has on his shelf. That's only the selection Mr. Eliot could scan while Jack poured the drinks.

"What are you doing? Reading my secrets?"

Jack hands Mr. Eliot a Scotch.

"Secrets?" Mr. Eliot asks, but then realizes Jack is being cheeky. "Do you always keep your secrets on full display?"

"Only when I want someone to see them."

Mr. Eliot's eyes glance over to the bookcase. "All you're missing are the Upanishads."

Jack smiles. "I can't give everything away on the first date." Jack clinks glasses and says, "Cheers," before Mr. Eliot reacts to what he just said. *Date?*

Mr. Eliot's eyes dance over Jack's body. Jack's beautiful body. Jack's bloody body.

"Your shirt's got blood all over it," Mr. Eliot says flatly.

Jack removes his shirt.

"Easily solved."

Mr. Eliot tenses. Jack's hands are around his neck. But, no, those aren't Jack's hands. Jack's hands are at his side. Someone else must be strangling him.

"The bleeding's stopped, but we need to get your cut disinfected."

Jack holds up his glass. "I'm working on that."

"Where are your bandages?"

Jack hands Mr. Eliot his drink. "Hold this."

Jack ducks into the bathroom, returns with a bottle of rubbing alcohol, a washcloth, and the bandages. He plops down in one chair. Mr. Eliot takes a seat on another. Jack has two chairs in his flat, one for him, and one for Mr. Eliot.

"Can I get that back?" Jack asks as he holds his hand out for his Scotch. He takes a big swig and then pours the rubbing alcohol on his forehead. He winces in pain, but then applies a washcloth before replacing it with a bandage. He holds one end of the bandage on his forehead and then hands the other end to Mr. Eliot.

"Do you mind?"

"No, not at all."

Mr. Eliot wraps Jack's head. He goes round and round until he reaches the end of the roll. "You look like one of the mummies in the museum."

"Which one?"

"The British Museum," Mr. Eliot intones. Which other museum would he be talking about?

"No," Jack laughs. "Which mummy?"

"Oh, I, uh . . . maybe . . . maybe . . . one of the Roman ones?"

"Is that a question?"

Mr. Eliot smiles. "No, definitely one of the Roman ones, the ones with the painted eyes."

Jack scoffs. "Are you trying to say something about my makeup?"

"Do you—I, uh, didn't know you wore makeup," Mr. Eliot stammers.

"I don't," Jack says coyly. "But it's good to know you haven't been looking at my eyes."

"Brownish green," Mr. Eliot blurts out.

"What?"

"Your eyes," Mr. Eliot continues. "Most people probably say you have brown eyes, but there are little flecks of green in them, especially when light hits them. So, they're brownish green. Not brown."

Tick. Tock. Tick. Tock. Brown. Green. *What does it matter?* Why does it matter what color Jack's eyes are? Jack probably thinks Mr. Eliot is a creep. He is a creep.

Jack places a hand on Mr. Eliot's chest.

"Your heart's beating fast." Jack swallows. "That was dangerous, but exciting, wasn't it? Back there at the club?"

His hand lingers, no longer clocking the beat, but trying to determine who it tocks for. "But we're safe here."

Mr. Eliot places his hand over Jack's.

"I know what you need," Jack intimates.

"What . . . and what is that?"

Jack stands, walks over to his bedside table, and lights a candle.

"A little candlelight."

Mr. Eliot exhales. Jack looks so lovely in the flickering glow, but then again, Jack looks lovely in any light. Jack turns down the covers on his bed. Turns down the sheet. Turns off the lamp, leaving them with only the flicker of the candle.

Jack carries the candle over to Mr. Eliot, places it on the table next to him.

"Let me help you," Jack breathes.

Jack undresses Mr. Eliot slowly. First his jacket. Then his shirt, his shoes, and his pants. All that's left is Mr. Eliot's underwear and what's left of his propriety.

Jack leans in. Their lips are close. Jack kisses him briefly, dipping his toe into the water, seeing if it's warm, welcoming. Mr. Eliot is passive, uncertain, trembling.

Jack whispers, "You're beautiful."

Mr. Eliot looks away, embarrassed.

"I—I'm not," Mr. Eliot mumbles. "But you are."

Jack leads Mr. Eliot to his bed. Mr. Eliot starts to climb in, but then Jack reminds him.

"Aren't you forgetting something?"

What? What could it be? Mr. Eliot has come this far. Jack has led him to the door again, but he's forgotten something.

Jack glances down at Mr. Eliot's underwear.

"Oh, yes, those," Mr. Eliot says as he shimmies them off.

Now it's Jack's turn. He undoes one button at a time, unfastening with a fancy flick, like a dancer finishing their footwork with a flourish to show you how skilled they are, how much they're in control. But with Jack, there is no dance. No, he's only taking off his pants. All that's left are his skivvies.

Mr. Eliot inhales sharply. "Aren't you forgetting something?"

Jack smiles, removes his underwear. "Better?"

Mr. Eliot nods. He's seen naked men before, but he's never seen one like Jack. It's not that Jack is fit, which he is. Mr. Eliot has seen nude athletic men, some in pictures and some in real life. But he's never seen a naked man standing before him with the same hunger he has in his eyes.

Jack climbs into bed with Mr. Eliot, caresses him. He kisses Mr. Eliot deeply, passionately. Only the flicker of the candle lights these lovers, but Mr. Eliot could swear it was a sunset. There's no air between them, and there's no air in Mr. Eliot's lungs, but he doesn't care.

Jack pulls back for a second. "We don't have to do anything you don't want to do."

"No, I want to," Mr. Eliot starts before wondering, "but isn't this all of it?"

Jack laughs. *Is he serious? He must surely . . .* but then Jack sees the earnest look of innocence on Mr. Eliot's face. He's sweet.

Jack goes in for another round of kissing. And then it's Mr. Eliot's turn to pull back.

"What should I do?"

Jack puts his finger to his lips. "Shhh. I'll show you."

His hand wades down to Mr. Eliot's crotch.

"Oh, that's—"

"Shhh."

Stars. Mr. Eliot remembers seeing stars. Was Jack teaching him astrology? He can almost remember seeing The Big Dipper, Aries, Cassiopeia, Cepheus, Circinus, Fornax, Hercules, Orion, Pavo, and Taurus. But Mr. Eliot smiles. Jack showed him many things last night, all the things he never learned at Harvard, but none of it involved astrology.

It had been a long time since Mr. Eliot had a good show and tell, although with Jack it was more of a show, don't tell. And how could Jack have told him about what awaited him? The purpose of poetry is to bring forth the beauty of the world with words. There are many other ways to explore the beauties of the world, though, and in this particular one, Jack was Mr. Eliot's most winning professor. Mr. Eliot liked his class so much he wishes he could get a Ph.D. in Jack's offerings. Mr. Eliot had studied for his Ph.D. in philosophy at Harvard. Again, that's not something he likes to reveal about himself this quickly. His reticence might have something to do with the fact that although he completed all his coursework, Mr. Eliot never returned to take the oral exam, and was thus not a doctorate. In that regard, he's more like a nurse, still capable but without the qualifications of a doctor. He came to England with his tail tucked between his legs, licking his wounds instead of bandaging them. But with Jack, there is no exam, oral or otherwise, that Mr. Eliot would ever skip.

Mr. Eliot's sleepy thoughts settle as he awakens fully and finds himself momentarily disoriented, but then he realizes where he is, lying naked in Jack's bed, his head on Jack's stomach, the dawn dappling through Jack's decorative, tastefully striped curtains. He smiles and doesn't move. No, Mr. Eliot will not move from this spot as long as he can help it. The light stripes the lovers, making them look like hairless, beige zebras. Is a zebra a black horse with white stripes? Or is it a white horse with black stripes? No, a zebra is both black *and* white striped. It does not begin as one and transition to another. It is another thing entirely. Trying to put the logic of a horse on his hide does no one any good. Mr. Eliot wonders whether he's a horse with stripes or a zebra. Has he been something else all along? Is he only now comfortable seeing himself as a zebra?

Jack is sitting up against the headboard, reading Mr. Eliot's journal. He notices Mr. Eliot stirring and gives him a little tap on the head with it. "Good morning."

Mr. Eliot twists his neck, but keeps pressed against Jack's stomach. "Hey, that's my journal."

"Is it?" Jack asks coyly. "I was wondering why you would keep someone else's journal in your jacket pocket."

Mr. Eliot's finger grazes Jack's stomach. "Is that why you wanted to undress me? To get to my journal?"

"It would have been a good enough reason. You have some good stuff in here."

Mr. Eliot reaches up slowly, playfully snatches the journal out of Jack's hands. "Thank you, but it's private."

Jack's eyes go wide. *Did he really just do that?* He smirks as he pinches Mr. Eliot under the covers, making him squeal. "More private than this?"

Mr. Eliot contorts, laughs as Jack tickles him.

"Oh, you rogue!" Mr. Eliot screams as he twists away from Jack. "This intrusion, now seeming sweet, will turn to bitter gall."

"You'd be a good Tybalt," Jack responds. "You have the passion for it."

Mr. Eliot smiles. Jack glances at the journal.

"Your journal. It's all so . . . deep. Don't you ever write anything more fun?"

Mr. Eliot scoffs, but then bolts up on his knees and pretends the bed is a bow. "Now when they were three weeks at sea. Columbo he grew rooty. He took his cock in both hands and swore it was a beauty."

Jack bursts out in laughter, but Mr. Eliot isn't done.

"The cabin boy appeared on deck and smeared the mast-o," he continues, and then flops on top of Jack, humping him. "Columbo grasped him by the balls and buggered him in the ass-o."

Jack is beside himself. "That's more my level."

Mr. Eliot glances over at Jack's bookcase. "It seems you operate on many levels."

Jack smiles. "And one day, we'll get you up to mine."

"Last night was amazing."

"Not bad for your first time," Jack says slyly, cozying up to Mr. Eliot and giving him a quick peck on the lips before snatching the journal back. "But we'll work on that."

Jack starts writing in it.

"What do you mean 'not bad?'" Mr. Eliot pouts before he realizes he has something else to pout about. "And, hey, what are you writing?"

"Nothing," Jack lies. "Passing grade, but definitely an 'A' for effort."

"That's my journal, not some public guest book."

Jack flings the journal over to Mr. Eliot.

"There," Jack says as the book plops on his chest. "Now your journal includes the poem you wrote for me."

"How do you know I wrote it for you?" Mr. Eliot teases.

"Ha!" Jack tosses back.

Mr. Eliot smiles. He looks at Jack, the striped sunlight lingering on his chest. Mr. Eliot would like to linger on Jack's chest, but then he remembers something in the back of his brain that tells him he needs to leave. *I don't belong here.* Mr. Eliot starts dressing. First, his underwear, then his pants, buttoning each button, but not with a quick dramatic flick. No. Mr. Eliot buttons his shirt. He thinks he's going to be sick. *What have I done?*

"Where are you going?" Jack asks.

"I'm still a little uncertain about all this."

"About what?"

Mr. Eliot considers telling Jack the truth, but realizes he can't say it to his face. "About . . . everything."

He tries to put on his jacket, but Jack stops him.

Jack holds Mr. Eliot's shoulders in his hands, unbuttons the buttons Mr. Eliot has just fastened. "Listen, it's obvious you have a tremendous gift here. You can't hide it under a bushel. You need to take it as far as it can go. You need to do whatever it takes."

Jack slides Mr. Eliot's shirt off, unbuttons his pants. "I'll be here for you. I'll help you."

Mr. Eliot hugs Jack. He holds him close, shuts his eyes. "Thank you, Jack."

It's a tender moment, but then Jack pushes Mr. Eliot back onto the bed.

Mr. Eliot needs more tenderizing.

"Don't thank me just yet."

14

Books. Rows and rows of books. All of Mr. Eliot's friends are here: the couple Robert and Elizabeth Browning, Emily Dickinson, John Keats, H.W. Longfellow, Gerard Manley Hopkins, Christina Rossetti, Percy Shelley, Lord Tennyson, Walt Whitman, William Wordsworth, and W.B. Yeats. He takes Emily by the hand and opens her. The smell of the paper greets his nostrils. It's a sweet smell, almost as good as Jack's sweat.

Mr. Eliot peruses a public library, but wishes he was back at Jack's, perusing Jack's library. *Perusing Jack.* He enjoys taking Jack into his hands. Enjoys reading him. But Jack can be so impenetrable sometimes. Mr. Eliot wants to know what Jack is thinking all the time, but Jack can only verbalize so much. And then there are the things they don't talk about but communicate in other means. Mr. Eliot delights in reading Jack's books. Of course, he's read most of them before, but he savors reading the very books that Jack himself has read. He likes to imagine Jack's eyes going from line to line. *What did Jack think when he read that one? Did he laugh here? I bet he did.* Jack has such a beautiful laugh.

Mr. Eliot has been spending a lot of time with him. In truth, he's been spending most of his free time with him, but sometimes they must part, if only to let their absence make their hearts grow fonder.

When that happens, Mr. Eliot returns to his first love, the library, where he roams the stacks, seeking a new, temporary infatuation.

Love. It's a word Mr. Eliot's been contemplating a lot lately. He thinks about a great deal of words with a great deal of frequency, but this is the one he's been tuning in to the most. Does he love Jack? It's hard to say. He's never been in love before. How can he identify something he's never experienced? All Mr. Eliot understands is that he'd like to feel this way a lot more. Perhaps that's why he let Jack talk him into giving a poem of his to Ezra.

Ezra Pound has been hounding Mr. Eliot for a full poem, but Mr. Eliot has resisted, until, that is, when Jack became involved. With Jack, he can't resist. Whatever Jack wants, Mr. Eliot is willing to supply. He can be himself with Jack.

Even when they go out to dinner, they don't have to stop being lovers. Even in public, they don't have to pretend they're with any other. Or at least, they don't have to pretend they're anything but proper English gentlemen, as long as they keep their discretions out of view. One of their favorite things is to go out to a fancy dinner at London's finest establishments, looking like penguins in their suits, not paupers evading pursuit. They remove their shoes beneath the table, cozying their feet next to one another. Like other birds in water, what appears calm and serene above the surface often belies frantic action below. They sip their Scotches, and sometimes put their feet in each other's crotches.

When they ride bicycles down the street, they sometimes pass an apple back and forth. To anyone observing, they look like good friends sharing a snack. But to Mr. Eliot, each bite he takes is out of Jack.

When Mr. Eliot emerges from the bank at the end of a hard day, Jack is there, to play. They often amuse themselves with this game where they pretend to be strangers. Jack joins Mr. Eliot, walking beside him in the throng of well-heeled men and their girlfriends, and then they nudge each other, trying to get the other to crack. The first one to crack has to carry the other on their back, as soon as they're out of sight of the well-heeled men, of course. Jack is usually the first to attack, and Mr. Eliot is usually the first to crack. He adores carrying Jack.

In so many other ways, Jack is carrying him, and Mr. Eliot savors returning the favor. Mr. Eliot carries so much weight on his shoulders. He can't stand the thought of Jack struggling. *Jack is so light.* It makes more sense for Mr. Eliot to carry him.

Today, as always, Jack makes the first move. He lets out a large, grotesque yawn, throwing his arms into the air, then grazes Mr. Eliot's backside on the way down.

Mr. Eliot laughs, but then catches himself and puts on his serious mask. Beating Jack is no easy task.

And saying no to Jack is no easy ask.

Mr. Eliot had taken a chance giving Ezra a poem of his. So, when it came time to find out whether his lady luck had been plucked, Mr. Eliot was happy to hear: "Here. Take a sip from my flask."

Mr. Eliot imbibes Ezra's liquid courage, hoping to conjure some of his own.

"Although I have to warn you," Ezra explains, "we might want something a little stronger."

Mr. Eliot shares a glance with Jack, shifts his stance.

Ezra plops a magazine on top of a table at George's. Their coffees shudder. Mr. Eliot stares intently at the magazine, ready for his dreams to shatter. It's a copy of *Poetry: A Magazine of Verse*. Pegasus flies through the "P" in "Poetry." There are many names on the cover. Mr. Eliot reads them frantically, hoping to see his, and dreading that if he doesn't, he'll feel like Medusa after Perseus cut off her head. It seems fitting to have Pegasus deliver the news. That legendary horse emerged from a pool of Medusa's blood after she was beheaded. Perhaps when Mr. Eliot fails to find his name, when his head is lopped off and the blood pools around his body, something equally impressive will spring from his macabre blob.

Edited by Harriet Monroe. Then the poets: Ajan Syrian, Arthur

Davison Ficke, Bliss Carman, Dorothy Dudley, Georgia Wood Pangborn, William Griffith, Skipwith Cannéll, T.S. Eliot.

That last one . . . that's him! There it is, right beside the name of his poem, "The Love Song of J. Alfred Prufrock." Mr. Eliot's eyes alternate between the two, trying to make sense of how both exist on the same page as these other poets . . . and in this magazine for poetry. Then he notices: "Chicago" down at the bottom of the cover. It says this magazine was printed in Chicago. Mr. Eliot chuckles. He's come to England to be noticed for his poetry, and now, his first poem is published in a magazine in Illinois. Chicago is only a state away from his native Missouri.

Harvard is three times as far from ol' St. Lou as Chicago, and London is many times more. He's come all this way, only for his breakthrough to happen close to home. Perhaps the farther he moves from where he came from, the more successful he'll become.

Ezra smiles. "I told you Harriet would come through."

Mr. Eliot squints his eyes. "But I thought nothing was definite."

"When is anything ever definite?" Ezra expounds. "She can be a fool sometimes, but she almost always listens in the end."

Mr. Eliot grimaces. "And I see that's where she placed me . . . at the end."

Jack shakes him out of his state. "She saved the best for last. Congratulations, Tom!"

"Yes, congratulations are in order," Ezra adds. "You can't retire from the bank yet, but it's a lot of money nonetheless."

"Yes, congratulations, Tom!" Vivienne shrills as she spills more tea into Mr. Eliot's teacup, and some on his lap.

"I'm sorry!" Vivienne yells. "I'm just so excited for you and your work." She touches Mr. Eliot on the shoulder. "You deserve it."

"And you serve it," Bertrand beckons, waving a teacup in the air.

"And why don't you show us why you deserve it, Tom?" Bertrand follows, a hint of hostility in his voice. "Stand up and read us all the famous lines from your famous poem."

"I'd hardly say it's famous," Mr. Eliot responds.

"But it will be," Jack joins in.

Vivienne holds her hands to her chest. "Oh, I'd love to hear you read it."

"Yes, a reading!" Bertrand bellows. "Be a good chap and give a reading of your surely soon-to-be-famous poem."

"Be a good chap and buy it, Bertie," Ezra snaps. "Everyone knows you can afford it. Don't be such a cheapskate."

Bertrand narrows his eyes. "I already have a copy."

"I have mine, too," Vivienne coos.

"Well, that's two," Ezra says flatly. "But now we need everyone else in this cafe, then everyone in London, and everyone in England to buy a copy. And maybe we'll sell it to some Krauts, too. Mr. Thomas Stearns Eliot is published. His poetry has a price. And everyone must pay for it."

Mr. Eliot smiles at Ezra's exaltation, but then notices the disappointment on Vivienne's face. She's always been so nice to him.

"Then perhaps a reading of something else?"

For a moment, everyone cranes their necks to see where the words came from. *Who said that?* Was it Vivienne? A stranger? There are a few tables nearby. Was it one of those men? Even Mr. Eliot doesn't realize the words are his at first. They don't sound like something that would come out of his mouth. Normally, doing a public reading is the last thing Mr. Eliot would want. It's never been in his nature. He's always been forced to do it, but perhaps now that he's published . . . he's becoming a force of nature himself.

"Perhaps . . . perhaps something unpublished then?" Mr. Eliot mutters.

Everyone turns to him. They see a new man sitting in Mr. Eliot's skin.

"Are you sure?" Jack asks.

Mr. Eliot can see the happiness on Vivienne's face. "Yes, I'm sure."

"All right, one poem," Ezra exclaims. "But the rest . . . you'll have to pay for."

Vivienne claps, but then realizes she's the only one and stops.

Mr. Eliot stands up on his chair. He's not a Bright Young Thing, but he has their confidence.

"As with many things in life, I hope this moment is a door I must walk through, a prelude to something else. The poem I am about to read was, in many ways, a prelude to 'Prufrock.' And so, without further ado, I give you: 'Preludes.'"

Rapt attention. A moment of suspension. The entire room awaits his words.

Mr. Eliot takes his journal out of his jacket pocket and recites:

I

The winter evening settles down

With smell of steaks in passageways.

Six o'clock.

The burnt-out ends of smoky days.

And now a gusty shower wraps

The grimy scraps

Of withered leaves about your feet

And newspapers from vacant lots;

The showers beat

On broken blinds and chimney-pots,

And at the corner of the street

A lonely cab-horse steams and stamps.

And then the lighting of the lamps.

II

The morning comes to consciousness
Of faint stale smells of beer
From the sawdust-trampled street
With all its muddy feet that press
To early coffee-stands.
With the other masquerades
That time resumes,
One thinks of all the hands
That are raising dingy shades
In a thousand furnished rooms.

III

You tossed a blanket from the bed,
You lay upon your back, and waited;
You dozed, and watched the night revealing
The thousand sordid images
Of which your soul was constituted;
They flickered against the ceiling.
And when all the world came back
And the light crept up between the shutters
And you heard the sparrows in the gutters,
You had such a vision of the street
As the street hardly understands;

Sitting along the bed's edge, where
You curled the papers from your hair,
Or clasped the yellow soles of feet
In the palms of both soiled hands.

IV

His soul stretched tight across the skies
That fade behind a city block,
Or trampled by insistent feet
At four and five and six o'clock;
And short square fingers stuffing pipes,
And evening newspapers, and eyes
Assured of certain certainties,
The conscience of a blackened street
Impatient to assume the world.

I am moved by fancies that are curled
Around these images, and cling:
The notion of some infinitely gentle
Infinitely suffering thing.

Wipe your hand across your mouth, and laugh;
The worlds revolve like ancient women
Gathering fuel in vacant lots.

Applause. And this time not only from Vivienne. Mr. Eliot has experienced the wild and thunderous applause of this room before, but never has it meant more. He's an explorer, being greeted on a new shore.

This must be what well-heeled men feel like all the time, he imagines.

Ezra leaps to his feet, leading Mr. Eliot's ovation.

Mr. Eliot reaches out his hand to Ezra, gives him a handshake, but then pulls him in for a hug. "I don't know how to thank you."

"Let's publish 'Prufrock,' this 'Preludes,' and whatever else you have in a collection," Ezra says enthusiastically. "That'll be thanks enough."

Mr. Eliot's mouth falls open. "A collection? You mean a book?"

"Good, it seems you're familiar with the concept," Ezra deadpans.

"Do you think I'm ready?"

"'Preludes' isn't as good as 'Prufrock.' What could be? But we can bundle them together. The point is . . . it'll sell. Just look around."

But Mr. Eliot doesn't need to look around, he can hear the adulation engulfing him, which makes Ezra's honesty all the easier to accept, especially since it aligns with his self-loathing.

"All right. Let's do it." Mr. Eliot swallows.

Tom tries to give Ezra another handshake, but finds a few tickets in his hand instead.

"Oh, and take these," Ezra explains. "Come with me to the ballet tonight. I'll make arrangements for you to meet the key people in the British Poetry Society. They're all asses, but they're influential asses."

The former incarnation of Mr. Eliot pipes up. "I don't think I'm ready for—"

"You're ready," Ezra pushes. "And it's important."

Mr. Eliot must have gone to Paris recently because there's a frog in his throat. "I'm not important," he croaks.

"You're right," Ezra explains. "You're not important, but your art is."

"That's not right," Jack interjects. "Tom writes the poems. He's important."

Mr. Eliot shakes his head. "No, Ezra's right. It's the work."

Mr. Eliot and Ezra exchange a look. It's the serious look of serious men who have a mutual understanding of their mutual seriousness. But to Jack, they both look silly, especially when Ezra monotones, "Ballet. Tonight."

"We'll be there," Mr. Eliot answers.

Ezra turns to leave, but then swivels back. "Oh, and I gave you three tickets. I had an extra. Someone else I planned to bring couldn't take this . . . seriously. Someone who wouldn't be able to adapt to influential asses. So, bring friends, but only people who can keep up."

Mr. Eliot and Ezra exchange another handshake, but then Mr. Eliot pulls him in for another hug.

Ezra pulls back. He forces their hands together.

"Handshakes are for gentlemen," Ezra intones. "Hugs are for handmaidens." Ezra cocks his head to the side. "Do you understand what I'm telling you?"

Mr. Eliot swallows. Yes, he understands what Ezra is saying all too well. Even at the ballet, there's no place for men like him. So, he must become something different. He must be the man of his work, and not a man of anything more. Especially not anything the well-heeled men would deplore.

Ezra turns on his heel and exits. Mr. Eliot looks at the door as if in a trance. His feet are firm in their stance.

But then Jack pulls him down to a chair to celebrate. "This is so exciting!"

"And unexpected," Mr. Eliot adds.

Jack reaches for Mr. Eliot's hand, but Mr. Eliot recoils. He glances around. "Not here!"

Jack's mouth opens in confusion and disgust. "Not here? We're at George's, surrounded by poets and drunks. We can't always stay hidden, Tom. That only empowers them."

"Them? Who is them?" Mr. Eliot interrogates.

"Everyone. Society. Influential asses. If we let them pretend we don't exist, then we never will. If they never understand us, they'll never accept us."

"They'll never accept us?" Mr. Eliot asks rhetorically. "I'm not sure that I accept us."

Jack's eyebrows lower. "You should think about what you really want, and tell me at the ballet tonight."

But Mr. Eliot doesn't hand him a ticket. A pained expression creeps across Jack's face. He looks out the window.

"You're a victim and you don't even know it," Jack scoffs. "Even though it's difficult, dangerous even, we need to sacrifice everything for the sake of people like us, now and in the future. If you close your eyes and hide, even if it's from evil, you only endorse that evil."

He stands to leave. "I can't close my eyes and I sure as hell can't hide."

"Don't forget your ticket," Mr. Eliot says sullenly, holding out Jack's ticket. What was he thinking? He has to take Jack.

Jack snatches the ticket and leaves, but lingers outside the door to the cafe. He watches Mr. Eliot through the window, hoping he'll follow him.

But Mr. Eliot marches over to Bertrand. He's already given one ticket to Jack, but he has a second ticket, a second chance. There will be well-heeled men at the ballet, and the most well-heeled man he's acquainted with is Bertrand.

"Would you like to go to the ballet tonight?"

Bertrand squints. "Well, you've gone from an embarrassment to an embarrassment of riches, haven't you?" But then he laughs and slaps Mr. Eliot on the back. Well-heeled men love to insult you, and then pretend their insult was intimacy.

Mr. Eliot tries to play along. He has to get used to playing along with men like this.

"I'd love to go with you, Tom. And congratulations. Your poem really was . . . something."

Mr. Eliot hands over the ticket. "See you tonight, then."

Bertrand bares his teeth. He's smiling, although his eyes don't seem to be. "It'll be a delight."

Jack jumps into a shadow as Mr. Eliot leaves. *What am I doing?* He just said he couldn't hide and now here he is, hiding. *But why?* He wanted Mr. Eliot to follow him. So, why, now that Mr. Eliot is exiting George's, why doesn't he reveal himself? Maybe he doesn't do it because he's not sure that Mr. Eliot will be looking for him when he leaves. And even if Mr. Eliot found him, what would Jack say? He's angry. He's upset Mr. Eliot wouldn't take his hand. He understands why, but sometimes understanding makes it all the more painful. Maybe he's afraid to show Mr. Eliot he's scared. Because if there's one thing he fears, it's Mr. Eliot. He's afraid of how he makes him feel. He's frightened he won't be able to show him how truly petrified he is of the things he said Mr. Eliot shouldn't be afraid of. It's not as simple as being brave. It's not as simple as disregarding other people's opinions.

Jack wants Mr. Eliot to see him as the type of person who could fly in the face of so much fear and animosity, but he stays hidden as Mr. Eliot walks away unbidden. He'll see Mr. Eliot at the ballet. *Yes, I'll be calmer then.* He won't be afraid to say or do something he shouldn't. Or at least, he'll be less afraid than he is now. Jack steps out of the shadow, but doesn't start after him. No, he spots a bench, saunters across the street. He's not used to sitting on benches. That's usually Mr. Eliot's territory. Jack is usually too busy, but for now, doing nothing seems like the best way forward.

15

Vivienne never sits. Someone always wants coffee or tea. And sometimes tea before coffee, but never coffee before tea. How queer would that be? She'd love to talk to more of the customers, but there are so many of them. It's hard to have any meaningful conversation with any particular one. There are a few of them who try, though. Bertrand, in particular, is usually very trying. He could get any girl, and it usually seems as if he has, but then other times, he comes into George's with eyes only for Vivienne. But Vivienne is wary of the glances of well-heeled men. No, she wouldn't take a chance with Bertrand's glances. She only has eyes for a slight, shy poet she's helped coax out of his shell.

Tonight, though, she gives into Bertrand's glances as soon as Mr. Eliot leaves. She needs to share her assertions with someone else.

"Bertrand, he's the greatest poet writing in the English language," Vivienne contends.

Bertrand's lip curls. "He's the greatest con artist writing in the English language."

Vivienne is taken aback. "You can't mean that."

Bertrand sighs, picks up his copy of *Poetry*. "I don't, really." He flips toward the end of the magazine. "I'm not sure I understand him, what he's trying to say."

Vivienne smiles. "I know what he's saying."

"Oh, yeah. And what is that, little miss literary critic?" Bertrand says as he cocks his head to the side. But Vivienne takes no notice of his rudeness. She's used to well-heeled men being rude to her.

She wipes the counter slowly and averts her gaze, as if it's a secret she shouldn't be telling, no matter how much she wants to. "Sometimes he acts like he doesn't notice me, but he writes secret messages to me in his poetry."

Bertrand's eyes go wide. This girl has a healthy fantasy life. No, scratch that, an extensive fantasy life. But he won't let that get in the way of a good time.

He leans in, glances around, and whispers, laying his faux camaraderie on thick. "Secret messages?"

Vivienne smiles. "Yes, only I understand them."

"Secrets, like what?"

Vivienne places her elbows on the counter, looks Bertrand right in the eye. She's been waiting for someone to ask her this.

"In the poem he just read. 'Wipe your hand across your mouth and laugh. The worlds revolve like ancient women gathering fuel in vacant lots.'"

Vivienne looks at Bertrand expectantly, as if she's explained everything. "Well . . . isn't that proof?"

The corners of Bertrand's mouth turn upward, belying his disbelief, but then he recovers. "I'm sorry. I'm not as advanced as you. It's all very hidden to me. Can you explain it?"

"Okay." Vivienne nods. "'Wipe your hand across your mouth'? I have a mouth. This is obviously a reference to his desire to kiss me."

"Okay," Bertrand says doubtfully.

"'The worlds revolve,'" Vivienne continues. "Revolve as in a circle . . . circle as in a teacup . . . I serve him tea almost every day . . ."

She flares her eyes. *Isn't it obvious?*

Bertrand nods his head warily. "I suppose I can see that."

"And 'vacant lots.' That had me confused until I remembered that Lot was that gent in the Bible, right? His daughter gave him wine and then . . . well, ladies don't discuss these things in public . . . But Mr. Eliot is asking me to give him wine . . . to loosen him up . . . and then, well, you understand what I mean."

"I see it clear as day," Bertrand says conspiratorially. "How could I not have seen this before? Have you talked to Tom about this?"

Vivienne shakes her head. "He's very shy, which is why he needs to use the code."

Bertrand throws his hands in the air. "Makes complete sense! You have this completely figured out."

"It just goes to show that you can truly understand someone if you take the time and really listen to what they have to say."

Bertrand licks his lips, at least in his mind. Should he tell her now? She's such an innocent lamb, and he can't wait to lead her to slaughter. "Vivienne, there's something about Tom you should know, though."

"What is it? I bet there isn't anything you could tell me about him I couldn't tell you. We're destined to be together. I've known that ever since he started coming here. So, what is it?"

Bertrand looks hungry. In England, it's tradition to slow cook lamb in liquid, or baste it to tenderize the meat. You add rosemary, garlic, onions, carrots, and, if you're feeling fancy, anchovies. Then you place the lamb in an oven for up to nine hours until the meat is practically falling off the bone. The most common cuts of lamb for slow cooking are shoulder, leg, shank, neck, and breast. Bertrand's choice of cut, however, is anything but common, and after sizing Vivienne up, he decides that he wants to eat her heart.

Cooking a lamb's heart is much the same as cooking her other organs, but you have to get your hands dirty and remove the tubes and gristle. Luckily, Bertrand doesn't mind getting his hands dirty. He loves it. But Bertrand doesn't have the time to slow cook this lamb. The ballet is tonight, so he must throw her into a pan and start frying.

"Oh, never mind," Bertrand bemoans. "It's more fun this way. Say! Tom and I are attending the ballet tonight, but wouldn't it be a fun surprise if you took my ticket? What do you think? The show starts at seven."

Vivienne squeals, "What do I think?" She clasps her hands above her head and pirouettes. "What does that tell you?"

Bertrand smiles. "It makes me so happy to see you so . . . happy."

He hands the ticket over. Vivienne embraces it with both hands.

But then Vivienne frowns. "You said it's at seven?"

"That's the time on the ticket."

Vivienne tries to hand it back. "I work until midnight. I'm sorry. I can't."

But Bertrand doesn't take it. "Why don't I watch the cafe for you?"

"Would you? Would you really?" *Can this be happening?* Is someone really being this nice to her?

"It would be my pleasure."

Vivienne kisses him on the cheek. "Oh, thank you! You're such a dear! Oh, but I must go home and change. I can't go to the ballet dressed like this. I'm sweaty and I have coffee stains on my skirt. Would it be all right with you if I went home and changed? Are you ready to work now? Can I go?"

"Please. Go now."

Vivienne starts to leave, but Bertrand catches her by the wrist. "And remember, if you're ever frustrated and need a friend, someone to talk to, someone to listen to you . . . even in the middle of the night, my door is always open. To you."

Vivienne hugs Bertrand. "Oh, thank you, Bertie. You're such a great friend." Then she jumps into the air and pirouettes, excitement rushing through her veins. She does a few more as she exits, and by the time she enters the street, she's become dizzy. The cobblestones shake and skip. They drift to the left, then snap back to the right. Right, then left. Right, then left. She needs to sit down and get her bearings until the world is more settled. But nothing is ever settled in The Wasteland.

Vivienne plops down on a bench across from the cafe, her head still spinning. She doesn't notice Jack beside her, but that doesn't stop her from talking to herself.

"Tonight is my chance. He's not married. No girlfriend. Handsome. Famous . . . well, almost famous. And best of all, I'm perfect for him!"

"Sounds like you've found someone special," Jack says.

Vivienne flinches but then relaxes when she sees Jack. "Where—ugh, yes. He's extraordinarily special. If only he realized how special he is."

"I understand how you feel. I've fallen in love with someone, too."

"Is it someone I know?" Vivienne asks.

"I should hope so," Jack answers with a smirk. "So, your beau. Is it someone *I* know?"

Vivienne leans back on her elbow. "I'll say if you do."

Jack shakes his head. "I shouldn't say. They wouldn't like it."

"Ah, a secret romance," Vivienne intimates. "I know all about that. But tonight, it won't be a secret any longer. Tonight is the start of making him tell the world how much he loves me."

Vivienne lays out a scene. "There will be dancing. Our love, lit from the lowliest spark, will grow into a flame."

"I wish we could dance," Jack bemoans.

Vivienne holds out her hand, beckoning Jack to stand. "Bend them to your will." She touches his shoulder and leg, begs him bend on one knee.

Jack dips.

Vivienne lets slip. "Tonight I'll make him want me a fraction as much as I want him. Soon, he'll say, 'Please marry me.'"

Vivienne gives Jack a quick peck. "Then we'll kiss, and I'll take his name."

She smiles, as if what she said is logical, simple, and, above all, normal.

But Jack knows love doesn't have to be normal. "I'll teach him of love, once forbidden to us. No more fear. No more guilt. No more shame." Yes. The love he felt up to now will seem tame.

Vivienne play-acts getting dolled up. "I'll get expensive perfume. A low-cut dress." She playfully tugs down her cleavage.

"Thanks for the pep talk, Viv."

"I wish you luck in love, Jack."

"I don't need luck, remember? Just bend him to my will?"

Vivienne chuckles.

They take off in opposite directions, on their way to the same destination.

16

Ballet chairs. Musical chairs. The four chairs in the ballet box are arranged in a square. Who will sit where? Who will be left out?

Mr. Eliot situates himself in one of the front seats.

Ezra enters. "Where's everyone else? The ballet is about to start."

"I'm sure they'll be along shortly," Mr. Eliot answers.

"Here I am," Jack says as he arrives.

He takes the seat next to Mr. Eliot, but Ezra intervenes. "Why don't you sit back here with me, Jack?"

But Jack doesn't want to. "No, I'd rather—"

Mr. Eliot reads Ezra's face. "Perhaps it would be for the best, Jack."

Jack plops down next to Ezra in the back row. "If that's what you want."

Ezra leans in to ask Mr. Eliot, "Whom did you give the other ticket to?"

"Bertrand."

"Perfect choice. I should have thought of that myself."

Then Ezra's eye spies someone. "Ah, I see some of those gentlemen I told you about. I'll set things up and introduce you at intermission. How about that?"

But Ezra doesn't wait for an answer. He disappears from the box as fast as John Wilkes Booth at a performance of "Our American Cousin."

Mr. Eliot and Jack sit alone, but apart, one in front of the other. Jack taps him on the shoulder. Mr. Eliot spins around.

"Your shoe is untied."

Mr. Eliot looks down. His laces are done up nicely. He even double knotted them.

"They seem to be—"

"I see your shoe is untied," Jack reiterates.

Mr. Eliot gets the message loud and clear. He bends down. So does Jack. Now, with the audience out of sight, they get to put on a play. Jack puckers his lips, sends a kiss through the air. Mr. Eliot catches it, holds up a program to his face, and sends a kiss back to Jack.

"This way, Miss."

An usher leads Vivienne into the box, and the two lovers spring back upright. Yes, upright. They're both upright gentlemen. There was nothing clandestine going on.

"Jack!" Vivienne exclaims. "Fancy seeing you here."

"It's good to see you. Where are you sitting?"

Vivienne spots the open seat on the other side of Mr. Eliot and says, "That's the one."

She tries to climb over him, but falls in his lap instead.

"Oh, my. I'm so sorry," Vivienne apologizes. "I get clumsy when I'm nervous."

Mr. Eliot flounders under her weight. "You may be in the wrong seat."

Vivienne slides over to the one next to him. "Well, yes, of course. I should be beside you."

Mr. Eliot tries to be polite. "I meant, perhaps the wrong box. Bertrand's in that seat, and he should be here any moment."

"Oh, that explains it then." Vivienne smiles. "He gave me his ticket."

"Whatever for?"

"So I could see the ballet, silly. But, really, so I could see you."

"See me?"

Vivienne's eyes go wide. "I never asked, though. What ballet are they performing?"

"'Cinderella,' I expect. It's what's on the posters."

"Oh, perfect," Vivienne says gaily and flashes her lashes at Mr. Eliot. "That's just perfect."

Mr. Eliot looks like he has something uncomfortable to say, but all he can get out is, "Vivienne . . .?" before she pounces on him.

"You must call me Viv. It's much more intimate, wouldn't you say? I see you all the time at George's, but I wanted to see you somewhere else. I mean, Vivienne is all right for contracts and things, but when you're whispering in someone's ear, it's much too formal, don't you agree?"

"Vivienne, there's something you should know—"

"I'll show you what I mean."

She leans in, whispers in his ear. What is she saying? All you need to know is that Mr. Eliot's mouth opens. He's shocked.

"You see," Vivienne says with glee, "it would have been inappropriate for me to tell you something like that unless we were on more familiar terms."

"Bertrand, is that a new haircut?" Ezra asks on his return, eyeing Vivienne curiously.

"No, I'm Viv. Tom's girlfriend."

"I like the sound of that," Ezra responds heartily.

"Girlfriend?" Jack questions.

Mr. Eliot brings a shaky hand to his forehead. He wants to correct Vivienne. He wants to console Jack. But Ezra seems to like the idea . . . and it seems like fate may favor their union because before Mr. Eliot can set the record straight, the curtain goes up. The ballet begins.

A pile of shoes is laid out on the stage. There are shoes of all different types, some heels, some flats. Some white, some black. There's a red shoe, and a green one, and a dirty one, and a clean one. But there are no pairs. Each shoe is on its own. Each shoe lies in a pile with many others, but there are no matches.

A woman in black lies beside the pile. She's limp, lying there on the ground, not stirring. A woman in blue lingers over her, not making a sound, but whirring. She caresses the woman in black, checks if she's all right, but senses that life has emptied out of her body. She holds the dying woman's hand to her face for a long, pained moment and then rises. She envelops herself in a rich, royal blue, a piece of drapery behind her, turning the curtain into a cape. Then she runs offstage. The drapery descends from above and becomes the most resplendent train, a giant, billowing cloud of fabric.

When the woman in blue returns, the scene has changed to a cafe. This must be a modern retelling of the fable. Cinderella is not tending to the whims of her sisters. In this version, she's a barista tending to the cafe's demanding customers. They order her around and she fulfills their wishes as best she can.

But even though the show is onstage, the drama is in the audience. Vivienne cozies up to Mr. Eliot. Jack bristles at her brazen display of affection, and how easily Mr. Eliot accepts it.

Vivienne's smiling. Her eyes bounce along with the dancers. Her mind pirouettes with them. *This is the start of something,* she anticipates. He's wonderful. So adorable. After the ballet, they'll waltz and sway. Then they'll go to a quaint cafe, perhaps a cabaret. They'll go on romantic walks. Have intimate talks. Friends will speculate. Are they dating? Will they do more than date? Have they found their mate? There's no need to be blue. Vivienne has found love. It's true.

Meanwhile, Jack writhes, at least inside. *Who does Vivienne think she is?* And more importantly, *Who is she to Tom*? Mr. Eliot has always put up so many barriers between himself and Jack. There's always been so much hesitation, so much perspiration, a lot of hand-wringing and heart-aching. Sure, there's been a lot of palpitation, but there's been so much trepidation, and fear. Mr. Eliot has always shown resistance. And Jack has always shown persistence. *Yes, this is the start of something,* Jack fears. It's like when you see a spider, but no web. You realize that one follows the other. So, while you don't know what web the spider will weave, you understand they catch their prey, and leave. Jack can already smell the stench of death.

It's plain to see . . . Mr. Eliot can't love her. *Is she on the make?* Either way, it's all one big mistake. He's on the verge of something. *Why does Tom need her anyway?* She's bound to lead him astray. Jack's on the verge of something, too, with Mr. Eliot, which just makes this whole charade maddening, and saddening. Jack is a proud man, but he's not afraid to crawl, to fight for what he wants, to brawl.

But he's also a man who understands when it's time to cut your losses. Should he leave Mr. Eliot now and let him make this big mistake? Or does his heart have too much at stake? He could leave him now. *Right now.* Love can be blind, but right now, Jack is out of his mind.

Mr. Eliot's eyes blink rapidly. Vivienne places her head on his shoulder. His hands twitch. What is he supposed to do with his hands?

This is the start of something, he figures. It's definitely the start of something, but what? Is she his girlfriend? *Do I want a girlfriend?* Ezra seemed to like the idea. Even without asking Jack, Mr. Eliot knows he hates it, but does it matter what Jack wants? Mr. Eliot has no future with Jack. He loves him, but what does love mean in The Wasteland?

Yes, this is the start of something. *This is the start of something adequate.* Vivienne is so . . . acceptable. Has he found a bride to hide him? She'll shop and clean. Cook haute cuisine. He'll be respectable. She'll fill the need and then, he'll be freed. She'll legitimize him, not compromise him. Love doesn't have to be true, it only has to be what's best for you.

But how will this drama end? The ballet is far from over, and now, there's choreography in the audience. Mr. Eliot places his arm around Vivienne, finally finding a place for his hands, which launches Jack from his seat. He exits the box in disgust.

Mr. Eliot is pained by Jack's departure. Mr. Eliot is the woman in blue. Jack is his woman in black. Mr. Eliot's face goes slack. He's a maniac. But what can he do? He's found a place for his hands, and he can't turn back.

On stage, Cinderella tries on slippers for the ball. Finally, she has a pair that matches, a pair that fits. Yes, Mr. Eliot realizes she'll end up orphaning one, setting in motion a course of events that causes people to lie and maim themselves. But right now, all Mr. Eliot can see are the shoes. *Yes, this pair will work.* And if the shoe fits . . .

17

Arm in arm. Smarm in smarm. Mr. Eliot and Vivienne promenade through the lobby. A well-heeled man nods to them. Mr. Eliot nods back. *Do I know him? Who introduced us?* He understands that men greet each other this way, but he's not used to it happening to him. But with Vivienne on his arm, it seems there's a lot he'll have to get used to.

Jack leans against a pillar, a Scotch in hand, eyeing the sappy couple. What does Mr. Eliot plan on doing? *Does he expect to fit in?* Jack could fit in here if he wanted to. Jack has a knack for making people of all stripes like him. You smile. You laugh at their jokes. You make small ones yourself. Not big jokes, only small, wry, observational ones. Jokes that let people know you're paying attention. There's nothing that scares well-heeled people more than the idea you might catch them slipping.

Mr. Eliot sweats. *What if they see I don't belong? What if they catch me slipping up?* Another well-heeled man, this one with a well-heeled woman, approaches.

"Are you enjoying the ballet?" the woman asks.

"Oh, very much so," Vivienne says. "Cinderella was my favorite story when I was a girl."

The man scrutinizes them. "Have we seen you here before?"

Mr. Eliot freezes. *What do I say?* He's never seen this man before, but doesn't want to admit it's his first time at the ballet. *Has it already been too long to answer? Have I been spotted? Can the man see me slipping up?*

"We thought you were familiar," Vivienne bluffs.

The man smiles, holds out his hand. "Archibald MacLeish, and my wife, Matilda."

Mr. Eliot shakes his hand, but doesn't introduce himself. *Why can't I do this?*

Tick. Tock. Tick. Tock. Each passing second counts down until the moment Mr. Eliot will be revealed for the imposter he is. Vivienne clocks Mr. Eliot's shock.

She curtsies. "Oh, yes, I'm Vivienne Haigh-Wood, and this man, who prefers to put his words on the page, is Mr. Thomas Stearns Eliot, the poet."

"T.S. Eliot? The poet!" Matilda gasps, holding her hand to her mouth. "I read your 'Love Song of J. Alfred Prufrock.' All of my friends have, it's all we talk about."

Mr. MacLeish grins. "T.S. Eliot. The man himself. How impressive."

Matilda puts her hand on her husband's back, gives him a small push. "My husband is a poet, too."

Hemingway swoops in, places an arm around Mr. Eliot. "Poets. Poets galore. Everyone's a poet, including your mother, the whore."

His other arm is busy holding a drink. He stinks of whiskey, but he's at least sober enough to recognize his belligerence. "I'm sorry, lady and gentleman. As you see, I enjoy the ballet. To some, it brings out the best, and to me, it brings out my . . . thirst." Hemingway takes another sip and winks at Matilda. "But with so many poets in attendance, shall we ask the dancers to delay the second act, and all give the audience a reading?"

"There you are, Tom!" Ezra exclaims as he approaches with three well-heeled men. "I'd like to introduce you to Lord William, Sir Richard, and Viscount Jameson, all esteemed members of the British Poetry Society."

Mr. Eliot squints. *Am I seeing double? Triple?* The men look remarkably similar. Most well-heeled men look alike in their suits, but there's something particularly odd about these particular men. They appear to be the exact same man, only twenty years apart in age. Viscount Jameson appears to be Mr. Eliot's age, around thirty-three. Sir Richard is Viscount Jameson twenty years in the future, and Lord William is the stately evolution of both men, an older gentleman in his seventies. The resemblance is uncanny. Dickens might say that Viscount Jameson has visited the Ghost of Christmas Yet to Come twice over. It's all that Mr. Eliot can envisage. Or perhaps he only focuses on that because he wants to see what *his* legacy will be.

What will my future look like twenty years from now? And another twenty after that?

"Will T.S. Eliot join the British Poetry Society?" Matilda asks curiously.

"That, I presume, is what we're here to assess," Lord William says solemnly.

Viscount Jameson nods to his other iterations. "Yes, we must see now, won't we, gentlemen?" He nods to Matilda. "Although it sounds like he already has one vote."

"Too bad she's not a voting member," Sir Richard jests.

"Yes," Viscount Jameson continues, aiming an arched brow at Mr. Eliot. "With that, and the popularity you're amassing, I'm sure you'll be admitted in a landslide."

Landslides cause excitement, but their main result is destruction.

"If only we focused on what was popular," Lord William sneers.

Sir Richard looks to Lord William. "Perhaps he's too popular, then?"

"Gentlemen, let's speak no more of the offensive art known as popularity," Ezra interjects. "Let Mr. Eliot's words speak for themselves. Let him give you a reading at the club. Normally I'd say people have to pay for the pleasure of Mr. Eliot's poetry, but I'm aware the club already has many copies of his current work, or else we wouldn't be having this conversation."

Viscount Jameson defers to Lord William. "Shall we schedule something?"

"I suppose so," Lord William intones.

Ding. Ding. The five-minute warning rings. The influential asses return to their seats. The dulcet, melodious tone was their cue to leave. Did they need all five minutes? No, their seats are close. They're not the type of men to climb stairs, and they have the money not to. They don't have time for that. They don't have time for many things, and at present, that means Mr. Eliot.

"Don't worry, they'll come around," Ezra estimates.

Jack peers upon the proceeding. The men had been far from chummy. But perhaps that's what Mr. Eliot deserves. Jack downs his drink, revolves around the pillar. He doesn't want his empathy directed in Mr. Eliot's direction.

Mr. Eliot rubs his head. *Did that really happen?* The men talked about him as if he wasn't even there. *Why didn't I say anything on my own behalf?* Ezra's explanation of their character had been correct. Yes, they were asses, but influential asses, nonetheless. Mr. Eliot took his first whiff of them, and he liked the smell. Is it a scent he can purchase? Can it be woven into his clothing?

But the sweet smell of success is often confused with another stench.

It's the same smell that men wore in the trench.

Mr. Eliot's life was a slur, and now, it's a blur. Ezra not only arranged a reading with the British Poetry Society, but also a few beforehand to prop up Mr. Eliot's confidence. Everyone wants him to sign copies of his poem. Everyone wants to be Mr. Eliot's friend. Back when there was no future to portend, Mr. Eliot thought his loneliness would never end.

Mr. Eliot starts spending nights out with the Bright Young Things. Perhaps it's the potion in Auden's tit flask, but he can never remember what they've been up to in their rendezvous. Perhaps that's the point of the potion. How many nights has Mr. Eliot spent out with them? How many readings has he done?

Even though Ezra might not agree with his choice of company, the Bright Young Things are remarkably adept at doing one thing, and that is to accompany.

Mr. Eliot walks up to a posh bookstore on Kensington High Street. *Have I been here before? Is this where I'm supposed to be?* The Bright Young Things seem sure.

"We're here to conquer!" Auden booms.

Joe zooms in the door. "Liberate the peasants!"

"Yes, let them feast upon our words," Mary adds.

"Yes, a feast," Auden says as he shoves Joe's head down on his crotch. "Let them eat . . . cake."

If this is the present they brought for the peasants, a feast is what they'll need least.

But Mr. Eliot isn't as boisterous as his compatriots. He stands outside the door to the shop. Ezra spots Mr. Eliot milling outside, and begs him enter. Vivienne clutches Mr. Eliot's hand. She's been clutching his hand a lot lately, smearing herself across all his blurs.

"Time to go inside," Vivienne prods.

There are dozens of people sitting on chairs and dozens more standing.

Hemingway sizes up the crowd, says to Ezra, "So, your boy seems to be doing well."

"Well, he's both a modernist and self-taught. I've seen one or the other, but never both together."

"Should I take offense at that?" Hemingway scoffs. "But that Prufrock thing was inspired."

"You should tell him that. It would mean a lot coming from you."

"I consider it a professional courtesy never to compliment another poet's work."

Vivienne leads Mr. Eliot up to them.

Ezra clasps his hands together. "Harriet's thrilled with the response it's been getting in the States. And she'd love to print something else."

"What he means to say is," Hemingway adds, "what will you write next? Got any more 'Prufrocks' in your pocket?"

"I . . . we . . . I thought we had the collection coming out." Mr. Eliot checks Ezra for confirmation.

"Of course, we do," Ezra reassures him. "What Hemingway is getting at, somewhat indelicately, is what will you write next that's as big as 'Prufrock'?"

"You've had your whole life to write your first collection," Hemingway explains, "but now the clock is ticking on your second."

Somehow, all the air has been removed from the room. Mr. Eliot wants to gasp, but finds he's frozen in place.

Ezra notices he needs to thaw him.

"He's right," Ezra agrees, "but tonight, don't worry about that. Just get up there and drum up attention for your first collection. Read 'Prufrock' for all I care. Make them think you're saving something special for the book."

"I am working on something new," Mr. Eliot postures, his confidence askew.

"Oh, yeah. What's it called?" Hemingway asks, trying to call his bluff.

"It's called 'He Do the Police in Different Voices.'"

"Well, I'm sure Harriet would love to publish whatever it is, whenever it's ready," Hemingway says.

"She'd like to, but Scofield might be a better choice," Ezra contemplates. "He's turned *The Dial* around."

"You turned it around, Ezra," Hemingway states. "He only put up the money."

Mr. Eliot stands in front of the podium. *How did I get up here?* A moment ago, he hemmed and hawed as he watched Ezra and Hemingway discuss his career. And now he's in front of the podium. *Did Vivienne lead me here?*

Jack enters the bookstore, stands in the back. Mr. Eliot tries not to acknowledge him, but he has all his attention. He hasn't seen Jack since the night at the ballet. The night Jack left. There's nothing more to say. But standing in front of the podium, Mr. Eliot supposes there's a lot more he's supposed to say. He's supposed to put on a play, a one-man monologue that displays how calm and confident he is in front of a crowd. He's supposed to read his poetry aloud, but he doesn't want to, because poems aren't meant to be read aloud. They're meant to be read on your own. You're supposed to read the lines at your own pace. It's not a race. You read a line, then reread it, if that is your need. You can look over a section, parsing it for meaning before moving on. Poetry is meant to be savored, but when read aloud, the crowd can only get a flavor. There's no space for a slow pace. Reading poems in front of an audience turns it into a performance, much like a ballet, or another form of dance.

Mr. Eliot recites:

> I have seen them riding seaward on the waves
>
> Combing the white hair of the waves blown back
>
> When the wind blows the water white and black.
>
> We have lingered in the chambers of the sea
>
> By sea-girls wreathed with seaweed red and brown
>
> Till human voices wake us, and we drown.

It's not the start of "Prufrock." It's the end. *Did I forget to read the rest?* Or was his mind wandering? From Jack to poetry and back . . . it's easy to see how his mind could wander. Mr. Eliot sweats. *Did I read the whole thing?*

Either way, it doesn't seem to matter. To this audience, these last words sing. They greet Mr. Eliot's conclusion with an enthusiastic ring, applauding. Mr. Eliot bows his head. He can't accept their praise. But the audience can't accept his modesty. They increase their applause, inflating Mr. Eliot's ego. They grow louder until he becomes prouder. They clap until he stands with his shoulders back, his chin held high.

But when he sees Jack, Mr. Eliot feels like the end is nigh.

Jack isn't clapping for him. He's the only one in the audience who isn't. The only problem is, Mr. Eliot needs Jack to clap. He needs Jack to be happy for him. Mr. Eliot doesn't need this audience's adulation. He just needs to hear Jack clap.

He wants to stand proudly in front of Jack, not only there in front of that audience, but everywhere. No, not in front of him. Beside him. The only thing is, Mr. Eliot knows he can't.

Jack knows the difference between can't and won't is a chasm, and he won't clap for that.

"He never seems happy, does he?" Ezra wonders to Hemingway.

Hemingway shrugs. "Happiness in intelligent people is the rarest thing I know."

18

Mr. Eliot hears restrained, polite applause from one pair of hands. *Is it Jack?* He looks around and sees only the influential asses of the British Poetry Society. Lord William, Sir Richard, and Viscount Jameson sit before him. Have they been his audience? *Or my tribunal?* Was Mr. Eliot just speaking? *Why is no one saying anything?* Mr. Eliot can't conjure anything to say, so his eyes wander the room. They're in some sort of club. Intricate intarsia images of itinerant British Empire expats exploring their indentured outposts inhabit the wood-paneled walls. They speak to the old-world opulence of a society that has raped and pillaged much of the world. It's genocide doubling as decoration. Pure taste. The chairs are covered in leather from animals whose meat has been discarded. What a waste. But the chairs themselves bear none of that weight. They're innocent. Chaste.

But there's nothing innocent about the glares Mr. Eliot is receiving. His tribunal stares at him.

"Well done, Mr. Eliot," Lord William acquiesces. "But we've all read your 'Prufrock' poem. We thought Ezra would have you read us something new. Something better."

"And where is Ezra? We thought he'd accompany you," Sir Richard states.

"It's quite unlike him to be late," Viscount Jameson joins in.

"I . . . I remember him mentioning an errand, but I'm sure he'll be here shortly," Mr. Eliot stammers.

In fact, Mr. Eliot doesn't need to remember which errand Ezra is on, because he's the one who set him on it. Realizing this reading at the British Poetry Society Club would be important, and potentially hostile, Mr. Eliot needed another shining face in the crowd, so he asked Ezra to find Jack and have him join them. Mr. Eliot knew Jack wouldn't come if he asked him. No, he's behaved poorly toward Jack ever since the whole Vivienne business started. *How could Jack not see?* How could he not see that this Vivienne business was just that, business? Yes, she was lovely at times, but she was no Jack. No one could ever be Jack, especially not her. All Mr. Eliot needs is Jack in the audience, clapping or not, and he can take on any Goliath.

"What are you working on now?" Goliath asks in the form of Lord William.

"Uh, yes. What I'm working on now . . . I am working on something, but it's only fragments."

Sir Richard peeks at the other two. "We've all seen a work in progress, haven't we gentlemen?"

"Proceed," Viscount Jameson prods.

Tick. Tock. Tick. Tock. Mr. Eliot takes in a big breath, trying to calm his nerves. He breathes out, lets his poem begin.

"'What shall I do now? What shall I do?'" Mr. Eliot starts.

"Is he reading a poem or just talking out loud?" Lord William asks the others.

"Reading. I'm . . . I," Mr. Eliot stammers, then continues. "'I shall rush out as I am, and walk the street. With my hair down, so. What shall we do tomorrow? What shall we ever do? The hot water at ten. And if it rains, the closed carriage at four. And we shall play a game of chess: The ivory men make company between us. Pressing lidless eyes and waiting for a knock upon the door.'"

Jack. *There's Jack!* Just outside the door. Mr. Eliot's heart swells. *Is he about to knock?* No, Ezra's trying to coax him inside, but they're having some sort of heated debate. The horse is so close to water. *Please drink.*

Perhaps it's seeing Jack, but Mr. Eliot soon finds himself at the end of his fragments. He finds himself at his best.

"'These fragments I have spelt into my ruins.'"

Mr. Eliot holds his journal up to his chest. If only it were a shield. He waits to hear whether these influential asses will embrace his poetry. He waits for Jack to reassure him their opinions don't matter.

"Is that it? Are you finished?" Sir Richard asks.

"Yes, thank you," Mr. Eliot answers.

"But it doesn't rhyme," Lord William says incredulously. "How can you call it poetry if it doesn't rhyme?"

"His 'Prufrock' rhymed," Sir Richard offers.

"Rhymes don't matter," Viscount Jameson says. "It's the emotion that counts."

"Well, I—" Lord William starts.

"I agree," Mr. Eliot interjects. "I'm sorry for interrupting you, Lord William, but I think it's important to note that although some poets may write to relieve themselves of the burden of emotion, I try to create something that lives for its own sake. Something that washes over the reader, creating its own emotions . . ."

Mr. Eliot peers out the window at Jack. "Defining its own truths."

Sir Richard's eyes follow Mr. Eliot's. "What's going on out there?"

"Why is that fruitcake talking to Ezra?" Viscount Jameson asks.

Mr. Eliot opens his mouth, but no words come out. Tick. Tock. Tick. Tock. He becomes pale, frightened.

"The one with the ruffled shirt?" Lord William asks.

"No, that's Ezra Pound," Viscount Jameson corrects. "He's all right. The other one's the queer. That man mistook me for a homosexual as I was strolling in the park one night."

Mr. Eliot looks like he's been slapped.

Sir Richard shakes his head. "They're getting a lot more brazen if you ask me."

"Maître d'? Maître d'!" Lord William calls out. He's known the maître d' for decades, but still calls him by his profession and not his name. The man scurries over, a smile plastered on his face from years of service.

"Yes, Lord William?"

Lord William points out the window. "You see that man there? The one next to the man in the ruffled shirt. He's a homosexual. Don't let him into the club. I forbid it."

But Ezra must have persuaded Jack to enter because as soon as Lord William forbade it, Jack and Ezra seek to invade it.

The maître d' rushes over to greet them. The front door is thirty paces away, but the maître d' makes it there in ten. He holds up his hand as soon as they enter. "I'm sorry, but the club is members only."

Ezra narrows his eyes, becomes flustered. He's not used to this type of treatment. "We're meeting someone here. Besides, I'm a member."

"Yes, sir," the maître d' says, "but this gentleman is not."

"He's my guest."

"Unfortunately, I have been instructed not to permit him entrance."

Jack glowers. "Instructed by whom?"

"I'm not at liberty to share that information, sir. But I can inform you that we don't allow his type inside."

Ezra throws up his hands. "He's not Jewish!"

He slaps Jack's back. "They assumed you were Jewish. I had the same confusion when I first met you. I—"

"Not Jewish, sir," the maître d' interrupts. "He's a homosexual."

Jack steps forward, angry. He comes so close to the maître d' that their chests almost touch.

Ezra's eyes bulge. He seizes Jack's left arm, but the right one pushes the maître d'. Ezra shoves his way between them, separating the two as Mr. Eliot runs over. Together, he and Ezra drag Jack out of the club.

"Homosexual? Homosexual! Half the men in this club are homos!" Jack screams through the doorway.

Mr. Eliot had wanted Jack there, but now he wishes Jack were anywhere else. His presence isn't welcome, that's clear. The last thing they want is a queer.

Out on the street, Jack shuffles them off. "Let go of me. I'm all right."

Ezra shakes his head. "The buffoons. There shouldn't have been any problem. Unless they have something to hide."

A tear creeps out of Jack's eye.

"Are you sure you're all right?" Mr. Eliot asks.

Jack looks at Mr. Eliot, then at the club. "They'll never let us in there, will they?"

Mr. Eliot gives Jack a pained expression that Jack mistakes for agreement.

"Let's get out of here." Jack starts to leave, but then notices Mr. Eliot isn't following him. "Tom?"

Tick. Tock. Tick. Tock. "I'm sorry, Jack, but I need to go back inside."

Jack stares at Mr. Eliot for a long beat. *This is hell.* He's looking him in the eye, but it feels like he's scrutinizing his soul.

Jack turns away in disgust.

"I'm sorry, too." And then he walks down the street.

Mr. Eliot starts after him, but Ezra intervenes, blocking his path. "Let him go."

Mr. Eliot steps around him, but Ezra grips his arm. "We have to go inside."

Indignation. Resignation. This is the state of Mr. Eliot's one-man nation.

Ezra props the door. Mr. Eliot plods through it.

"Thank you for your help, Mr. Pound," the maître d' sounds. "Mr. Eliot. I do apologize for the disruption."

Ezra brushes past him. "You're an ass."

"Did they throw him out?" Sir Richard asks.

"Yes," Mr. Eliot states simply.

Lord William cocks his head. "Do you know that man, Mr. Eliot?"

Mr. Eliot pauses for a moment. "No."

Judas! a voice inside Mr. Eliot's mind screams. Is it Mr. Eliot's conscience? Perhaps it's the Lord himself noting Mr. Eliot's betrayal. Did Jack foresee that Mr. Eliot would eventually betray him, as Jesus had with Judas?

"It was all a misunderstanding, gentlemen," Ezra answers. "Everything's all right."

"You need to be careful," Viscount Jameson instructs. "They can look normal."

Lord William nods his head. "I can always tell. It's a sense I have."

"Lord William thought you were the homosexual, Ezra!" Sir Richard exclaims. "Why are you wearing that dreadful shirt?"

Ezra puts his hand to his chest, fluffs a few of his ruffles. "This? I thought it was fashionable."

Lord William frowns. "What is fashionable will never last."

"By definition, one would say," Sir Richard sniggers.

Ezra pays them no mind, he's used to their quirks. "I'm sorry I'm late, gentlemen. But I see you've started."

"We've done more than that," Lord William corrects. "Mr. Eliot read us two of his fashionable poems."

"Lovely," Ezra exhales. "Shall he read a third or are you able to render your verdict?"

"Third?" Mr. Eliot panics. "Can't they recommend me to the selection committee on what I've already done?"

Sir Richard puts his hand to his chin. "Ezra, you introduced us to him the other day yourself."

"Didn't you tell him who we are?" Viscount Jameson asks.

All three men look directly at Mr. Eliot.

Lord William scowls. "We three are the selection committee."

Mr. Eliot glares at Ezra. He led him into the lion's den, but hadn't told him about the lions.

"Apologies," Ezra says solemnly. "Very well then, let me do the honors. Tom, this is Lord William, chairman of the British Poetry Society, and a member of the Nobel Prize selection committee as well.

Sir Richard is the current Nobel Laureate, well done there, and chairman of the British Nobel nominating committee. And this is Henry, Viscount Jameson, an exceptional poet in his own right."

Ezra extends his hand toward Mr. Eliot. "Gentlemen, this is the poet I introduced to you at the ballet the other day, the one I've been telling you about, Mr. Thomas Stearns Eliot."

Lord William purses his lips. "Yes, we're well aware."

"Which poem did you read?" Ezra asks Mr. Eliot.

"'Prufrock.'"

Ezra nods. "Good, and then the second one. Which was that?"

"We weren't informed of the title," Sir Richard states.

"'He Do the Police in Different Voices,'" Mr. Eliot says.

"'He Do the Police . . .'" Lord William wonders, but trails off.

"Is that by our mutual friend Dickens?" Viscount Jameson asks.

"Dickens?" Lord William scoffs. "You never met Dickens! He was dead long before you were born."

"I meant 'Our Mutual Friend' by Dickens," Viscount Jameson says, licking his wounds.

"Yes, that's right," Mr. Eliot answers.

"Yes, Dickens," Lord William says, "now that's a man who didn't care what was fashionable."

Sir Richard tempers his response. "I'm not sure if everyone would agree with you on that."

"Fact is not something to agree upon," Lord William snipes. "But literature and poetry do have subjective elements, I suppose. All tied to the emotion of the reader, as you previously alluded, Mr. Eliot."

Lord William, usually so stoic, seems stilted. "I'll confess to being shocked by some of your images. Shaken to my core." But then he regains his composure. "I suppose each generation must burst through the calcified shell of the previous one. And you might be the man to do it."

"Might?" Mr. Eliot asks.

Lord William juts his chin. That wasn't an invitation for him to speak.

"Yes. Might, Mr. Eliot. Although your poems are fashionable, sometimes fashions change. I charge you, though, with creating something that will stand the test of time. Something serious."

"Are you married, Mr. Eliot?" Sir Richard asks.

Mr. Eliot searches for an answer. "I . . . uh, no, I'm not married. What does that have to do with this?"

"I'd caution you to show this committee a modicum of grace, Mr. Eliot," Viscount Jameson scolds.

Mr. Eliot is flustered. *Marriage? Grace?* Why are these men talking about things that have nothing to do with his poetry?

Ezra takes a small step forward. "He's quite serious with a lovely young lady, though."

"Is she pretty?" Lord William asks.

Pretty? Why would she need to be pretty? Mr. Eliot doesn't know how to answer.

"Very pretty. Beautiful, even," Ezra says, stepping in again.

"Ah, yes. To be young," Lord William says wistfully, but then he catches himself. He lowers his head, puts some gravel in his voice. "My advice: settle down, young man. These are unsettling times. We need our public figures to set an example of stability, decorum, and seriousness, don't you agree?"

Mr. Eliot squirms. "Of course."

Lord William winds up. "So, show us you're a serious man with serious poetry . . . and then we'll reconsider your application, how about that?"

"Thank you for your time, gentlemen," Ezra seethes.

"Our pleasure," Lord William says as he stands and leaves.

Sir Richard and Viscount Jameson rise to their feet.

"Do you plan to marry this woman?" Viscount Jameson asks.

What would a serious man say? What do serious men do?

"Uh, yes," Mr. Eliot answers.

"Good man!" Sir Richard exclaims.

19

Mr. Eliot wears a funeral suit. It's his wedding day. Vivienne insisted they get married as soon as he proposed. Did he propose, though? Mr. Eliot told Vivienne what happened at the British Poetry Society. He said he read his poems, and then they asked if he was getting married. Mr. Eliot said yes. What else would he say?

Mr. Eliot never asked Vivienne to marry him, but what did that matter now? Vivienne took his story as a proposal and started planning their wedding without him. Everything happened so fast. Soon they had a location and a date. There was no reason to wait. Vivienne didn't even need to buy a wedding dress. She'd bought one a year earlier, just in case.

"So many women make crazy decisions when they marry," Vivienne explained. "Better to make those decisions beforehand than leave them to some whim or fancy, don't you agree?"

Mr. Eliot nodded, but didn't agree in the slightest. Best not to create waves, though. Waves take time, and he only has time to focus on his next poem. The fragments he read to the British Poetry Society whirl in his mind. "He Do the Police in Different Voices"? No wonder they hadn't taken him seriously. He needs a better title. He needs a better poem. He needs to be serious. Serious men commit themselves to their craft. Serious men make commitments. And that's why he's here.

"I do," Mr. Eliot answers the priest when he asks whether he'd like to take this woman as his wife. Marriage is all about commitment. But that doesn't mean he has to be happy about it.

As the attendees shower the newlyweds on their way out of the church, Mr. Eliot glowers. Ezra, Hemingway, and Bertrand pelt them with rice and smiles. So does Mr. Prufrock. *Mr. Prufrock?* Mr. Eliot whips his head around as he passes him. *How did he get here?* But as soon as he turns around, Mr. Prufrock is gone. He must have sailed away on this sea of shining faces.

The only person not smiling, other than Mr. Eliot, is Jack. Jack stands across the street. He did not attend the wedding. *Why did he come?* Did he come to toast the couple at the reception? Or perhaps roast the couple?

Why did I come? Jack doesn't seem to understand either. He assumes Mr. Eliot doesn't want him there.

How could Mr. Eliot get married in front of Jack? Everyone hopes to get married with the person they love. The trick, though, is to get married *to* them, and not just have them present at your wedding. Maybe that's why Mr. Eliot is dressed for a funeral.

"Where's that bow tie I got you?" Vivienne asks.

"I thought I'd wear a tie instead," Mr. Eliot answers.

"But I wanted you to wear the bow tie. You look like you're attending a funeral, you realize that?"

"No, sorry. I didn't," Mr. Eliot lies. "I'm just sick, that's all."

"Don't worry. I was nervous, too. But we got through it, didn't we? Me and you?"

Mr. Eliot swallows and nods.

"I've known since we first met, that we would sing the 'Song of Life' duet."

She takes Mr. Eliot's hand in hers, inspects their matching wedding bands. "With this ring I do thee wed."

"That's what you said inside," Mr. Eliot responds, perhaps a bit too tersely.

"And I meant it," Vivienne says. "Did you?"

Mr. Eliot can see he's hurt her. He can see that he needs to say "Yes, a thousand times yes," but all he can say is, "I like you, Vivienne. I like you a lot."

"Is that all you've got?"

Mr. Eliot gazes into her eyes. "I embrace the bond. The ties of gold. My love goes well beyond what I have told."

It's not a lie. He does embrace the bond. He understands what a serious commitment this is. That's why he's doing it. And his love does go far beyond anything he's told her. How can he tell her how deep his love is? The ocean can't fathom its depth. What does it matter if his love is not for her? Many men don't love their wives.

But Vivienne doesn't realize it's a lie. She just likes the poem.

"Did you write that for me?"

"Of course, dear."

Vivienne coos. "Look at you and me, we're two lovebirds. I love you desperately."

The corners of Mr. Eliot's lips turn upward. "Did you write that for me?"

Vivienne nods and jumps into his arms. She makes Mr. Eliot carry her all the way to his flat and across the threshold. *This must be what a bride feels like on her wedding night*, Mr. Eliot has thought before, but now he knows for sure. But even when Mr. Eliot puts Vivienne down, he doesn't feel like he's shed any weight.

"Shall I make you a plate?" Vivienne asks, standing near the kitchenette.

She removes her dress. First one strap, then another. She shimmies out of the lacy white gown until she's in her skivvies. Surely, she had someone help her get into the dress, but she doesn't need any help getting out of it.

Vivienne stands there, nearly naked in front of Mr. Eliot.

"Vivien Eliot," she says.

Mr. Eliot cocks his head. "What?"

"Vivien Eliot. Vivien. V-I-V-I-E-N. It's shorter than Vivienne with an N and an E at the end, but it sounds the same and you never did get around to calling me Viv as I asked. But I guess marriage is all about compromise. So, how about we compromise? We'll drop two letters for now and then work on those other pesky ones in the future. We could call it a fair trade. I took your last name so I might as well give you a few letters of mine if that's what you really want."

Mr. Eliot exhales. "Compromise. I like it. Vivien."

"Or Mrs. Eliot if you hate it."

"No, I like Vivien fine."

Vivien . . . what other changes will this marriage bring?

Vivien steps forward. "Well, Mr. Eliot, are you glad we waited? It seemed unnecessary, but it makes tonight special, doesn't it?" She brushes her fingers along Mr. Eliot's jacket, teases her lips against his collar.

Mr. Eliot bristles. He hears a noise, a ringing. *Is it a whistle?*

"Would you like something to drink?" Mr. Eliot asks, trying to change the subject. "Some champagne, perhaps?"

"No," Vivien balks.

Mr. Eliot and Vivien gawk at each other for an uncomfortably long amount of time. Vivien's ready to celebrate the vows they've sworn. Mr. Eliot looks like it's time to mourn.

Vivien saunters over to the bedside table, turns off the lamp. She lights a candle. The candlelight flickers over her body as she fingers her underwear. Slowly, ever so slowly, she takes it off, places it delicately on the bedside table. She turns down the cover. She turns down the sheets. The only thing she isn't turning down is Mr. Eliot. She lies there ready, like a flower waiting to be plucked. Vivien wants to get fucked.

But Mr. Eliot is no gardener. He makes no move toward her.

"What's wrong?" she asks.

Where should he begin? Where did he go wrong? "I don't know if this is where I belong."

Vivien stands, caresses Mr. Eliot's face.

"Compromise, Mr. Eliot. I've made you my husband. Now make me your wife."

She loosens Mr. Eliot's tie, removes his jacket, then his pants. She kisses his neck, caresses his crotch. The candlelight flickers their silhouette onto the wall.

Click. The lamp turns on. The silhouette scatters. Mr. Eliot steps back, disgusted and afraid. The moment is gone. He runs to the bathroom, slams the door.

Vivien puts on a robe and a brave face. She implores through the door, "It's okay, love. You just had a bit too much to drink, that's all."

That's all . . . it's not that Mr. Eliot has had too much to drink, it's that he hasn't had enough. Enough . . . *when will it ever be enough?*

Mr. Eliot cracks the door open. "I need a drink."

Vivien doesn't know what to say.

"I . . . um, I'll be back soon, okay?" Mr. Eliot stammers.

"I can pour you something here if that's what you want."

Mr. Eliot shakes his head. "No, no. I need to go out. Clear my mind."

Vivien moves toward the kitchenette. "We have wine, champagne—"

"I don't want anything here." Mr. Eliot catches himself, corrects, "I don't want anything we have here. I want something . . . stronger."

"Shall I come along?"

"No, you stay here. Relax. I'll be back soon, I swear."

Vivien puts on her nightgown. "All right, if that's what you want."

Mr. Eliot puts on his pants and jacket. He walks to the door.

"I love you," Vivien says earnestly.

Mr. Eliot turns back. What should he say to her? He knows he should say he loves her. It's that emotion, isn't it? *Love?* People get married because they love one another. But then again, people get married for a whole list of reasons that have nothing to do with love. Mr. Eliot wants to love Vivien. She's given him the biggest gift anyone could have.

Mr. Eliot walks over to Vivien, grabs her shoulders. *I love you. I love you!* He wants to scream the words at her, but it would break her heart if she knew he didn't mean it. She's looking back at him so lovingly. She's so sensitive, empathetic. Mr. Eliot would never want to break her heart.

"I'm so glad you're my wife, Vivien," Mr. Eliot mumbles.

"Thank you," Vivien replies, humble.

He kisses her on the forehead. Then stumbles out into the jumble.

20

Down, down into the ground, into whatever pit of hell Mr. Eliot is leading himself. Each step leads Mr. Eliot downward. He pauses as he approaches Bertrand's door. *Is it open?* Mr. Eliot would hate for Bertrand's door to be open. He would hate for Bertrand to be entertaining some well-heeled young lasses and beckon Mr. Eliot inside. Is there somewhere he can hide? Some back stairs he can take to get out of his building? Out of his mind? Out of his marriage? Mr. Eliot tiptoes closer and closer to Bertrand's door, and then he sees the knob. It's closed. *Thank heavens.* Although the heavens surely won't be thanking him back.

Mr. Eliot crosses the street into the park. Jack. He needs to find Jack.

He tramps into the trees and screams, "Jack! Jack?"

"Tom!"

Mr. Eliot turns around. Jack rises. He's been sitting on a bench in the park, the one Mr. Eliot used to occupy.

"What are you doing here?"

"I was . . ." He glances at Mr. Eliot's building.

Mr. Eliot beams. "Would you like to have a drink with me?"

Jack smirks.

Down, down the street. They must be discrete. Mr. Eliot leads Jack into the trees. No, not in the park, but in the woods of an Irish pub. They sit in a secluded booth in the back. The entire establishment seems secluded, though. The only other person there is the bartender. Two beers sit in front of them. They're cold. And the beers that sit in front of them are cold, too.

"Why did you marry her?"

Mr. Eliot eyes the exit. "You know why."

Jack taps his fingers on the table. Tap. Tap. Tap. "Congratulations."

Mr. Eliot sips his beer. "Thank you."

Jack notices the bartender eyeing them warily. "Come here often?"

"First time. I'd noticed this place before, but never went inside. It didn't seem too busy."

Tap. Tap. Tap. "There's a first time for everything, I guess."

Mr. Eliot takes another sip of beer.

"Have you ever been here?"

Tap. Tap. Tap. "No, I don't like places like this."

"Places like what?"

Jack gestures around the room. "Wood-paneled. Old-fashioned."

"We can go somewhere else if you like."

Jack takes a big swig and slams down the glass. "Oh, yeah. Can we?"

A spurt of beer shoots out of the glass onto the table.

The bartender calls over to them. "You boys all right?"

"We're peachy, aren't we?" Jack says, throwing his arm around Mr. Eliot. Jack smiles, clinks Mr. Eliot's glass on the table, and takes another big swig.

But when the bartender turns back, Jack takes his arm away. It was all a front, like so many things in The Wasteland.

"You say we can go somewhere else?" Jack asks accusingly. "I've been trying to convince you to go somewhere else with me for how long now? I lead you to the club. I do everything right, but you can't be bothered. And now you've gone ahead and married this woman, but you bring me here, even when I make it clear I don't like this place. And you have the nerve to say that we can go somewhere else?"

Jack leans in close, thumps his finger on Mr. Eliot's chest. "I want to go to the Pansy Club. I want to go to the Pansy Club with you. I don't like these wood panels and old fashions. I hate it. And they hate me right back."

Mr. Eliot exhales. "All right, let's go."

"Let's go. Let's go. You'll follow me there and then poof. No."

Mr. Eliot stands. He downs his beer in one go, one big swallow. Why did he do that? *How did I do that?* He places the empty glass down on the table.

"So, are you coming or not?"

Mr. Eliot rubs the back of his neck.

Down, down the street. Time for a treat.

Red. The red door. It's the door Mr. Eliot has stared at before. But today, Mr. Eliot won't just stare at it. No, today he's walking through it. He strides right up to the bouncer. There's no metal grill. And the bouncer isn't gruff, or tough. He's a spritely old man in his seventies sitting on a chair. He's warm and welcoming, eliciting the air of a grand affair.

"Welcome! Welcome to the Pansy Club." He nods to Jack. "It's good to have you back."

Jack nods to the man as they enter. First one foot, then the other. Mr. Eliot crosses the threshold, waits for something to happen. But, no, he doesn't change. There's no lightness or heaviness. This place hasn't changed him. Or at least it hasn't had the opportunity to yet.

The club before him has an eerie resemblance to the one of his imagination. A giant golden globe on a golden stand gleams golden light, dappling the room in intricate dots. It lights up the room's corners and crevices, or at least it would if Mr. Eliot could see into them. The primary distinction between Mr. Eliot's imaginary version and the club, in reality, are all the men who occupy it. Mr. Eliot's jaw drops. He never imagined there were so many men like him. *Are these all the men in London who share his predilection? Maybe all of them in the world?*

Jack touches Mr. Eliot's shoulder. "I'm sorry, it's usually busier."

Busier? *Busier!?* "How could this place be any busier?"

"Gladys must have already performed."

Gladys. Gladys Bentley. That name sounds familiar. "Is that the name on the marquee?"

"The one and only."

Mr. Eliot notices the empty grand piano in the middle of the room. There's no one sitting at it. And there's no one onstage. Or rather, everyone is. All the patrons ogle each other. They strut and perform, even though they're only waiting for their next drink. Will they have to buy their own? Or will someone buy it for them?

Jack whispers in Mr. Eliot's ear. "Is this one on you, or me?"

Mr. Eliot takes a moment to understand, but then comes to his senses. "On me. It's on me."

They belly up to the bar. Luckily, unlike the club of his imagination, the Pansy Club has bartenders, but at this moment, it seems as if they've all disappeared. Or at least Mr. Eliot can't make any of them see him.

Jack raises his hand. A handsome young man turns his head. Lots of handsome young men have been turning their heads to look at Jack ever since they entered the club, but this one serves alcohol.

"What'll you have?"

Mr. Eliot starts to speak, but Jack cuts him off. "Two gin and tonics, please."

"Anything for you." The bartender winks at Jack.

"Service here can be spotty," Jack says. "So, it's best to leave a big tip."

"Is Jack talking about his big tip again?"

Jack turns and greets Frederick, with Daniel in tow.

"Oh, it's you, you old crow," Jack says playfully.

Frederick looks Mr. Eliot up and down. "You finally got your sugar daddy to come in the club with you?"

Daniel slaps Frederick on the shoulder. "Don't mind him. He's too sour for a sugar daddy."

Jack scouts the room. "Looks like we're late for the show."

Frederick throws his hands in the air, bends his wrists. "What do you mean? The show just arrived."

Jack laughs. "How silly of me."

Frederick touches Mr. Eliot's chest. "You're the married one, aren't you? The one from the other night?"

"Ooh, I love the married ones," Daniel coos.

Jack lowers his chin. "Today. He got married today."

"Today?" Frederick screams. "We can have a stag party!"

"Does it count if he's not a bachelor anymore?" Daniel asks.

"Oh, be fun," Frederick demurs. "If it's not a stag party for him, it can be a stag party for us!"

"The confirmed bachelors!" Daniel shouts.

"A fag stag," Jack jokes.

"Here are your drinks, gentlemen," the bartender interjects.

Frederick pouts. "Only two? But there are four of us."

Jack leans across the bar, touches the bartender's shoulder. "Two more, please."

Now it's Mr. Eliot's turn to pout. *Why did Jack touch that man?* They seemed intimate.

"Don't be jealous," Frederick says, his eyes clocking Mr. Eliot's. "Nada to vada in the larda. What a sharda!"

Jack and Daniel laugh, but Mr. Eliot furrows his brow. *What did Frederick say?* Mr. Eliot peeks at his gin and tonic. He hasn't even taken a sip yet. Perhaps the beer from the pub is finally hitting him?

Frederick looks at Jack. "He can't parse Polari?"

"Polari?" Mr. Eliot mouths.

"Yeah, Polari. Do you speak it?" Daniel intones.

Frederick gestures wildly with his hands. "Is this the first time the Queen's English is catching your Polari lobes?"

"Has he even had a bit of hard?" Daniel asks.

"I can attest that he has," Jack says. "And no flies."

Frederick leans in. "What have you done with him? And don't be strange."

Daniel's eyes light up. "Does he have coliseum curtains?"

Jack slaps him on the shoulder. "Shut your screech."

"I thought he was just a mauve," Frederick nods.

Daniel shakes his head. "No, I knew he was an omee-palone."

"He looks daffy, though," Frederick notices.

"No, this is our first drink," Jack corrects. "Our first drink here, at least."

Frederick bites his lower lip. "How long has it been since you two . . ."

Jack bats his eyes. "A lady never tells."

"Jack, a lady?" Frederick demurs. "My harris."

"Your rosie," Daniel snorts.

"Oh, cheeky now? Nosy now?" Frederick says as he puffs out his chest.

"Okay, calm down," Jack says, separating the two. "Don't make me play Hilda Handcuffs."

"Oh, please. Can we?" Daniel asks coyly.

"Nanti that, you twat," Frederick swats.

Jack notices that Mr. Eliot is completely and utterly lost. "How much of that did you understand?"

Mr. Eliot shakes his head sheepishly.

Jack turns to the others. "Shall we pop his Polari cherry?"

"Only the Polari one?" Frederick asks.

"Jack already got the other," Daniel teases.

Frederick clasps his hands together, as if in prayer. "My dear Jack always does what he pleases."

Jack shrugs off their derision. "Nada to vada in the larda. What a sharda," he says slowly.

Mr. Eliot stares at him blankly. "I didn't understand it the first time."

"No, yes, of course," Jack explains, "but I wanted to repeat it so you might catch the rhythm, the rhyme.

"Is this how you speak to one another all the time?"

"It's how we speak to one another with no one else being the wiser."

Frederick scoffs. "Don't give away all our secrets."

Daniel purses his lips at Frederick. "Don't be a drag."

Jack continues. "Nada means nothing. Vada is seeing. Larda, like a larder."

"You know," Frederick crows, "where you store the raw meat?"

"Do you like your meat raw?" Daniel entreats.

Jack shrugs off their diversion. "What a sharda. What a shame. So all together it's 'He's got a small penis. What a shame.'"

"Well, when you explain it, it all sounds rather boring," Frederick says.

"Much, much too serious," Daniel rejoins. "But Fred's right. If that bartender's got a little winkle, there's no need to worry about Jack going with him."

"Which tells us a lot about you, deary," Frederick says.

Jack slaps Frederick on the shoulder. "You slaggy, kerterver cartzo."

"What does that mean?" Mr. Eliot asks.

"I'll tell you later," Jack says as he collects himself. "Polari. It's a language, but not a lingo." He catches himself. "Not a foreign language, you see? It's a language for people like you and me."

Mr. Eliot sees. He sees Jack standing before him. He sees Frederick and Daniel. He sees a sea of men, all here together. *So many men.* Every club has its secrets. And Polari, it seems, is one of this club's biggest. Are there more words to teach him? Or are they done? Words. So many new words with so many new meanings. Mr. Eliot sees the golden ceiling shimmering above him. It's exactly like he imagined. It bounces the golden light down on the men's faces. He keeps waiting for the gold to drip, but the oil paint in this club stays firmly on the canvas. It's real. And he's here. A part of it. Mr. Eliot keeps waiting for Mr. Prufrock to appear. He's seen so much of Mr. Prufrock's world, so much that was scarier than this place.

Mr. Eliot looks relaxed. He has a strong posture, his shoulders back. He looks like an animal that's escaped captivity, finally free.

And that's when everything stops. Somehow, everything and everyone in the club comes to a complete standstill. The bartender holds up his shaker mid-shake. Mr. Eliot scans the crowd, sees two men longing for one another, mid-ache. Mr. Eliot stands there, the only one of them who can move, awake.

"Tom. I'd like you to refer to me as Tom. Is that all right with you?"

But who is he talking to? Is this the moment where Mr. Prufrock appears? Is this the moment when Mr. Eliot learns this was all another fantasy?

Mr. Eliot looks straight ahead and—

"Tom. I asked you to call me Tom, not Mr. Eliot."

Mr. Eliot stands there, his chin upright. He—

"Tom stands there. Tom's chin is upright," Mr. Eliot corrects.

"Tom corrects."

I . . . all right, I'll call you Tom.

21

Black. The lights go out. *Is it an attack? A raid? Is it time to run?* Are the night's festivities done?

A spotlight illuminates a black stage. Black skin. White suit. Gladys Bentley owns the spotlight. She wears a white top hat and tails.

Tom stands with his mouth open. Mr. Eliot, now "Tom," a man with aplomb, a man whose confidence is a bomb. Tom squints his eyes. They had adjusted to the darkness but now have a hard time seeing with so much light.

Even before she opens her mouth, Tom can tell: this is a woman who knows who he is. Gladys Bentley is a portly woman who looks utterly regal. She's not a queen, though; he's a king. And this king can sing. The musicians pull a few strings. A violin, a cello, the room gets mellow.

And then Gladys speaks. "Hello."

The room erupts. Whoops, hollers, the men adjust their collars. Things are about to get rowdy.

"Howdy," Gladys greets them again.

The audience greets her back.

"We love you!"

"Sing 'Prove It On Me Blues'!"

"Sing whatever you want to!"

"I thought I'd sing something new," Gladys purrs into the

microphone. She nods to the musicians. The piano kicks in, then the strings.

Gladys croons a bawdy tune:

> You see, now I'm a bull dagger.
>
> I wear a dress, I look haggard.
>
> Can't wear no dress. Can't be no actor.
>
> I wear a suit. I stand my full stature.
>
> Better a bull dagger, than a simple, black . . .

Gladys stops the lyric short. The crowd goes crazy. She holds them in the palm of her hand, continues:

> Don't tell me to wear no dress. Don't be no nagger.
>
> Just drink with me. Drink until we stagger.
>
> Drink until we stagger. Drink until we stagger.
>
> Just drink with me. Drink with your daddy bull dagger.

Tom claps so hard you could call it a slap. Slap. Slap. His hands clap with a loud smack. She's wonderful. His deep, growling voice is soothing but flirtatious.

Gladys exits the stage to greet her subjects. Tom rushes over.

"Gladys . . . Mr. Bentley . . . you're heavenly."

"Thank you, sugar. You're sweet," Gladys says as she touches Tom on the cheek.

She saunters away, swimming through her adoring subjects, a big, black buoy on a white-capped sea of congratulations.

Tom turns to Jack. "She was . . ." But he's at a loss for words.

"Marvelous?" Jack offers. "Remarkable? Sensational?"

"Yes, all those things, but also . . . inciting, er, I mean . . . exciting." Tom shakes his head. "No, I mean inciting, too."

"Inciting, huh? Bound to bring out all that you've been hiding?"

Tom blinks rapidly. His shoulders are tight. "I fear my hiding has only begun."

"Only begun?" Jack asks. "Well, then there's bound to be more fun."

"More fun. More fun," Tom singsongs. "More fun until we see the sun."

Jack smiles, looks at Tom. He's joking. He's jolly. *Please, God, don't make this a folly.*

"How long have I been waiting to get you here? And now that we are . . . I only want to take you home with me."

Yes, Jack wants to show Tom his penis, or at least that's the first thing Tom sees when they enter his flat. There. Up on the wall. Tom has seen the man in the painting's penis before, and now he's here again. *Am I a whore?* Tom hopes the painted man won't be the only nude man he sees this evening. But much as Tom wants to eye Jack's natural figure, he wants to ogle something bigger. Jack's bookcase.

Tom pushes past Jack to take in hundreds of leather-bound tomes.

"I want to discern what's moved from before. What's changed . . . shifted. You know?" Tom says excitedly as if he's out of breath just looking at the stacks.

"Is there anything, in particular, you're looking for?" Jack asks.

"Give me a minute . . . a moment, please."

Tom's eyes strain. This is hard work. He's concentrating so hard it causes pain. But it will all be worth it when he figures out what's different and he can put his mind at ease.

"Scotch?" Jack asks, but then puts his finger to his lips. "Sorry, the queen has asked for silence."

Jack pours two Scotches as Tom stands there, stares. He is a hunter in a blind, waiting to pounce.

Tom strolls up to the bookcase, removes one bound in green leather.

"The Upanishads. You acquired the Upanishads."

It creaks as Tom opens it.

"I'm right. This book is new. Hardly broken in."

"I've taken it around the block once or twice," Jack says as he gets close to Tom. "But yes, I've yet to fully . . . devour it."

Jack kisses Tom, places the book back on the shelf. "For safekeeping."

Tom gulps. "It's always good to be careful."

Tom kisses Jack. He leans in with all his weight, pressing Jack's back to the stacks. Jack writhes in ecstasy as Tom kisses his neck.

But then Tom pulls back.

"What's wrong?" Jack asks.

"No, I, uh . . . nothing's wrong. I . . . uh . . ." Tom stutters. Something is wrong, or at least something was wrong. Now, Tom sees a place for him to belong. Tom stands upright, strong.

"I'd like you to be my boyfriend."

Jack's jaw is tight. "You'd like me to be your mistress."

Tom can see he's caused him distress.

"No, not my mistress . . . my . . ." Tom takes a step back, considers the books, then Jack. "You can see we're supposed to be together, can't you?"

Jack averts his eyes. Yes, he can. *That's what makes all this so difficult.* Jack weighs his options. Should he be considerate or callous? He's torn, so he picks scorn.

Jack squints. "What's it like to be married?"

"I don't know," Tom says. "It all happened so fast. It was all a bit harried."

"And how exactly would being boyfriends work?"

"I . . . I don't . . ." Tom starts. "I hadn't given it much thought."

"It seems you haven't been giving a lot of things much thought lately," Jack attacks.

Jack's words smack Tom across the face, putting him in his place.

Tom shakes his head. "Why did you bring me here? To punish me? That's clear."

"Punish you? Yes, everything I do is to punish you. Do you like it? Are you unnerved? Feel out of place? Out of your mind? Are you questioning why you came here? What you're doing? Who the other person is screwing?"

"I'm sorry, I—"

"You married Vivien!"

Tom exhales. This night had been a dream, but now it's a nightmare. Jack stands across from him. He's upset, angry, hurt, and confused. But mostly, he feels used.

Jack wipes a tear from his eye. "I know I asked you to come back here tonight, but I . . . I . . . you should go."

Tom swallows a mouthful of air and emotion. What should he say? What could he say that will make Jack let him stay?

"If I could have . . . I would have married you today."

The words pass through Tom's lips quickly. The words came so fast, without much thought. Did he mean it?

Jack leans away. "Do you mean it?"

Do I mean it?

"I do," Tom says as he searches his heart. "I really do."

Tom saunters over to Jack's bedside table, turns out the light. "I want to pretend that this is our wedding night."

"Well, tonight is *your* wedding night," Jack jokes.

"I guess I deserve that."

"No, you deserve so much more." Jack takes off his pants, his jacket.

Tom follows suit, removes his. He turns down the covers, the sheets. It's time to see what's underneath.

Tom climbs onto the bed, spreads his legs. He lies there, ready, like a flower waiting to be plucked. Yes, that's right. Tom wants to be fucked.

Luckily for Tom, Jack has a green thumb, and many other willing body parts, too.

"What would you like me to do?" Jack asks seductively.

Tom puts his finger to his lips. "Shhh. I'll show you."

Tom's hand wades down to Jack's chest, then his crotch.

Tom smiles. "That's no winkle."

"You learn Polari fast."

"Shhh."

22

Nightgowns. *Why do they call them nightgowns?* They're so delicate and white. *Why don't they call them whitegowns?*

Vivien stands before a display rack, trying to discern which one will best display hers. She holds one up in the air. It has long ribbons and lace trim. She puts it back, pulls out another. Will this one make her look slim? It's covered with embroidered butterflies.

Vivien turns to the shop girl. "Do you have this in my size?"

"Let me check in the back," the shop girl replies.

Vivien puts the butterflies back on the rack. If only she could return the ones in her stomach, too. *Why didn't Tom come home last night?* He said he would. Vivien's been unsettled ever since she last saw him. She waited up all night, until early morning light. How she had hoped Tom would come through that door. That would have been a sight.

The shop girl returns from the back. "This should fit you."

Vivien holds it up, then against her bosom. "Yes, this will do nicely. Thank you."

But then Vivien's face crinkles. "Do you like it, though?"

The shop girl scrunches her nose. "It's . . . uh, fluffy, I guess. Is this about the price?"

"No," Vivien responds. "If it's worth it, I'd pay double."

Vivien holds it against her bosom again. "I guess, does it make me look feminine?"

"Oh, yes, very feminine, madame."

The corners of Vivien's lips turn down. She places the nightgown on the counter, turns back to the rack.

She fingers a few more choices. *How about this one?* No, too lacy. *How about this one?* No, too racy. *How about this one?* No, it's all wrong, much too boxy. It makes her look like a . . . Vivien holds it up to the light, examining it. Then she holds it up to the shop girl.

"How about this one?"

"To be honest, we've had a lot of trouble getting rid of it. The shoulders are too square. Not very feminine, madame, if you ask me. But there are a lot of other options."

Vivien smiles. "I'll take it."

"You will? I . . . I'm sorry about the shoulders, but as I said, we've had trouble getting rid of it. I could let you have it for half price."

"No, that's all right," Vivien responds. "It's worth it."

Yes, it's going to look nice on her. Until, of course, it's done its duty and Vivien can do hers. Tom and Vivien are going to be the perfect couple. She'll make sure of that.

Vivien spreads the nightgown on her bed, and then lies down beside it.

She giggles and rolls over, wrapping the nightgown around herself.

The perfect couple indeed.

Knock. Knock.

"Who's there?" Vivien asks.

"It's Ezra!"

Vivien almost answers, but then remembers to hide the nightgown in a cabinet on her way to the door.

Vivien flinches when she finds Ezra hunched over in the doorway, his hands straddling the frame. "Oh, you startled me."

"I'm sorry. I got so tired of standing upright. It's been quite the night."

"Would you like some tea?" Vivien asks.

"I'd love a cuppa, but more than that, a seat."

"Yes," Vivien says. "Of course. Please come in. I should have the tea ready in a moment."

Ezra falls into a seat. "I wanted to wait until later in the day because . . . well, you know."

Mr. Pound looks around. "Where is . . . where is he?"

"Oh, he's out getting supplies," Vivien lies.

"When will he be back?"

Vivien pours water into the kettle. "I'm not quite sure."

"Well, how long do you suppose?"

"Later today, I presume," she says.

Vivien turns on the stove, but Ezra turns on the heat.

"How long has he been out?" Ezra asks.

Vivien prepares the tea leaves. She doesn't want to answer. And even if she did, what would she say?

"How long has he been gone?" Ezra asks with increased intensity, the same tone as a king on a throne.

"Since last night, I guess."

"Out since last night getting supplies? That's . . ." But then Ezra notices the pained look on Vivien's face, realizes it was a lie. She just needed something to say, something to let her hide.

"Do you have any idea where he is?"

Vivien shakes her head no.

"Well, fortunately for you, I do."

Yes, Ezra knows exactly where he is.

Knock. Knock. "Who's there?"

"Someone who needs to clear the air!"

Tom and Jack gawk at one another. *Who could that be?* What could that mean?

"Just a minute," Jack says.

Tom and Jack lie naked in bed. They look like they've been caught. Their faces, red.

Tom nudges Jack, who begrudgingly dons a robe. It's silk, soft. He ties it shut, giving him a waist. Tom looks at Jack in the morning light. He likes how the robe fits him. He likes how it slopes over his rounded shoulders. He likes how maybe it's a bit too short to answer the door in, but Jack does anyway.

But before Jack opens the door, he signals to Tom. He needs to hide. Tom bolts up. Where should he go? Jack doesn't know. Where can he go so their night together won't show?

"The bathroom," Jack whispers.

Tom scurries into the bathroom, shuts the door. He tries to be as quiet as a church mouse. But would God let this mouse into His church knowing what he's done?

Jack opens the door, throws his arms around Ezra.

"Ezra, what a lovely surprise!"

"Do you have tea?" Ezra asks and slithers out of Jack's grasp. "I didn't stay long enough to get a cup at my last stop."

Jack pours some water into a kettle, puts it on a burner.

Ezra sits down at Jack's table, looks around. "So, where is he? It's important."

Jack shrugs a bit too slowly. "Who do you mean?"

Ezra slumps over, puts his head on the table. "I should have stayed for a cup with Vivien. I can't deal with this type of drama so early in the morning without a cup of tea."

"You were at Vivien's?"

"I was at Tom and Vivien's," Ezra corrects. "Silly of me, wasn't it? To look for a man at his flat the day after he's married."

"Downright hilarious if you ask me," Jack says stoically.

Ezra chortles. "You could be a comedian if you wanted."

Jack plays along. "You really think so?"

Ezra's face goes flat. "No, I don't. So, where is he?"

The water boils.

"I need to go to the bathroom," Jack says.

"Have you hidden your answer in there?"

"Would you like to accompany me and find out?" Jack says as he plays with the sash on his robe.

Ezra smiles weakly. "I'll wait right here, thank you."

Jack walks over to the bathroom, slides inside.

"It's Ezra. He wants to talk to you."

"What's he doing here?" Tom asks.

Jack throws up his hands. "I don't know, but he said it's important."

"Well, I can't go out there dressed like this, now can I?"

Indeed, he cannot. While Jack wouldn't mind if Tom pranced about his flat naked, Ezra might not be as appreciative.

Jack slips out of the bathroom, makes his way over to a cabinet, grabs a pair of pajama pants, and heads back. He flashes a smile to Ezra as he hands them to Tom.

"This will be some magic trick," Ezra groans.

"Ta-da," Tom says sheepishly as he emerges wearing Jack's green-and-white-striped pajama pants.

"Can you please put on a shirt?" Ezra asks. "I can't do business with you unless you're wearing a shirt."

Tom cocks his eyebrow. "Business? What do you mean 'business'?"

Ezra pulls a wrinkled contract out of his jacket, along with a pen, and sets them down on the table before him.

"This business," Ezra states matter-of-factly. "The business of being a professional poet."

Tom marches over to the table. "What have you done?"

"What did I say about a shirt?"

Jack tosses Tom a dress shirt. Tom throws one arm in, then the other.

"So, what business are you talking about?"

"Button it all the way up, please."

Tom huffs but buttons the shirt quickly. "All right, now answer me. What have you done?"

Ezra irons the contract with his hand. "The more appropriate question is, what have you written? I sold your poem to Horace."

"Who's Horace?"

Ezra moans. "Horace Liveright of Boni & Liveright. Do I need to explain everything to you? They bought your poem."

"Poem? Do you mean my collection?"

"No, of course not," Ezra explains. "Your collection is on its way. They're buying your next poem."

"Next? Everything I've written so far is in the collection."

"Didn't you say something about a 'He Do Police . . .' or something or other?"

"That's—I'm not finished with it. It's only fragments."

"I suppose you better get working then."

"I, uh . . . I can't . . . I just . . . I'm still figuring out what I want to write," Tom stammers.

Ezra slides Tom a pen. "How about you start with your signature? Horace wants a contract now. The poem can come later."

Tom shivers. Did someone open a window? He looks around. No, no open window. *No way out.* "Couldn't he wait until tomorrow at least?"

"Maybe he could, but I can't. I'm a little drunk, and I don't want to be. Better to make it the whole way or nothing, know what I mean? Horace is a little drunk, too. I left him back at the bar."

Tom hesitates. "I just—"

"You'll make a year's pay. Just sign the damn thing."

Jack steps forward. "He said he won't sign it."

"Tom, I completely understand if you want to listen to your wife," Ezra says and then rubs his eyes. "Oh, wait. That's not Vivien. Who is this man?"

"He's my . . ." Tom starts. "He's my Jack."

"Yes, I know very well who he is," Ezra deadpans, then stands. "We both did things last night we wish we hadn't. Now, maybe some good has come out of it, but it's time to move forward."

He picks up the contract. "Shall I return this to Horace? Tell him to file it where the sun doesn't shine? I want to keep coming to you with opportunities like this, but let me know if I should stop."

"No, I'll sign it," Tom says. He bends over, puts ink on paper. He signs his name: T.S. Eliot. It's a name he's written over and over, but this time each letter was difficult to scribe. It wasn't harder than writing his next set of words will be, though. Tom has signed a contract for a poem he hasn't written.

"How long do I have?"

Ezra shrugs. "Shall I say a week?"

Tom gulps. "Make it two at least."

"Two then."

Tick. Tock. Tick. Tock. The clock is ticking.

Whiiiiiiieeee. The tea kettle whistles. The tea is ready. If only Tom was.

"Just my luck," Ezra says. "I'll see if they can make me a cuppa back at the bar."

"I suppose we can use it for our baths," Jack says. "If you'll excuse me, I'll take mine now."

"I imagine you need it," Ezra rejoins.

Jack puffs out his chest, strides over to Ezra with his hand clenched around the hot kettle. "Excuse me. What did you say?"

Ezra cowers. "No, excuse me. Please. It's the brandy. I'm sure you understand?"

A bit of brandy will make anyone randy.

Jack smiles with his teeth, but not with his eyes. "Thank you so much for your visit. I'm sure you can see yourself out."

Jack takes the kettle into the bathroom, slams the door to punctuate his exit.

Ezra pockets the contract as Tom escorts him to the door.

"Listen, I don't want to . . . interfere," Ezra says, winding up, "but you need to be more discreet."

"About what?" Tom asks as innocently as he can.

Ezra looks at Tom blankly. "About Jack. You shouldn't be here. You should be with your wife. You married her yesterday for Chrissake. You realize I went over to her place, to your place before I came here? Almost let it slip that I knew where you'd be."

"You told her where I was?"

"I almost did but thought better of it. She didn't know where you were. I said you were probably at the bank, trying to get some sort of bonus for working on your wedding day and that I would go and make sure."

"You said what?"

"What was I supposed to say? You can sort that out with her yourself, but if you keep this up, you'll ruin your nomination to the British Poetry Society."

"My poetry seems to do that all on its own," Tom says, deflating.

"What are you talking about?" Ezra asks. "They love your poetry. They're just not sure about you. They don't want another Auden on their hands."

"What are you talking about?"

Ezra rubs his eyes. How can he be clear? "They canceled Auden's nomination because they found out he was a queer."

Tom looks at Ezra, waiting for him to reveal he was joking. Surely, there's more nuance, more to the story. Tom inhales sharply. It's one thing to know something is true, and another to see it proven.

"Horace is waiting for me. Go home to Vivien."

Ezra exits, but forgets to shut the door in his haste.

Tom stands there, frozen. He can't move. He's numb. He feels nothing. No, that's not right. He does feel something. Fear. The fear every queer understands all too well.

Tom puts his hand on the door. When one door closes, another opens, but this door is already open. He already has his opportunity in front of him.

He needs to get away from here. Away from this moment. Away from fear. Away from Jack. Tom realizes if he walks through this door, there might be no turning back. Jack might never forgive him. Some wounds are too big for bandages. But he has to go now. He has to go now before Jack comes out of the bathroom, or else he'll never be able to leave. Jack won't even need to say anything, he'll just need to stand there. Be there. Be Jack. And Tom won't be able to part with him.

Tom takes one step forward, then another, then another. He closes the door behind him with a click. Tick. Tock. Tick. Tock. His heart beats fast, keeping pace with his feet as they race down the stairs into the street.

Jack opens the bathroom door with a creak. He takes one step out, then another, then another. He's meek, wounded from his encounter with Ezra, wounded from past encounters with Tom. But Jack exits the bathroom ready to be a good host, ready to be a good boyfriend, ready to be what Tom needs most.

But where did he go? Why would he go?

Tom, a man with aplomb, a man whose confidence is a bomb, a man who has exploded Jack's heart.

Jack stands alone in the middle of his flat. It's the moment he expected would come, but that doesn't make it any less shocking. He was ready to be there for Tom. He was ready to be calm. You can only put yourself out there and be disappointed so many times before there's no heart left to break. How much more of this can he take?

Jack removes his robe, lays it down on his bed. Then he lies down beside it. The perfect couple. *We were going to be the perfect couple.*

He wants to yell at Tom. He wants to scream. There's so much to be said, but right now, Jack just wishes he was dead. If he was dead, he wouldn't have these emotions any longer. He wouldn't sense his love for Tom growing stronger and stronger.

Jack wants to be stronger. That's why he practices judo, but he's been learning *kintsugi* from Mitsuyo Maeda as well. Simply put, kintsugi is the Japanese art of fixing broken things with gold, but it's so much more than that. The point of the gold is not only to fill cracks and join pieces back together again, it's to highlight the object's imperfections and make them shine, literally. When a bone is healed, it's stronger than it was before. And with kintsugi, objects are more beautiful after they're broken and mended. A formerly simple bowl is given prominence on the dinner table. A ladle used for stirring is used for serving. Things aren't discarded, they are made better, stronger because of their struggle. Their past gives them an exalted purpose.

If only kintsugi could mend Jack's broken heart.

23

Strange men and women stare at Tom. Elephants walk on the couch. *Who's flat is this? What are these things?* Tom had put his key in the lock. It had fit, but this is not his flat, or rather, it's no longer his flat alone anymore. Vivien's touch is everywhere. Vivien's things are everywhere. A colorful stained-glass lamp. A crystal chandelier. A silver urn on the coffee table. A coffee table. And every conceivable surface is covered with fabric. The windows have long curtains that go all the way to the floor. A tapestry covers one wall, all the way to the door. The mantle has a red runner with gold tassels. On top of the runner, white porcelain candleholders are decorated with edelweiss. A couch is draped with a red sheet and has elephants embroidered on its pillows.

Tom's grandfather clock is no longer the patriarch. The walls are lined with portraits of the men and women of Vivien's past. Tom doesn't know much about Vivien's lineage, but he now sees it on full display. *Is that wallpaper?* He can hardly tell. The portraits of Vivien's ancestors are crammed so tightly he can't see the wall behind them. Tom senses all their eyes on him. *This is hell.* He's in the middle of a surgery gallery, his innards on full display, his pain on parade for everyone's pleasure.

But his desk is still there, next to the window. Tom sits. From this vantage point, he can't see the rest of the flat. He can only see outside, out onto the city. The gray city. The gritty city. The shitty city.

Yes, the shitty city. He can write about that. Tom takes his journal out of his desk. *Black water. Gray skies.* Yes, that's perfect. He can write about this state of mind. He can write about The Wasteland.

Click. A key in the lock. Tom puts away his journal, quick. The door opens. Vivien enters with packages.

"You're home!" Vivien says. "Can you give me a hand?"

Tom hops up, nabs a green box with pink ribbons out of Vivien's hands, and another covered in lace.

"What did you buy?"

"Oh, a few things we needed," Vivien explains.

Tom looks around for a place to set the boxes down. He balances them in one arm while he moves a candelabrum on the dining room table.

"What were you doing?" Vivien asks.

"Oh, I was . . . I was at the bank, working," Tom explains.

Vivien frowns. "No, I wasn't asking about last night. I was asking about when I arrived. Were you writing?"

"I was."

Vivien smiles. "How exciting. What are you writing about?"

"Oh, um, this and that. I didn't get very far along."

"Sounds lovely," Vivien says. "Did you get the bonus?"

"Bonus? What do you mean, 'bonus'?"

"From working at the bank on your wedding night."

"Bonus!" Tom squeals. "Yes, that bonus."

"Oh, good. I hoped we'd be able to afford all these things."

Tom's face falls. "Oh, no. I didn't get a bonus from the bank."

Vivien looks at all the things she's purchased. "No bonus?"

"No, bonus. Just onus, unfortunately."

"Then how will we—?"

"I sold a poem!" Tom remembers.

Vivien jumps up and down with joy. “You have? Why didn’t you tell me that?”

“It just happened this morning.”

“This calls for a celebration!” Vivien announces as she kisses Tom on the lips.

She pulls away and says, “Let’s go!”

“Go where?”

“Everywhere.”

She seizes Tom’s hand, pulls him out the door. The next thing Tom remembers is sipping champagne with Vivien and a few well-heeled men in the bar of a hotel near Trafalgar Square. Then he’s at the Victoria and Albert eating bonbons. A taxi takes them past Big Ben as they crisscross the city.

Tom and Vivien lounge in a private box at the ballet.

“What are they doing today?” Tom asks.

Vivien shrugs. “I don’t know. I only asked the box office for the best seats.”

As the ballet begins, the dancers prance onto the stage. They whirl and twirl. Vivien mirrors their motion. She points to members of the audience, whispers in Tom’s ear who she imagines they are. Her opera glasses stay pointed at the audience, not the stage.

Vivien opens her purse, takes out a small medicine vial, but that only describes the container and not its contents. She adds two drops of liquid to a glass of wine. Plop. Plop.

Tom raises an eyebrow. “What is that?”

“Only a dab of ether, dear.”

“Vivien!” Tom says too loudly before he notices he needs to restrain his reaction. The audience turns to the show he’s putting on instead of the one on stage. Everyone is looking at him. Their eyes linger for only a moment, but to Tom, it’s an eternity. Their corneas tear into his flesh. It’s like he’s at home again with Vivien’s ancestors judging him. The souls of the past peering into his.

Vivien downs her drink, licks her lips. “It was only a taste.”

But it was only one of many tastes.
Tom and Vivien dine.
There's more drinking, more wine.
When will Tom write? When will he ever find time?
Tick. Tock. Tick. Tock.

"I'm sorry to disrupt our dinner," Tom says, "but I must do some writing." He pulls out his journal, starts scribbling.

"Don't mind me," Vivien says. "As long as we're together, we're together."

She looks at Tom, writing furiously, and then at two teenage girls across the restaurant. They're staring at them, or at least they were. They turned their heads as soon as Vivien spotted them. They're shy.

Vivien knows a lot about shy girls. She used to be one. She's familiar with what shy girls think about. She remembers what shy girls talk about. And she can tell that right now, all they're talking about is Tom. Every few seconds, they glance over. Every few seconds, their minds dance with what it would be like to approach Tom . . . to meet him . . . to ask for his autograph. Could they manage to ask? And if they did, would he laugh?

Vivien could use a good laugh.

"I hear Munich is lovely this time of year," she says.

Tom doesn't respond. He just keeps writing.

Vivien downs her drink. "Sorry, don't mind me."

Tom looks up, half-smiles before returning to his journal.

Vivien rummages through her purse, a striped, beaded bag with a silver ring for a handle.

"I love this bag," Vivien says. "So chic, don't you agree?"

But she's talking to herself. Should she invite those girls over? They'd love it, but she's not so sure about Tom.

Vivien looks for companionship in her handbag and finds it in the form of a tarot deck.

She lays out the cards on the table in front of her. What will they say? What will they tell her?

A man lies face down on the sand, having run out of air and life. Ten swords stick out of his back. This is not a good sign. But it couldn't be related to her life, could it? No. She and Tom are getting along swimmingly. *We are, aren't we?* He seems happy. *Doesn't he?*

"This must be about Munich, darling," Vivien says, trying to explain the card away. "I hear there's a lot of fighting there between the Nationalists and Communists. I mean, we just had a war, and they just lost one, and I understand why they're upset, but they're fighting each other all the same. I mean, what will they do next? If they keep this up, will they start a war to end all wars or something like that? Some people say war is unavoidable, but I think we can avoid it if we really want to. I mean, this poor Egyptian sailor couldn't avoid his death, but I think we can. No one could want a real war. Not a war with guns and bombs and all that. Not again. Don't you agree?"

Vivien looks at Tom expectantly. Doesn't he have anything to say about that? Will he say anything at all? She doesn't mind if he writes in his journal. She loves it when he's writing his poems. She loves that he's a poet, but he could at least do her the courtesy of responding every now and then.

"Well, haven't you anything to say?"

Tom peeks at the tarot card. "He's Phoenician, not Egyptian."

"What? What did you say?" Something about a Phoenician?

Vivien inspects the card. "Where does it say where the man is from?"

But Tom doesn't respond.

Vivien places the card down. She'd like to frown, but she doesn't want the shy girls to see.

"Oh, I guess I have been running on, haven't I? I'm just so excited. Bertrand was telling me about the battles between the Nationalists and the Communists in Germany and that England and other countries should stay out of it. Let them sort whatever's going on between them amongst themselves, don't you agree? He's so intelligent. Don't you agree?"

Tom murmurs into his journal. "By whose standards? Yours or mine?"

He doesn't even look up. And it's probably best that he doesn't because then he'd see how much he wounded her.

"You're so funny sometimes," she lies. Sometimes shy girls need to be strong. They need to hide their emotions. They need to overcome. And sometimes they need to come over. And that's exactly what the two teenage girls across the restaurant do.

"Can we have your autograph?" one of them asks.

"I'm sorry, all we have are these napkins," the other demurs.

"We left our copies of your poem at home."

"We didn't expect to run into you."

Tom signs their napkins.

"Thank you so much for introducing yourselves," he says.

The girls curtsy on their way out like they've met the queen, and in a way, they have. Tom is their royalty.

Tom gives them a big smile as they exit.

Vivien smiles, too, waiting for Tom's eyes to meet hers, waiting for a moment where they're both smiling at each other. But Tom goes straight back to his journal.

What should she do? Should she continue with her tarot? Should she turn over another card? A few words here and there, is it that hard?

"Bertrand's taking me to meet him this evening. Well, maybe not him, but people like him. Well, maybe not like him, but in his club."

Tom sets down his pen, blinks his eyes. "Meet who? What club?"

Vivien smiles. "Sir Oswald Mosley. He's got this club called the British Union of Fascists. They don't want anything to do with Germany. Bertrand said something like that. I'm sure they're not for another war either."

Tom looks at Vivien blankly. "Vivien . . .?" *Does she realize what she's saying?*

"Yes, dear?" Vivien asks eagerly.

Tom lets out a huff of air and then gets back to his writing. "Oh . . . never mind."

"Tom?"

"Yes, Vivien?" he asks with a tone.

It's the tone a father takes with his children. *Tom would be a good father, wouldn't he? What would it be like to raise the children of a poet? Marvelous, wouldn't it be?* They'd play in the park. Climb trees. Their father could write, push them on swings. They could have picnics. Vivien would prepare the most fantastic picnics. There would be apples and cheese and fig jam and bread . . . but she won't get any of that if she keeps being a shy girl.

"I've been meaning to talk to you about . . . children. When will we have children running around the house? I mean, how much fun would that be?"

"Absolutely not. No children. Not yet," Tom utters with little consideration, almost as if she had asked him if he wanted any butter.

Absolutely not? Never? How could that be? You get married. You have children. She didn't ask Tom if he wanted kids before marrying him because, well, who doesn't want children? But there are many things that people do once they're married that Tom and Vivien aren't doing.

"Tom?"

Tom sighs, but doesn't look up from his work. "Yes, Vivien?"

"Do you ever . . . are you ever compelled to take advantage of me? I mean, I'd understand. And you wouldn't be taking advantage of me, not really. I don't understand why people say it like that. It's not unnatural or anything. Lots of people have certain desires. I might even want something like that myself. It's possible, you know."

Tom sets his pen down, leans back in his chair. *Is it finally time?* Finally time to clear the air? He's been wanting to tell her this for the longest time. It's something that he's always known, deep down. Marrying Vivien made the fact even clearer.

"The body is the enemy of the soul," Tom says solemnly. "Our relationship must remain pure, holy."

There. He said it. And it's true, isn't it? We only have one body and that body belongs to God. *Yes, that's right.* There will be time for progeny. But first, Tom must work on his legacy. He puts his head down, gets back to writing.

"I will tell you when the time is right."

Vivien slides her napkin off the table, wipes her mouth with it. She snatches Tom's glass of wine, takes a sip. He doesn't even notice.

"Oh, yes . . . of course."

24

Tom gets close to the glass, curious to see if they have anything new. He sees paper covers on the poetry. Leather covers on the real literature. Or at least that's what some people still maintain. Poetry. Prose. It's all literature, although Tom can't help but notice the difference between how the two are presented in bookstores.

Nevertheless, his eyes roam widely. He sees D. H. Lawrence's "Tortoises," Robert Graves's "The Pier-Glass," Nancy Cunard's "Outlaws," Aldous Huxley's "Leda," Ruth Pitter's "First Poems," and "The Second Coming" of W.B. Yeats.

Tom's face falls. They're all poems he's read before.

"Can you imagine your poetry in the window?" Vivien asks.

"Yes. Yes, I can," he says plainly.

Vivien empathizes with the longing in his eyes.

Big Ben chimes. It's time. A shopkeeper appears on the other side of the glass. He places a new book on the shelf, a tan mass.

It's a simple cover, just one word in the title, but something doesn't need to be complicated to have impact.

It reads "PRUFROCK" in black capital letters.

Tom's head jerks back. "Is it? How did . . .?" He can't quite figure out what to ask Vivien.

"Ezra told me what time they put out new books," she says as she takes his hand. "He thought it might be good for us if the surprise came from me."

A surprise in need. A surprise indeed.

"Come on," Vivien announces as she pulls him inside.

Tom grabs the display copy from the shelf. It has his name in the lower right corner, and on the inside cover, the full title, "Prufrock and Other Observations."

Tom's smile is as wide as the Nile.

But the shopkeeper treats him like bile. "Sir! Put that back!"

Tom flinches, he's not filching it.

The shopkeeper snatches the book out of Tom's hand, places it back on the shelf. "That's for display only," he chides and walks away.

"I'd like to buy T.S. Eliot's book, please," Vivien says, but the shopkeeper doesn't hear her.

Vivien plants her feet, cups her hands around her mouth. "I'd like to buy T.S. Eliot's book, please!"

Why is she shouting? Is it all a tease? The other shoppers, busy as bees, stop buzzing around. They freeze.

The shopkeeper returns, puts on his customer service face. "How can I help you, madame?"

"I thought I was clear. I would like to purchase T.S. Eliot's book."

"I'm sorry, but we're sold out."

"Sold out!" Tom yelps. He covers his face with his hands, not knowing how to contain the emotion.

"Yes, sir," the shopkeeper responds warily. "And I ask that you refrain from becoming hysterical. It's been a hard enough day as it is telling everyone not to worry about their slot on the waiting list."

Tom throws his hands in the air. "Waiting list!"

"Sir, if you continue this outburst I shall ask you to leave."

"Don't mind him," Vivien reassures the shopkeeper. "There's a waiting list?"

"Yes, right," the shopkeeper continues as he leads them to the counter. "We've had a waiting list for days. Debated whether or not to put out the display copy. Thought someone might try to steal it, but tradition is tradition."

He places a ledger in front of them. "But if you sign here you—"

Bang. The shop door slams shut. A man runs away down the street.

The shopkeeper dashes to the door to find the display copy of "Prufrock" has grown legs.

"Dammit!"

He trudges back to Tom and Vivien. He squeezes his eyes and mouth into a smile, but his nostrils are flaring. "That's unfortunate." He inhales sharply. "So, can I place you on the waiting list?"

"Yes," Vivien agrees readily, signs her name in the ledger.

But then she flips a page and signs again.

"I'm sorry, madame, what are you doing?" the shopkeeper huffs.

"Oh, I'm starting the waiting list for his second book."

Tom looks at Vivien warily. "But I haven't written a second book yet."

"Yes, I know that," she says. "I'm informing them I'd like to buy it when it comes out. Drum up demand, as they say."

The shopkeeper rolls his eyes, takes a step back. It's not worth the fight. "So, is there anything else I can help you with today?"

Vivien spies a stack of Robert Graves's "The Pier-Glass" and takes one off the top.

"Yes, I'll take this . . . for now."

Vivien hands Tom the tome on their way out of the shop.

"For you. A present to my husband. I planned on it being your book, but this will have to do for now."

"Thank you," Tom replies graciously, even though he's already read it. "I shall cherish it."

"I only ask you do one thing in return."

Should he even ask what it is? He doesn't want children yet. And he can't do the other things Vivien wants him to do to her either. Perhaps he should be polite and ask her though. *Would harm could it bring?*

"What is it?"

Vivien is deadly serious. "I'd like you to push me on a swing."

Back and forth. Back and forth. On top of a hill. Tom pushes Vivien back and forth beneath the bough of a tree. Her face is alight with joy. Tom's glad he can make her happy. He realizes he's not the ideal husband, but he's being the best husband he can be, isn't he?

Tom pushes her with one hand while the other holds Robert Graves's "The Pier-Glass." He's read it before, but now, with Vivien, on this hill, pushing her back and forth, he sees it with a new set of eyes.

He reads:

Lost manor where I walk continually
A ghost, while yet in woman's flesh and blood;
Up your broad stairs mounting with outspread fingers
And gliding steadfast down your corridors
I come by nightly custom to this room,
And even on sultry afternoons I come
Drawn by a thread of time-sunk memory.

Empty, unless for a huge bed of state
Shrouded with rusty curtains drooped awry
(A puppet theatre where malignant fancy
Peoples the wings with fear). At my right hand
A ravelled bell-pull hangs in readiness
To summon me from attic glooms above
Service of elder ghosts; here at my left
A sullen pier-glass cracked from side to side

Scorns to present the face as do new mirrors
With a lying flush, but shows it melancholy
And pale, as faces grow that look in mirrors.

Is here no life, nothing but the thin shadow
And blank foreboding, never a wainscot rat
Rasping a crust? Or at the window pane
No fly, no bluebottle, no starveling spider?
The windows frame a prospect of cold skies
Half-merged with sea, as at the first creation,
Abstract, confusing welter. Face about,
Peer rather in the glass once more, take note
Of self, the grey lips and long hair dishevelled,
Sleep-staring eyes. Ah, mirror, for Christ's love
Give me one token that there still abides
Remote, beyond this island mystery,
So be it only this side Hope, somewhere,
In streams, on sun-warm mountain pasturage,
True life, natural breath; not this phantasma.

A rumour, scarcely yet to be reckoned sound,
But a pulse quicker or slower, then I know
My plea is granted; death prevails not yet.
For bees have swarmed behind in a close place

Pent up between this glass and the outer wall.
The combs are founded, the queen rules her court,
Bee-sergeants posted at the entrance-chink
Are sampling each returning honey-cargo
With scrutinizing mouth and commentary,
Slow approbation, quick dissatisfaction—
Disquieting rhythm, that leads me home at last
From labyrinthine wandering. This new mood
Of judgement orders me my present duty,
To face again a problem strongly solved
In life gone by, but now again proposed
Out of due time for fresh deliberation.
Did not my answer please the Master's ear?
Yet, I'll stay obstinate. How went the question,
A paltry question set on the elements
Of love and the wronged lover's obligation?
Kill or forgive? Still does the bed ooze blood?
Let it drip down till every floor-plank rot!
Yet shall I answer, challenging the judgement:
'Kill, strike the blow again, spite what shall come.'
'Kill, strike, again, again,' the bees in chorus hum.

Back and forth. Back and forth. Give and take. The wandering. The obstination. The obligation. *Did Vivien mean to give me this poem?* It seemed random. But now all he can hear are the bees, and their hum.

Or is it the sound of water? Is he hearing the babbling brook from his Garden of Eden? No, it's just the bubbling from his bathroom.

Mr. Eliot glowers. Vivien showers.

The water stops with a squeak. The floorboards creak. And Vivien comes to bed, but she doesn't want to sleep. She's dressed seductively in the nightgown she bought at the shop earlier, or at least she's as seductive as she can be in a boxy sheath. She opens up the green package with pink ribbons, pulls out red gauze. She saunters over to the lampshade, drapes the red gauze on top. First the lamp on one side of the bed, then the lamp on the other, casting the room into a crimson glow. She walks over to the table, takes a rose out of the vase, and places it on Tom's pillow with both hands.

Then she arranges herself even more carefully. She splays out on the bed, trying as hard as she can to look casual. Her left arm is perched behind her head. She drapes her right arm toward Tom's side, the one with the rose. Her legs are bent. She holds her knees tightly together, although she wants them to be parted.

Tom needs to shower. He escapes to the bathroom. *How long can I stay in here?* An hour?

Water. Squeak. Floorboard creak. Tom emerges, surveys the scene. *Hell.* The room is the color of hell. Did he have too much to drink? Had it gone to his head? *When did the room turn red?* He notices the red gauze on the lampshades before he sees Vivien on the bed. Red gauze. *It's like the cravats that Jack has on his lampshades*, he remembers. And then he sees Vivien. A grave expression comes over his face. *She's trying so hard.* She's trying so hard to be his wife. If only he wanted to be her husband. That would make everything so much easier.

"I'll tell you when it's time," he says.

Tom stomps over to his side of the bed, rips the red gauze off the lampshade, turns out the lamp, and climbs into bed.

Ow! Tom yelps. He forgot about the rose.

Vivien stifles a giggle. He forgot that beautiful things can have thorns.

Vivien lies motionless as Tom turns away from her, licking his wounds. The room is still red. The lamp on her side is still covered with gauze. But Tom's side has sunken into darkness.

What's going on in his mind? What's he dreaming about? Vivien would love to wander around Tom's brain, either awake or asleep, and understand what's going on. What has she done wrong? *Why won't he tell me?* It's driving her mad.

Vivien pulls the red gauze off her lampshade, keeps it in her hand as she goes over to the kitchen. She pours herself a glass of wine, but doesn't drink it, at least not yet. She rummages through her purse, pulls out a vial of ether, and sets it down next to her wineglass. She wants to see red, so she uses the gauze as a blindfold.

Then her right hand reaches out cautiously. *There it is.* She grasps the vial. Her left hand probes for the wineglass. She pours in the whole bottle of ether.

She licks her lips, says, "Please give me a friendly drop," and then swallows the entire concoction in one fell swoop.

Vivien takes the blindfold off, staggers back to bed. She's woozy. Perhaps too woozy.

Thy drugs are quick.

Has she drunk too much? Will she die? *What is this horrible state of mind?* But then she remembers. This is what she wanted to get rid of. This is why she's taken the ether.

She waits for the ether to take effect. She prays it's quick, because when drugs are quick, everything else slows. She didn't expect the world to be this slow, though. *Has she drunk too much?* No, she's swilled the right amount. Enough to give a quick thrill, but not kill. She's consumed enough to fall asleep quickly. Enough to sleep, but not to dream.

25

Tom can't sleep. He can't stop thinking. *What did Vivien expect would happen? What was she doing in the kitchen? Is she asleep right now?* Or just pretending like he is? Tom wants to fall asleep, but can't. He can't wait for this night to end. He can't wait for his brain to shut down, to stop screaming at him. Why is it keeping him awake? Why won't it leave well enough alone? Vivien had tried again . . . and when she tried he thought of Jack. Why can't he stop thinking about Jack? He needs to forget everything about that man. He's no good for him. No good for his career. That's clear.

Tom sits upright. His posture is poised, tight. He looks over at Vivien, who takes slow, deep breaths. She's sleeping. The moonlight streams in, wafting through the window, bringing dreams. Or are they schemes? Tom has an idea, one that will surely get Jack out of his head. Yes, he knows exactly what he needs to do.

Tom shuffles down a cobblestone street, furtive, suspicious. It's a road he's walked down many times, but he's about to do something he never thought he would do. He hopes he doesn't see a soul, hopes there's no one around to witness him lose his. The lights of a taxi appear before him. Tom ducks into a shadow. As the car passes, he glances inside, but it's too dark to see. But no matter, Tom doesn't care who's in there. The taxi turns a corner until it's out of sight.

Tom steps out of the shadow and sees: There they are. The trees.

He's entered this park many times before. He strolls past the bench where he usually sits.

Tom soaks in the moonlight. But there's no moonlight in the trees, only shadow. Tom straddles the edge, takes one step forward, then another. He leaves the park. Enters the dark. Trill. What is that? The sound of a lark? Tom can't tell. There's no light, no spark. So much night.

Tom wanders under the plumage of a large oak tree, but that's not what he's come here to see. He blinks his eyes. They still haven't adjusted yet. Will there be anything here worth seeing? Will there be anything here worth being? There's still so much to see in these trees. And that's when he sees him, on his knees. That neck. Those ears. That jaw. Those eyes. Tom can see everything. Moonlight. Shadow. His eyes have adjusted. He can tell it's a man he's acquainted with just by looking at his back. He can tell it's Jack.

"Jack, is that you?" Tom asks.

"Tom?"

Jack stands up. A frightened blob blends back into the night.

Jack gets close to Tom, wanting to make sure it's him. "Why are you here?"

"I don't know. I guess I had a whim."

A whim. A whim. Jack understands why Tom came here. He's not dim.

"I know why," Jack says.

"You do?"

"I do. And this place is not for you."

But it is. He senses it. It's the place where he's wanted to . . . where he's wanted to come for a very long time. Perhaps he can take this as a sign, though. Tom came here to forget Jack, but apparently, God had other plans in mind.

"Let's get out of here," Jack whispers.

But before Tom can respond, Jack has whisked him out of the trees. Out of the sleaze. They disembark. Out of the park. Out of the dark.

"Where are you taking me?" Tom asks.

Jack clenches his jaw. "Well, we can't go back to your place, now can we?"

"You're right, there's no . . . space," Tom responds sheepishly.

Where to go? Where to go? Back to the trees?

Tom tilts his head to the side. "Can't we go back to your flat?"

"Oh, you'd like that."

Tom looks down, frowns. "Yes, I would."

They're walking so fast, but when Jack sees he's hurt Tom, he slows down. He takes his hand and places it on the back of Tom's neck. "My mother is visiting, or else we'd go there."

"Your mother?"

"Believe it or not, I have one."

Tom laughs.

Jack looks at him in the moonlight. "I know somewhere."

Jack leads him down a small street leading to a small hotel. It looks ancient. The grime has built up over time. The roof looks caved in. Or was it bombed? It's thoroughly run-down, although that would presume there was someone running it. There are no signs of life.

They enter through the front door, but there's no one at the counter. Jack peers over it.

"Sometimes he's asleep," Jack says. And he's right. A funny little man is curled up in the fetal position on the floor. Jack reaches over him, snatches a key from the wall.

"He won't mind," Jack says softly.

Softly. Softly. They tread softly down the corridor, leading to a bright red door. Tom looks at the other doors in the hallway. This is the only red one.

"Are you sure this is the right one?"

Jack inserts the key, turns it to the right. Click. That did the trick.

Jack looks at Tom. "The real question is . . . do you want it to be the right one?"

Jack enters. After a few steps, he's gone, disappeared into the dark. Tom stands before another doorway, looking into a black pit.

A match flares, illuminating Jack's face, illuminating the space, this . . . place.

The light goes out. Tom shuts the red door behind him, marches toward the flame. He can no longer see Jack, but he can sense where he is, and that's where he wants to be.

Hands grope. Mouths meet. Tom tastes Jack. He's sweet.

Jack pushes Tom backward. He lands on something springy, a bed. Tom blinks his eyes. When he was kissing Jack they were closed, but now, on the bed, are they open? Are they closed? Does it matter? Is he focusing on this too much? It's hard to focus on something you can't see.

"You want a stranger? Is that why you were in the park?" Jack asks. "I can be a stranger."

Jack thrusts himself on Tom. Tongues thrash. Bodies mash. Tom's eyes adjust. He looks around the room. It's trash. There's a chair turned over on its side. The bed doesn't have a sheet. A tiny shape scurries across the floor. Tom closes his eyes. Some things are better left unseen.

Tom doesn't see stars this time. Only bars. The ones on the windows. Why anyone would want to break into this place is anyone's guess. Although perhaps the bars aren't meant to keep people out.

Tom lies in Jack's arms, staring up at the ceiling. Like him, it's buzzing, pulsing.

"Let's get up," Jack says.

"No, can't we stay here a while?"

"Yes, but first we have to be good boys and make our bed."

Jack stands him up, lays their clothes down. He spreads out their jackets, lines up their pants, covering every corner of the mattress.

"There. That's better," Jack says. "We don't want all the creatures of the night cuddling us, now do we?"

Creature of the night. Is that what he is?

Tom wanders over to the window, sees a slowly pulsing red neon sign below. Pulse. Pulse. Impulse. Repulse. The two are so similar.

"Do you have a cigarette?" Tom asks.

"Would you like a cigarette? I didn't know you smoked."

"I don't," Tom says. "But I've heard it's something that people do, after . . ."

Jack grazes his hand on Tom's back. "I wouldn't get too caught up in trying to chase what other people do."

"I just thought it might calm me down."

"Why would you ever want to be calm?" Jack asks as he pinches the pink area between Tom's legs.

Tom squeals, doubles over. He glares at Jack, smiles, and laughs.

Jack tumbles onto the bed. Tom joins him, ready for another rumble. He kisses Jack's neck. He gives his cheek a peck, then cuddles him.

"I like this place," Tom says.

"Well, I'm insulted," Jack jokes. "Because that means you have very low standards."

"No. I . . . here. With you. I like being here with you."

"Then stay here with me," Jack says with cautious hope.

"You know I can't do that."

"I know you don't want to. I know that you're too concerned with trying to be something you're not."

For just having experienced so much pleasure, Tom is surprisingly numb. He realizes Jack is right. "So, what do we do then?" he asks.

"We? Who says there's a we?"

"I do," Tom says.

Jack turns to his side. Tom couldn't have said what Jack heard him say, could he? The two men lie face to face, the neon light buzzing the air between them.

"I do, too," Jack says. "And I wish that was enough."

He kisses Tom on the lips, but faces away, putting his weight on his other hip. Tom throws his arm around Jack, nuzzles his nose into the back of his neck.

"We have to try to make this work," Tom says.

Jack smiles, but it turns into a grimace.

"Yeah, we'll make it work. Sure we will."

"I know you don't trust me," Tom says. "You have every right not to trust me." He runs a hand through his hair. "I don't even really believe it myself."

Jack laughs. "Well, now I'm filled with confidence."

"Do you trust me?" Tom asks.

Jack contemplates the question. "No," he says flatly. "But I do love you."

Tom moves onto his back. Tick. Tock. Tick. Tock. His heart races. He breathes in . . . and out. In . . . and out.

"Are you going to say it back?" Jack quacks.

"I love you," Tom says, the words slipping past his lips. "I thought you already knew that."

"Just because I know it doesn't mean I don't enjoy hearing it," Jack says as he laughs, turns around to face Tom again.

"So, what will we do?" Jack asks.

Tom shrugs. "I don't have a clue, but I look forward to figuring it out, with you."

"Do you trust me?"

Tom squints his eyes at Jack. He can barely make out his face in this light, but Tom swears he could write a chapter on every feature.

"I do," Tom says.

"Good."

26

The candle flickers. It dances. The people around it dance, too. In truth, they're sitting, but it could be considered a dance of sorts.

Vivien cozies up next to Tom. And Jack sits beside Amy Lowell, a sturdy lesbian from Massachusetts.

Vivien examines Jack and Amy, and then leans in to pounce. "So, how did you and Amy meet? Have you been seeing each other long? It's so great that the two of you could join us."

"We haven't really—" Amy starts.

"Ezra introduced us," Jack says.

"Yes, I came to London to see him," Amy adds.

"You came all the way to London just to see Ezra Pound?" Vivien asks.

Tom places his hand on Vivien's, but it's not intimate, it's an intimation.

"We haven't discussed it much, dear, but you do realize he's one of the most important living poets in the English language, don't you?"

"Of course, I know that!" Vivien lets loose, but then reins herself in, restrains herself. "Of course, dear."

"I wondered if he'd even meet with me," Amy says. "So, I brought a letter from Harriet Monroe."

"She's the editor who published 'Prufrock,'" Tom explains.

"I'm fully aware of who she is," Vivien says curtly.

Amy commiserates with Vivien. "Men. They don't give us the benefit of the doubt, do they?"

Vivien smiles. Amy is the friendly face she needs right now. "And how did your meeting with Ezra go?"

"He was more into my money than my ideas, unfortunately."

Vivien shakes her head. "Of course, he was."

Jack tries to change the subject. "You met Tom at Harvard, didn't you?"

"Ah. Yes. Let's talk about my brother."

"I'm sorry. I didn't mean to—" Jack tries to apologize.

"Your brother?" Vivien asks.

"Yes, he's the president of Harvard University," Amy explains. "Although he might as well be the president of the United States for how much people like to talk about him."

Vivien squeezes Tom's arm. "People don't recognize the brilliance beside the man, do they?"

Amy's eyes soften. "Well said, Vivien."

Vivien looks at Tom quickly and then asks Amy. "So, what will you do now that Ezra has rebuffed your advances?"

"Well, I'm happy that you've all come to my rescue on this trip. It hasn't been easy without Ada being here with me."

"Ada? Who's she?" Vivien asks.

Tom glares at Jack, his cheeks flush. "What are you working on now, Amy?"

Amy pauses, not sure which question to answer first.

Jack joins in the misdirection. "Yes, what brilliant work is Ezra overlooking?"

Amy eats up the attention. "A biography of Keats, actually. Well, not a biography, but a chronicle."

"A chronicle? Like a diary?" Vivien asks.

"Something like that," Amy explains. "I have the events of his life mapped out with near day-to-day precision. I'm attempting to recreate what he must have been thinking as he went about his daily life, trying to shed light on aspects of his personal life that led to his professional development, but Ezra says I editorialize too much."

"Why editorialize at all?" Tom asks.

Amy looks confused.

"Why try to get into his mind at all? You should just let his poetry stand on its own merit."

Amy squints at Tom. "Ezra, is that you in there?"

Vivien laughs.

"It already stands on its own merit," Amy says. "I'm only trying to reach a deeper understanding of his work."

Tom interrupts. "Deeper understanding? That's not for you to decide."

"It's for me and others to interpret," Amy retorts.

Jack looks apprehensive, stands suddenly. "I need to go to the bathroom."

They all look at Jack curiously.

"All right," Tom says.

Jack looks at Tom intensely. "I'd like you to join me, please."

"I thought only women did that," Vivien jokes.

Jack scrunches his face, turns on his heel.

Tom sets his napkin down on the table. "If you'll excuse me."

Jack holds the door to the bathroom open as Tom steps inside.

Jack looks pitiful. "I'm sorry. This was a stupid idea. I should have realized she'd bring up Ada. I needed to talk to her beforehand, get her in on it. I wasn't thinking."

Tom leans in, gives Jack a passionate kiss. "It's going swimmingly."

Jack smirks. "Then why am I drowning?"

"Do you know how to swim? Would you like me to teach you?" Tom jokes.

Jack musses Tom's hair. "Please do, then I can drown you."

Jack kisses Tom but then pulls away abruptly. "Should we be leaving them alone together?"

Jack seizes Tom's hand as they dart out of the bathroom, back to the table.

What are they talking about? Has Amy already revealed the true nature of her relationship with Ada?

"I don't write poetry anymore," Vivien says, "but I do love it so."

Tom sighs with relief, perhaps too loudly. Vivien peeks toward him right in time to see their hands move apart. *Were they holding hands? Or just standing close together?* Then she notices Tom's hair. *Why is it mussed?*

"Appreciation of poetry is rather a rare quality," Amy says, snapping Vivien back to their conversation.

Tom and Jack sit.

"Yes, some things are vastly unappreciated, aren't they?" Vivien asks.

"And poetry is the most so," Amy adds. "It is, in my mind, absolutely quixotic to suppose that most people have any real appreciation of poetry at all. Most people have none."

"I couldn't agree more," Vivien says. "Yes, I for one, find that poetry is—"

"One of the highest functions of the human brain?" Amy says, trying to finish Vivien's thought and continue with her own. "But it appeals only to people who have it instinctively. Or those who have slowly and gradually trained a small faculty to a greater knowledge and appreciation. Most people are too stupid, or too lazy, or both. They don't pay attention to . . ."

And that's when Vivien stops paying attention to her. It didn't seem like Amy needed Vivien's attention to continue anyway. Vivien has more important things to pay attention to. Like hair. Tom's hair. *Why is it mussed?* She never would have let him leave the house that way. And it wasn't that way when they were seated. She didn't see him play with his hair. It must have happened in the bathroom. *What happened in the bathroom?* Had he rubbed his head? No, Tom's too fastidious to touch it in a bathroom. It's just not clean. *They have mirrors in there, don't they?* It's a nice restaurant. Not French, but Italian. So, still nice.

She's sure they have mirrors. *Should I go check it out?* No, it's not worth the trouble, especially since she can easily correct it.

Vivien dips her napkin in her water. She uses it to tamp down Tom's hair.

There. She fixed it.

If only everything with Tom was that easy. On their way home, Vivien wonders what she could do differently. Every night she tries to do the same thing, and every night Tom rebuffs her. Vivien is caught in the cycle of Samsara. It's a cycle Tom has been talking a lot about recently. He always brings it up close to bedtime. He always brings it up when Vivien tries to be his wife. Vivien wants to break the cycle. She wants their relationship to have meaning. She wants to mean something to him.

She lights candles in the bedroom, but she's done that many times before. She forgoes draping the room in red light because that usually makes Tom see the other kind of red.

Tom sits fully clothed on the edge of the couch. He sits upright. His face and posture are tense. He looks cornered, ready to flee. He eyes the exit.

Vivien puts on her new negligee. She thought she had Tom figured out with that boxy number, but since that didn't work, she bought one that made her feel sexy. She's gone from nightgown to negligee. This isn't new, though. It's just part of the cycle. Buy negligee. Test negligee. Return negligee. Nothing happens that would make it unreturnable. Then buy another one. Repeat the cycle.

Vivien adds five drops of ether to a glass of wine. Five drops. She usually does five. She glances at Tom. Adds three more. *Break the cycle.* Break the cycle. She must do everything she can to break the cycle.

Five drops. Then three more. Vivien downs the glass. Let's see what tonight has in store.

She enters the living room, trying to walk seductively, but she's shaky. Is it from the nerves or the ether? One combats the other, but the side effects are the same. She puts a record on, sending a sultry blues number wafting through the air.

"Have you listened to any of the records I bought?" she asks.

"No . . . I haven't. What's this one called?"

"Let's see."

Vivien looks at the record spinning. Spinning. Spinning. Round and round. She can't catch the name. It's moving too fast. She lifts the tone arm, screeching the music to a stop. She picks it up, but it keeps spinning, spinning. Vivien blinks. The entire room is spinning. She still can't read the title.

"It's a blues song," Vivien says, hoping Tom won't ask any follow-up questions.

She sets the record back on the platter. Tom's clocks chime. *It's time*, Vivien reassures herself. Time to make music. Time to put the needle in the groove. Vivien does so, and the sultry blues number starts over again. No, she doesn't want to start over. She wants to pick up where she left off. Vivien tries to move the needle, but every time she picks it up and drops it down, the song starts over again. The record is stuck in the cycle, too.

Vivien closes her eyes. Breathes in and out. When she opens them, she sees two things: Tom and a bouquet. Vivien loves roses. She loves having a bouquet prominently displayed on the dining room table. But these are not roses. Roses haven't worked. These are *Psychotria elata* and they look like lips. Red lips. Red lips like Vivien's red lips. *Men love red lips, don't they?* Vivien hasn't been successful on her own, and now she's depending on the alluring power of flowers. The florist told her they grow in tropical rainforests. It's a rare plant. It's not easily plucked. Vivien hopes she'll have more luck.

She takes one of the red lips in her hand and then tosses it to the ground.

"Oops," she says, although it's clear it was no accident. Vivien stoops, tries to pick it up seductively, arching her back and pouting her lips.

She smiles, places the floral lips in her teeth. She extends her hands in front of her, mimicking claws or paws . . . and growls.

Tom howls. Laughter emits from his lips like lava out of a volcano. But he stops when he realizes how much it's hurting her. Vivien's chin trembles. Her simpering turns to whimpering.

"I'm sorry. I must have a headache. I'm not in my right mind," Tom says apologetically.

"I can fix that."

Vivien saunters over, straddles Tom's legs, lowers herself onto his lap.

Tom swallows, squirms like a worm wriggling out of the grasp of a curious toddler. He stands quickly, dislodging Vivien from his lap. She falls to the floor as Tom retreats behind the couch. He wants to run. He needs to find Jack.

Vivien picks herself up off the ground. It's time to break the cycle.

"I don't think that—" Tom starts.

"Tonight!" Vivien screams with assertiveness and spite.

"Tomorrow would be—"

"Tonight!"

"We've talked about this. It's just that I—"

"Tonight!"

Tom sweats, frets, considers a few epithets, knows whatever's about to happen will only lead to regret.

Vivien leaps over the couch and kisses him. He turns his head, but she grabs his face, stabs her mouth on his. She only lets go to unfasten his pants.

Tick. Tock. Tick. Tock. *It's finally time*, Tom worries. Time to do his husbandly duties. He can no longer run from Vivien . . . but maybe he can still find Jack. He closes his eyes tight. He stands motionless, as if in a trance, but then grips Vivien, turns her around, and bends her over the couch.

Is it finally happening? Vivien anticipates. But then Tom enters her forcefully. A wave of emotion passes through her, but it's not elation. It's desolation, pain.

"Stop. Stop!" she strains, but Tom doesn't.

Vivien struggles, but he holds her down, ripping her negligee. This is what she wants, isn't it?

"No! No, Tom. No!" Vivien screams through sobs, shaking her head.

But Tom doesn't listen. His mind is somewhere else, imagining someone else.

Vivien stops struggling, tries to join Tom. She tries to imagine she's somewhere else, too. She tries to focus on anything other than what he's doing to her. She tries to escape the rape, if only in her mind.

Her negligee. Her negligee is ripped. *There's no returning it now.*

The cycle is broken along with so many other things.

27

Mr. Prufrock polishes a glass. It's only a small spot, but it bothers him a lot. He scrubs at it furiously until it's gone. *Ah, there it is.* All clean. Mr. Prufrock sets the glass down, completing the place setting. But then he lifts his head, sees what's happening to Tom's perverted vision of the Pansy Club. The zeppelin crashes to the ground. Gold paint drips from the ceiling. There's destruction all around.

"Mr. Prufrock, are you here? Yoo-hoo."

Reverend Hammond appears behind the bar, then sees Mr. Prufrock, scrambling to save the place settings from the ceiling falling down on them.

"There you are," Reverend Hammond says. "What is this place?"

"A pavilion of perversion," Mr. Prufrock says seriously.

"So, what are you doing here?"

Mr. Prufrock gestures to the chaos. "Do you see what's happening? I wanted to show you what he's been up to. I need your help."

"With Tom?"

"Of course, with Tom. Why else would I bring you here?"

Reverend Hammond looks around. Drip. Drop. Gold falls from the ceiling. When will it ever stop? "But what can I do?" he asks. "I'm but a minor player. Hardly more than some references in his private correspondence."

"You're too modest. I've been making good use of you," Mr.

Prufrock says. "You're important. We just need to make sure this isn't a passing fancy, a momentary fling. He can't stay on the path if it's this place he's remembering."

"Won't he outgrow this on his own?" Reverend Hammond asks.

"You've seen what he was thinking about when he . . . well . . . you remember."

Reverend Hammond recoils. "As if the act itself wasn't enough of a sin."

Mr. Prufrock shakes his head. "I almost had him on the right path. He was fulfilling his duty to God and his wife, but then he had to . . . think of that deviant, that Jack fellow."

"He's a lost lamb," Reverend Hammond commiserates. "One of God's chosen who has strayed from the path of righteousness. A prodigal son. And we all know God doesn't mind sacrificing his son for the benefit of others. We should stone him."

"We've already been giving him the stick," Mr. Prufrock says. "How about we entice him with a carrot?"

Tom stirs. Vivien whirs. *How can he sleep?* She wishes she could. She needs a respite from his spite.

Tom's hand reaches high in the air. He's reaching for something with all his might.

Inside his dream, faces beam. Fans scream. A crowd waits outside the Queen's Theatre. A limo arrives. Is Robert Frost gracing us with his presence? The door opens. A man steps out. Who is he? It's not Mr. Frost, but he's immaculately dressed in a tuxedo and long tails, accompanied by a woman dripping with even more exquisite evening wear. She's wearing a pearl necklace, but her dress seems to be wearing one as well. The white pearls decorating it shimmy and sparkle as flashbulbs light up the night.

The crowd calls out to them.

"Mr. Eliot! Mr. Eliot!"

"Can you sign my book!"

"Over here! Can I get an autograph?"

Mr. Eliot looks up at the marquee announcing "Murder in the Cathedral by T.S. Eliot. Opening Night! Sold Out!"

"Mr. Eliot! Mr. Eliot! How do you feel?" a reporter asks. "You've achieved so much success!"

Mr. Eliot squints. The flashbulbs are quite bright.

"Tom. I told you to call me Tom."

The reporter looks at Mr. Eliot cockeyed.

"No, I told you to call me Tom," Mr. Eliot says to no one in particular. "Stop it. Call me Tom."

Tom looks up at the marquee. The period at the bottom of the exclamation point falls to the ground, but it doesn't make a sound. It just flops there, plops there. Drops there, like a speck of paint.

This dream isn't going as Mr. Prufrock planned.

Tom turns away from the theater. Across the street, on a bench, illuminated by a lone streetlamp, sits Jack.

Vivien lowers Tom's hand to his side, then paces about the room. She can't get the evening's events out of her mind. She's his wife. Why does he put her through so much strife? Vivien paces around the room, holding a knife. She doesn't understand what compelled her to pick it up, but now, it seems like the natural thing to do, in case he wakes up, and tries for round two.

Even though Tom is asleep, he still threatens her. She moves the knife from one hand to the other. She can't do this. She can't be here. She needs to leave, if only for a little while. *But where*? It's the middle of the night. She won't be any safer out there than she is in here. The only people out this late at night are exactly the type of people you want to avoid. *But that makes it easier, doesn't it?* If you know you should avoid everyone, there doesn't need to be any judgment involved. There doesn't need to be any thinking involved, only pure, simple, instinctual evasion. That sounds much easier than being in a room with Tom.

Down. Down. Vivien escapes the onslaught of her thoughts by climbing down the stairs. She can't wait to get outside. Outside where it's safe. She passes through the warm, welcoming lower floor on her way to the door, but a woman's scream stops her in her tracks.

Vivien spots a partially open door leading into a flat. The woman sounds like she's in pain. Vivien looks down at her hands, but she left the knife upstairs. She stares at the door, makes her hands into fists. They'll have to do.

Vivien charges into the flat. "Stop it!"

But the scene she envisioned doesn't match the one she enters. Bertrand stands in front of an elegantly dressed woman who is bent over, cackling with laughter. Bertrand must have said something particularly hilarious, but whatever it was, it's been lost now as he turns his attention to his new guest.

"I'm sorry, were we making too much noise?"

The woman continues cackling unrelentingly.

"Can I get you a drink?" Bertrand asks. "Although be warned, I must have given her too much. I can't imagine the story I was telling her was this hilarious."

Vivien squints her eyes. Was Bertrand regaling with a tale over a pint of ale? Or is there more to this cocktail? Her fists relax, but she's still tense. "Yes, I suppose."

Bertrand pours Vivien a beer, hands it to her. "This is odd, isn't it? Me pouring you a drink? Usually, it's the other way around."

Vivien takes a sip, which turns into a gulp, and before she knows it, she's downed the whole glass.

She sets it down on the coffee table. "Things don't always happen the way you expect them to, do they?"

Bertrand is stunned, but intrigued. His chest puffs out. A slow smile creeps across his cheeks.

"I'm sorry," he starts. "Where are my manners? Please. Let me introduce you to Lady Ottoline Morrell."

Lady Morrell stops cackling, but stays sitting. "Charmed, I'm sure."

Hot blood is still coursing through Vivien's veins. "I thought something was . . ." But she trails off, not wanting to finish the thought.

"And you decided to join in, did you?" Bertrand asks.

But Vivien doesn't have a pithy response. All she has is fear in her eyes.

"You see, Lady Morrell is a patron of the arts. She has a lot of stress regarding the degree to which she is monetarily endowed, and I was proposing solutions to alleviate her of that stress, shilling by shilling."

Lady Morrell giggles.

But Vivien doesn't understand what he's insinuating, only the broad scheme he's indicating. Relief. Relief from stress. *Sweet relief.*

"Could you help Tom and me?" she asks. "We've been having a lot of trouble lately."

"I suppose I could come up with a few solutions," Bertrand replies hesitantly.

Good. Bertrand will help us, Vivien hopes. They need to try something new. Something new to fix what's askew.

Vivien tries to rouse Tom.

"Tom, are you happy?"

He's not sleeping, but he's paying her as much mind as if he were, sitting across from her in Pierre's as they wait to order.

Vivien peeks at him longingly.

Tom peers over his menu. Why does he even look at the menu? He already knows what he wants, but it gives him something to look at until the food comes. Then he can look at that instead. He's had a lot of trouble looking at Vivien lately. He's had a lot of trouble speaking to Vivien lately, too, and that's why he doesn't answer when she asks if he's happy.

"I mean, I'm not happy," Vivien continues. "And I realize we haven't been . . . happy together."

She tries to choke back her emotion, present her plea logically. "Married people are supposed to be happy. At least for a while. Of course, we're supposed to fight every now and again. But we're supposed to be happy sometimes, too."

Tom would love to be happy. He'd love to be happy with Vivien, but he doesn't see that happening any time soon. *So, why should she be happy either?*

"What do you want from me, Vivien, that I haven't already given you?" he asks coldly. "Do you need more money?"

Vivien's left hand trembles. Her throat scratches like there's something trying to make its way out.

"I want help . . . we need to get some help," she says. "Help with our marriage. From someone."

"Who?"

"I don't know," Vivien says, although she already has someone in mind. "A minister? A doctor? A psychiatrist? Maybe someone like Dr. Freud? I'd settle for a bartender at this point."

Tom bows his head, returns his attention to the menu. "Well, let me know how it goes."

Vivien bends forward ever so slightly. "What do you mean, let you know how it goes?"

"Tell me if they fix your problems."

Vivien is cold. She checks the door leading to the street. It's shut. So are the windows, but she can still feel a draft pass through her.

"We both need to go, darling," she says calmly. But her mind isn't calm. She sees the solution, but Tom can't see the problem.

"Maybe we could see Bertrand," she says tentatively. "He's a doctor—"

"Bertrand? Why Bertrand?" Tom asks accusingly, lowering his head to scrutinize Vivien. "He's a doctor of mathematics. Do you even understand the difference between—"

"And he's a psychiatrist. He's—"

"He's a philosopher, at best."

Vivien holds her trembling hand with the one that's not. "And he's spiritual. Definitely spiritual. Plus, he's fond of cafes."

"Cafes? What does that have to do with anything?"

Vivien presses her lips together, shuts her eyes for a moment, regaining her strength. "I mean he likes to go to the same places we do. We have similar interests."

Vivien lets her hands drift apart. They're steady. "He could help us. It's worth a try."

A waiter walks up to them. "So, what'll it be?"

Vivien looks at Tom square in the eye. "Yes, Tom. What'll it be?"

28

A vaguely erotic painting hangs over a large Victorian couch. A naked woman is swept up in the wind, covered by a pristine, white cloth. Vaguely erotic. Those two words seem to describe Bertrand better than any others. It's no surprise he decorates his flat the same way he decorates his demeanor. Bertrand fluffs two pillows on his couch.

Ding. Dong. The doorbell rings. Bertrand opens the door to find an anxious woman.

"Vivien, my love. Come in. Come in."

Vivien lies down on the pillows.

"You look distressed, my darling," he says sweetly, "but lovely beneath the emotions."

Bertrand pauses, choosing his words carefully. "Perhaps lovelier because of the emotions."

He kneels beside her. "Yes, the power of your emotions brings out your loveliness, like a flower pushing through concrete."

Vivien perks up. "Flower? What kind of flower?"

"Why, a rose, my dear." What woman doesn't love a rose?

Vivien sinks back into the couch. "I love roses," she slurs. She must be looped on ether. She sways back and forth. "Oh, Bertrand, I don't know what I shall do."

"Money is such a burden, isn't it? But patronage of the arts can set you free like it's done for Lady Morrell."

"Patronage? No, we don't seek to support other artists. We have enough trouble supporting ourselves, thank you."

Bertrand grimaces, but tries to hide his confusion behind an air of curiosity. "Well, if it's not about money, then why are you here?"

Should she tell him? Vivien searches his eyes. *He's being awfully nice, isn't he?* He seems like he'd understand their plight.

"It's about . . . our marriage," she says cautiously.

Bertrand hides a smile. This will be even more delightful than he expected, won't it?

"Tell Bertrand about it, my dear," he says as he takes her hand in his. "Unburden your heart."

"Are you sure? Would that be all right with you?"

Bertrand nods. "You're in good hands."

Vivien's gaze becomes unfocused. Is it the ether or the current state of her marriage? "I married him to stimulate him."

"Stimulate . . ." Bertrand says, really selling the idea that he's listening, that he cares. "Tell me more." But Bertrand can only play this part for so long before he gets bored.

"To bring some life into him. I—"

"To bring him back from the dead, like Dr. Frankenstein, yes?" Bertrand jokes. *Vivien was getting awfully boring, wasn't she?* And besides, some animals like to play with their prey before they eat them.

Vivien squints. "Well, that wasn't the allusion I had in mind, but something like that . . . sure."

"And it hasn't worked, has it?" Bertrand asks, cozying up to Vivien on the couch. "Despite your obvious physical and mental charms, and they are considerable. Don't you have any mind about that, my darling. Despite all that you offer, he still remains a cold dead body laid out on a granite slab."

Vivien's left hand shakes. She brings it to her forehead. "Something like that." She tries to stand up, but Bertrand places his hand on her shoulder, holds her down.

"Sit down. Lie down, my dear."

Vivien opens her mouth to speak, but Bertrand preempts her. "Lie back."

Vivien feels the couch embrace her. Should she let Bertrand crack the mysteries that chase her?

He places a finger over her lips. "You're married, but he won't sleep with you."

"How did you know that?" Vivien asks.

"I can tell," Bertrand intones. "Marriage is hard. A problem waiting to be solved," he says sympathetically, then sidles up next to her, pressing his crotch into her side. "Can you feel my hard solution?"

Is celibacy too steep a price to her? Should she let Bertrand entice her?

"Yes," Vivien ekes out in an uncertain tone.

Memories of the last time she was on a couch with a man seep into her mind. Will Bertrand bend her over the back of it like Tom did? She's apprehensive, scared, but it doesn't seem like he will. She detects Bertrand's attraction to her as he presses up against her leg. As much as she would normally be repulsed by this situation, it's oddly comforting to have a man fancy her. Tom's never seemed attracted. Cordial, yes. Friendly, yes, although that has gone away, too. Why would he marry her if he didn't want to ravish her? Vivien wants Tom to ravish her, but not the way he did. That was painful. It was the most painful thing she's ever experienced, and not just because of the physical force, but the mental toll. His contempt was more painful than his cock. Vivien wants it to feel like love, although the line between those things is blurring.

Vivien closes her eyes. "Would you like to make love to me?"

Bertrand answers the question by placing his tongue upon her neck, licking it with a quick flick. But it's not Bertrand's tongue, it's Tom's. At least that's what Vivien imagines as the man she's with starts removing her dress and becomes the man she wishes he was. Because it's not Bertrand unbuckling his pants. It's not Bertrand climbing on top of her, entering her gently. It's Tom. It's Tom as long as she keeps her eyes shut. It's Tom making love to her. It's Tom unless her eyes call her brain a liar.

"I love you."

Tom only responds with his body, continuing to show her the love she so richly deserves.

That's for the best, Vivien estimates. Better for her ears not to call her a liar either.

Fluffed pillows. Windswept woman, but she's no longer covered by a white cloth. Now the sheet barely covering her bosom features brightly colored specks and stripes streaking out in all directions.

Ding. Dong. Open door. Tom makes his way to the couch.

"Tom, my love. Come in. Come in."

Tom lies down on the pillows. "This is what I'm supposed to do, isn't it?"

"Yes, of course, especially since you seem distressed," Bertrand says sweetly, "but strikingly handsome beneath the emotions."

Bertrand pauses but knows exactly which words he'll say next. "Perhaps more handsome because of the emotions."

He kneels beside Tom. "Yes, your willingness to show your emotions, if only for a moment, brings out the best in you. It shows that you're strong, like concrete."

Tom sinks into the couch. He wishes he were powerful. It's nice to hear someone say he could be.

"Oh, Bertrand, I don't know what I shall do. Why am I even here?"

Bertrand takes Tom's hand in his. He almost flinches, but it's nice to be touched by a man.

"Tell Bertrand about it, my dear. Unburden your heart."

Bertrand massages Tom's shoulders. It doesn't matter that he's doing it from the front, it's nice. Soothing. Should Tom tell him? Bertrand's eyes look kind. He's being awfully nice, isn't he? Tom hasn't had another man be this nice to him since Jack.

"It's Vivien," Tom says. "I simply can't cope with her."

Bertrand smirks. "Ah, the curse of a . . . woman's love."

Tom squints at Bertrand. *What was that about a woman's love? Why did he pause before he said that? Does he know? If he does, why is he still rubbing my shoulders?*

"I wish several women loved me." Tom says, trying to play up his manliness. "If several women loved me, that might make the . . . practical side of love less evident to each of them."

"I know exactly what you mean." Bertrand smirks. It's one of his annoying quirks, but to Tom, it doesn't come across as annoying, but endearing. Jack smirks in the same way. It's a knowing smirk that says he understands what Tom is talking about. And if anyone understands the practical side of loving women, it's Bertrand, isn't it?

"Are you familiar with Aristotle?" Bertrand asks.

The question surprises Tom. "I love his 'Poetics.'"

"I didn't realize he wrote poetry."

"No, his 'Poetics,'" Tom intones, making sure Bertrand heard him correctly this time. He has read it, hasn't he? "His treatise on dramatic and literary theory."

"Ah, yes," Bertrand says. "I meant, are you well acquainted with Aristotle, the man? The way he was. Well, really how all the Greeks were. Are you familiar with that?"

Tom's not entirely sure what Bertrand is referencing. "Please. Illuminate me," Tom says cautiously.

"Oh, well. I'm surprised. If you're familiar with his work, I mean," Bertrand winds up. "Aristotle himself talked about what it was like being a woman with a man. What it was like to be a man being a woman with a man, I mean. Sexuality wasn't as rigid as it is now. In fact, they thought the more people of both sexes that fall in love with you, the better. That's interesting, don't you agree?"

Bertrand scrutinizes Tom's face carefully, but Tom's trying not to show any emotion. His mind is racing. What does Bertrand know? Is Bertrand talking about what Tom assumes he's talking about? And even if he is talking about that, is he talking about that . . . in relation to Tom? Is he flirting?

"I might know what you're talking about," Tom says warily.

"Do you see that as a solution to your problems?" Bertrand leans in. "Perhaps the perfect solution?"

Bertrand's question comes out airily, but to Tom, the words can only be interpreted scarily.

Tom swallows hard, tenses.

"Ah, I thought I loosened you up," Bertrand whispers as he continues to rub Tom's shoulders.

Tom opens his mouth to speak, but Bertrand cuts him off. "Lie down."

Should he let the couch embrace him? Should he unpack the mores that encase him?

Bertrand places a finger over Tom's lips. "Women want more than you're willing to give. So why don't you lie back and receive . . . my wisdom."

Bertrand sidles up to Tom, pressing his crotch against him.

"Sometimes you should keep the door open, and sometimes you should keep the door shut. If you know what I mean."

Yes, Tom knows all too well. Hide your true thoughts. Never get caught.

"You can't find a life that's fulfilling," Bertrand says sympathetically, and puts his hand on Tom's chest. "Life can be so rigid, so hard. A problem waiting to be solved."

He bites his lip, glances down at his crotch. "Would you like to hide my hard solution?"

"Yes," Tom squeaks. He's more certain than ever.

It's been so long since he's been with a man . . . and by man he means Jack. He's only been with Jack . . . and he only wants to be with Jack. It's nice to have Bertrand fancy him, but not as nice as being with . . . wait . . . who says he can't be?

Tom closes his eyes. "Would you like to make love to me?"

Jack kisses Tom on the lips, Tom's eyes squeezed tight to embrace the illusion. Tom and his inhibitions melt into the couch. He see stars on the inside of his eyelids, both from the pleasure and because he's keeping them held shut so tightly.

"I love you."

"Perhaps Vivien should join us next time," a voice offers. Tom knows it's not Jack, but that doesn't matter at the moment. It doesn't matter because the voice might be right.

Yes, Vivien should join us.

That's the solution.

The Bolos are on full display. Queen Bolo is now the windswept woman, but true to the painting, she's no longer confined by her regal finery. She's barely clothed, just cloth covering her bosom. King Bolo wears his crown adorned with a miniature grandfather clock, two horns sticking out the sides, one shaped like a telephone receiver and the other like the horn on a record player. But they're not the only things sticking out from his body, and for good reason. Columbo has joined them. He's stark naked aside from his jester's hat, making King Bolo's arousal grow larger and larger by the moment.

Pillows are fluffed. Doorbell is rung. King Bolo is hung.

Tom can't help but stare at the painting as Bertrand leads them inside. The Bolos didn't used to be in that painting, did they? He remembers so many things about his last visit to Bertrand's, but this isn't one of them. Tom would ask about the transformation, but if he's the only one seeing them in the painting, that would lead to a difficult discussion, and this discussion will already be difficult.

"Vivien. Tom. My loves. Come in. Come in."

Tom and Vivien both try to lie down on the couch, but quickly find that there's not enough room for both of them.

"You both look more relaxed since the last time we were together. Still distressed," he says sweetly, "but radiant beneath the emotions."

Bertrand doesn't pause this time, but goes directly into his spiel. "Perhaps more radiant together because of the emotions.

But he does kneel beside them. "Yes, the power of your emotions brings out your radiance . . . radiances, like a flower . . . or concrete . . . or . . ."

Bertrand's usually suave demeanor must have the day off, or maybe he hasn't been in this situation before, which is hard to fathom.

"Oh, hell," Bertrand says. "Like a flowerbed in a concrete parking lot."

"That sounds about right, doesn't it?" Tom asks as he turns to Vivien. But she doesn't respond right away. Tom wonders if she's nervous, but there's no room for nerves when you're looped out on ether.

"Oh, Bertrand," Vivien says, not replying to Tom, but starting a thread of her own. "We don't know what we shall do."

Tom is excited and nervous. He wants to lick his lips, wick away the sweat forming around his mouth. Or is he salivating?

"We've tried everything," Tom blurts, "but we can't seem to . . . get along . . . together."

Bertrand wedges himself between them on the couch, lays his hands on their laps.

"Tell Bertrand about it, my dears. Unburden your hearts."

Bertrand massages their legs.

Vivien crosses her arms. "He used to like my honesty and joie de vivre."

"Joie de vivre?" Tom explodes. "I wish she didn't have to strangle the life out of me."

Bertrand rolls his eyes, retracts his hands from their thighs. It'll be hard enough getting them on the same page, let alone the same bed.

"What would you say is holding you back from connecting?" Bertrand asks.

"I thought she understood we needed a special arrangement," Tom says.

Vivien sighs. "I thought the no-sex thing was only until marriage, not no sex ever!"

Tom looks away from her, but his tone is biting. "But we've had sex, haven't we?"

Vivien doesn't answer, but not because she doesn't have a thing or two to say on the subject. She retreats into her own little world, inside where it's safe.

Bertrand picks up on her reticence, tries to come between them, or at least more so than he already is.

"So, the two of you have come to me as a third . . . party. A mediator, you might say. To help you carefully facilitate your incompatible urges."

"Yes, that's right," Vivien agonizes.

"Would you like me to fill your gap? Create a safe passage through your sexual turmoil?"

"Yes, we would," Tom says. Vivien sees the eagerness in Tom's face. She wants to make him happy, but she's nervous about this whole arrangement, even though she's the one who arranged it.

Bertrand places his hand on her thigh again. "It's all very modern. The whole thing. I'm like an electric adapter, if you will, that can plug into both outlets and convert from one current to another."

Bertrand notices Vivien's pinched lips, Tom's tense shoulders.

"This is what you came to me for, isn't it?"

"Something like that," Tom and Vivien say simultaneously as they lock eyes. When was the last time they looked at one another?

Bertrand places a hand on Tom's thigh, massages both of them. "The only question I have is, who's Westinghouse and who's Edison?"

Tom and Vivien are stupefied. What is he talking about?

Neither of them opens their mouth to speak, but Bertrand puts his fingers to their lips as if they had. He's anxious, nervous. Bertrand wants this. And that means he'll have to pull out all the stops.

He speaks like he's in a trance. "Life is difficult. You don't know what is right. You don't know what is wrong. Other people won't understand. So, tell my hands what's wrong."

Tom and Vivien share a glance. Should they let his hands embrace them? Should they attack the fears that disgrace them?

Bertrand pulls Vivien in for a kiss, eyeing Tom to make sure nothing is amiss. Then he kisses Tom, eyeing Vivien to make sure she won't explode like a bomb.

Then he makes a triangle of tongues, a three-way kiss.

None of them can move their head, only their lips and, soon, their hips.

They are a triptych folded in on itself, an Eden of earthly delights.

Flesh flies in front of their eyes. Their mouths become too full to speak.

The Bolos occupy themselves as well. Queen Bolo joins in on the fun, sandwiched between King Bolo and Columbo as they try to eat each other, or at least that's what it looks like.

The Bolos match every move Tom, Vivien, and Bertrand make.

Every position. Every orientation. Every aberration.

29

White tie. Tails. An Order of Merit. What a carrot. Tom surveys an adoring crowd. He stands behind a podium wearing his finest, which now includes an Order of Merit from Queen Elizabeth. She may be the one wearing the crown for now, but Tom can see a coup brewing. His subjects are ravenous.

He's gotten used to being around fancy people. No, not people. Royals. He understands how to act around them, how to speak around them, and now he's expected to give quite the speech. He is receiving an award for his use of language, mind you.

His subjects wait expectantly for him to start, everyone except the King of Sweden, that is, who's absent for the first time since the Nobel Prizes were founded. Should Tom be offended? The king has sent the crown prince and princess to hear him speak. They're still royalty, like him. They'll have to do.

"When I began to think of what I should say to you this evening, I wished only to express very simply my appreciation of the high honor which the Swedish Academy has thought fit to confer upon me," Tom begins. "But to do this adequately proved no simple task. My business is with words, yet the words were beyond my command. To profess my own unworthiness would be to cast doubt upon the wisdom of the Academy. I must therefore try to express myself in an indirect way, by putting before you my own interpretation of the significance of the

Nobel Prize in Literature. Poetry is usually considered the most local of all the arts. Painting, sculpture, architecture, music can be enjoyed by all who see or hear. But language, especially the language of poetry, is a different matter. Poetry, it might seem, separates peoples instead of uniting them."

Although his words are somber, the caucus becomes raucous. Everyone is on their feet. Applauding. Making sure Tom knows it's him they're lauding. Their jewels sparkle. So many happy faces. Such a shining moment.

Tom will remember this for the rest of his life. It's sacred.

But then, suddenly, the applause stops. Why did they stop?

Tom looks down. He's naked.

What happened to his white tie? His tails? His Order of Merit?

There's a rustling in the crowd. Then snickers.

Lauding is replaced by laughter. Tom's face goes red. He can't bear it.

Tom turns away from the audience, introducing them to his backside. He looks for an exit. An escape. He wants to run. But where will he go?

Stage right. Stage left. Stage fright. Tom's bereft.

Click. Click. Tom's hands are cuffed.

Two policemen take Tom in their arms. *Where did they come from?* They lead Tom off stage, but not backstage. They drag him right through the audience, past his peers, everyone howling with demonic jeers.

Tom is awash in cold sweat, but he feels dirty. What will he do now? There's no use contemplating such an existence. There is no after . . . after experiencing something like this. Are they leading him to the police station? They may as well lead him to his funeral since he's just been publicly executed. The audience set him up on the stockade and then beheaded him by laughing theirs off.

Tom is humiliated. His head is bowed. His face is flush. His tears gush.

He can hardly see the street as the officers guide him out into the cold Stockholm night.

Tom wipes the tears from his eyes and then realizes . . . he wiped tears from his eyes. Where are his handcuffs? Where are the police? Where are those guys?

Tom stands alone. Cold. *What's going on? Where did I go wrong?*

He looks around. Stockholm is a ghost town.

Tom needs to find warmth. He needs to find cover, or else he'll freeze to death.

He paces one way, then another. *Which way to go?* He doesn't know.

And that's when he sees it, down a long alley across the street. A small red light glows.

Tom runs toward it. Down the alley. Down the wet cobblestones. The red light grows and glows. As he grows closer and closer, he can see that the red light isn't coming from a bulb. It's being reflected onto a wall, from around a corner. Tom hurdles toward it with increasing intensity. He has to reach warmth. He has to create warmth. That's the only way to survive.

He approaches the corner, ready to speed around it, but then slips and falls. Tom hits his head hard on the street. His limp body somersaults around itself, scraping and bruising much more than his ego.

Tom lifts his head, finds himself at the entrance to an alley of decadence.

Men and women of all shapes and sizes cavort around prostitutes in cages, some behind bars, some in store windows, some under gas lamps, all showing off their wares, all dancing alongside their denizens. Some have no physical constraints around them, but all exist in a cage.

In a doorway, a contortionist twists into a human pretzel as a small crowd gathers to eat her.

A whoosh of heat passes over Tom as a shirtless fire-breather walks by wearing stilts and little else.

Tom stands. His shadow from the gas lamp dances away in the dark, just one of many black streaks on this wet cobblestone street. Blacks. Oily blacks. *Has this street always been oil painted?* But it's not only the street. It's also the walking, talking bags of meat. Everyone and everything drips with oily liquid.

As Tom wanders down the alley, he sees a man on his knees with his back to Tom. He's blowing a john. The man writhes with pleasure and releases his sin into the prostitute's mouth. Then the prostitute turns to Tom. Would Tom like a turn? The prostitute doesn't have a face, but the demon occupying his body does. He hisses, his long black tongue flicks out, and then he turns back to the john, slithering and curling his tongue around the man.

Tom staggers back, runs down the street in disgust.

But Tom's footfalls aren't the only ones making their way down the alley.

Click. Click. A tapping. A tick. Tick. Tock. Click. Clock. Footsteps approach, punctuated by the sound of a cane, tapping in time to the steps, cane rapping, counting down.

Where is it coming from?

The gas lamps along the street flicker.

The fire-breather blows fire out of his ass.

Two lesbians make out until they see Tom spying on them. One pulls away, contorts into an impossible twist. Her feet stand on her head. She smiles at Tom for approval, and when he gives none, she frowns. The other woman, now disgusted by both of them, struts off.

Click. Click. The cane tapping gets louder. Tick. Tock. It's time.

"Is this what you want?" Mr. Prufrock leans on his cane. "If not this one"—he points at the lesbian as she returns her feet to the ground—"which one?" He gestures to the parade of prostitutes, all the while holding Tom with a scornful gaze.

"You're doing this?" Tom asks, but it's not a question. It's an accusation.

Mr. Prufrock has a stony expression on his face.

"Was it everything you imagined?"

Tom shakes his head. "Why are you doing this to me?"

"We can make beautiful things together, Mr. Eliot."

Tom stirs in his sleep. He's muttering.

Jack leans in, trying to decipher it. He smiles. His heart is fluttering

Tom's words become more distinct, but he's stuttering. "I can make . . . beautiful. I . . . I don't need . . ."

Jack smiles, but then Tom's words come out quicker, louder. He's sputtering.

"I can make things beautiful! I can make things beautiful!"

Tom's scared, and he's scaring Jack. Jack plants his hand on Tom's chest. He's trembling.

"I can make things beautiful! I can make things beautiful!"

Jack shakes Tom awake.

"I can make! I can . . ."

Tom stops as he takes in his new surroundings. He's relieved, but disoriented.

Jack touches Tom's face reassuringly. "The wonder of the mind is that it can make anything at all."

"What . . . what are you . . . what do you mean?"

"You kept saying over and over again, 'I can make things beautiful.' So I said—"

Tom perks up. "The wonder of the mind is that it can make anything at all."

The laugh lines around Jack's eyes come out to play. "I see you're fully awake then."

Tom sits up. Yes, he's fully awake. And now he's remembering. He couldn't go home after the . . . session with Bertrand. He couldn't go home with Vivien. He needed to go . . . someplace where it's safe. And that's how he ended up at Jack's, but how he ever thought Jack's was safe is beyond him now.

Is this the path he's chosen? Is this who he wants to be?

Tom drags his palms down the sides of his legs. He looks sickly.

"Are you all right?" Jack asks.

"I think I'm going to vomit."

But he doesn't just think it. He knows it will happen.

Tom bolts out of the bed in a beeline to the bathroom.

He retches into the toilet, making him feel like a wretch himself. He tries to empty out all the contents of his stomach, along with his entire memory of that dream.

Jack tries not to take Tom's sickness personally. Normally, he'd come to Tom's aid in matters such as this. That's why he let Tom in last night. But for the moment, he lets Tom take care of his own problems. Jack doesn't want to clean up all of Tom's messes.

Even so, he still asks, "Do you need any help?"

"No, I'll be fine in a minute."

Jack takes the opportunity to look through Tom's jacket. *There it is.* Tom's journal. Jack opens it, roams the pages with his eyes. He reads the inner workings, sees the inner thoughts. Every day. Every fragment. All bound in one tome. He tries to make out the lines that are crossed out. *What does it say?* What are the thoughts he's ashamed of?

Jack flips through the pages. *Where is it?* He's looking for something. *Where's that poem?* The one he wrote for him.

Ripped pages. Torn memories. Jack examines the shredded stubs of pages that have been removed from Tom's journal. He must have been too ashamed of it, too ashamed of Jack. But Jack doesn't need to read the poem. He remembers it.

Sometimes people need to be reminded of what they're ashamed of.

Jack plucks a pen and writes. Black ink dances on the blank page, turning it into a performance, a stage.

Tom exits the bathroom, enters stage left.

"What are you doing?"

Jack doesn't look up. "I'm writing your poem."

"You're writing my poem?"

"Yes, the one you told me."

Tom takes a seat next to Jack, looking over his shoulder. He wants to see if it really is his poem. They say beauty is in the eye of the beholder. Is the same true for poetry? Will whatever Jack is writing be a mirror for Tom? Will he be able to see his own beauty? Or will it reveal his ugliness?

Tom reads:

> Now when they were three weeks at sea
>
> Columbo he grew rooty.
>
> He took his cock in both hands
>
> And swore it was a beauty.
>
> The cabin boy appeared on deck
>
> And smeared the mast-o
>
> Columbo grasped him by the balls
>
> And buggered him in the ass-o.

It may be written as finished poetry, but it was not meant to be consumed as such. Tom would never want his vile blatherings written down, and that's why he removed them from his journal.

But for a moment, all that Tom can focus on is Jack's technical proficiency in scribing the poem from memory.

"How did you . . ."

"You didn't expect me to remember that little bit of brilliance?" Jack asks.

It's impressive. It's exactly as Tom remembers it. But it can't stay in his journal. What if someone reads it?

Tom reaches over Jack's shoulder for his journal, but Jack moves it out of the way.

"What are you doing?" Jack asks.

"I'm reclaiming what's mine."

Tom tries again, but Jack holds him back.

"I'm not done with the poem," Jack says.

"What do you mean, not done? You wrote it down perfectly."

"Thank you for the compliment," Jack says with his signature smirk. "But I want to make sure it remains that way. It only needs one more thing."

"Oh, yeah?" Tom asks incredulously. "And what's that?"

"A promise. What's been torn . . . now must be sworn."

Tom tries for the journal one more time, but Jack blocks his arm, knocks him over. Tom struggles as Jack pins him.

"I know you," Jack says. "You'll rip it out as soon as I hand it back. And I want you to promise me you'll keep it in there . . . promise me you won't erase it again."

A tear wells up in Jack's eye. He might not be talking about the poem.

Tom stops struggling, and not only because Jack has him pinned.

"Fine."

"Do you promise?"

The tear is no longer welling in Jack's eye. It's there.

"I promise," Tom says solemnly.

30

They say home is where the heart is, but it's also where you keep everything else you own. And it's probably where your wife is.

Tom slogs up the stairs. His hand pauses a few inches from the knob. *Is she home?* Maybe she's gone shopping. He turns the knob carefully as if he's walking on thin ice, which he is. He opens the door slowly, but there must be a window open. He feels a rush of air. And that's when he smells it, that sweet smell of sweat and books. The smell of Jack. And if he can smell Jack, Vivien surely will, too.

"Tom, is that you?"

Tom races over to his desk. He needs to get Jack off him, but before he does, he needs to lock up his journal. There are some stinks you can wash off, and others you need to hide. *Where's the key? Where's the key?* Tom checks his pockets for the key to his desk drawer. *Jack didn't take it, did he?* No, he didn't. Tom finds the key in the corner of his front jacket pocket surrounded by lint. It's been a while since he locked his journal away, but now, he needs to. It's a risk he can't take.

He stashes the journal with a click of the key.

"It is you," Vivien says, standing near the kitchen with a knife in her hand. "I thought maybe we were getting robbed."

"No, nothing of the sort," Tom says as he makes his way toward the bathroom.

"Are you all right?" Vivien asks. "Would you like a cup of—"

But Tom shuts the bathroom door behind him.

Vivien twirls the knife in her hand. It's a shame. If it were a robber, she would have liked to use it.

Vivien stares at Tom's desk. She moves the knife from one hand to another. Should she?

She walks over to it. She can hear the water running in the bathroom. There's a good amount of thrashing going on in there. *What did Tom put in his drawer?* What is he stashing in there? It's locked, but she knows how to open it. Yes, you could use a key, or you could use something cleverly.

Vivien lodges the knife between the lock and the drawer, pushes down hard. The lock opens easily. *If only Tom were this easy to crack.* She holds the journal in her hand for a moment. Should she read it? Should she betray Tom's trust?

Trust. Lust. Tom seems to have neither for her. Why should she have both for him?

Vivien scours the pages. There has to be an answer.

Her mind rages, eager to find the cancer.

There it is.

A poem quite unlike the others.

A poem that reveals Tom's druthers.

A poem that says Tom and Jack are more than brothers.

Vivien needs to confront Jack, but where? Somewhere she can ensnare. Perhaps at Pierre's?

Pierre's has the best tea, and there's nothing better than a good cup of tea. It's warm. It smells good. Makes you feel good. The only thing better than a cup of tea is a refill.

Vivien watches Jack refill his tea, and check his watch. He's been waiting, and hasn't been enjoying his tea as much as he should.

Vivien approaches Jack's table at Pierre's wearing a long black coat done up with a large buckle. Her tall boots lead to loose riding trousers. Is she trying to dress like a man? But nowhere does she look more butch than her armband. A white bolt of lightning cuts through red.

Jack looks at her curiously, asks her jokingly, "Have you been drafted into the British Union of Fascists?"

But there's nothing jocular about Vivien's reply. "No, not drafted. I enlisted."

Jack laughs until he realizes she's not kidding.

"But those people . . ." Jack says until he realizes there's no good way to describe them without insulting her.

"It's a very nice club," Vivien says, sits. "We want to return England to its former glory, stop the immigrants from taking our jobs, changing our culture. It's never nice when someone takes something that's yours, now is it?"

Jack averts his gaze to his tea. "I do love the tea at Pierre's, don't you?"

Vivien turns over an unused teacup on the table, pours herself some.

"As I said, it's quite nice. We sing songs, and we all get to wear fancy getups like this."

Vivien takes a sip, then dumps the remaining creamer in her cup. But it's not enough. She motions to the waiter, lifts the creamer, and then adds two eye droppers of ether. She's not hiding it from anyone anymore, least of all from Jack.

"They are something . . . aren't they?" Jack says coolly.

"Well, I got all dressed up for a meeting, but it turns out the meeting was yesterday and I completely missed it. It's just as well, though. I forgot to make my sign."

"What did you need a sign for?" Jack asks.

"Oh, we were about to go for a lovely walk in the park, all holding signs. I planned for mine to say, 'Stop the conspiracy of international Jewry.' That has a nice ring to it, don't you agree? It's such a shame that I got the day wrong. I would have loved a nice walk in the park. Have you ordered yet?"

No, he hadn't. Had he looked at a menu? If he had, after Vivien's tirade, he's forgotten it. If he had any hunger, he's lost it.

"No," Jack says. "I was just having some tea."

The waiter brings more creamer.

"We'd like to order," Vivien says to him.

Jack puts down his menu. "No, nothing for me."

"It's all right," Vivien says. "I'm used to eating alone."

She scans her menu, but she already knows what she wants. "I'd like a croque monsieur."

"One croque monsieur for both of you?" the waiter asks. "Shall I bring two plates?"

"No, we're not sharing," Vivien says seriously.

The waiter nods, leaves.

A carriage passes on the street. A bird tweets in the park. Jack and Vivien can hear everything that's going on in the neighborhood because neither one of them is saying a word.

Some children have staring contests. Jack and Vivien are having one with silence. But in this game, the winner isn't necessarily the one who holds out the longest. No, they're playing for something with much higher stakes.

"I wasn't sure you'd come," Vivien says slyly.

Jack smirks. "Well, sure. Why wouldn't I come?"

"I don't know. Most people might be ashamed . . . or afraid. But I guess neither of those apply to you."

If Jack has anything to hide, he won't let that show now. "What are you talking about?" he asks with a sincere tilt of his head.

Vivien's jacket is a few sizes too large, but that gives her ample room to hide things. She reaches inside, pulls out Tom's journal, and sets it on the table. Jack's eyes flare for a moment, but then he reigns in his emotions. Vivien delights in Jack's fright.

"How's Amy?" Vivien asks, changing the course of conversation.

Jack squirms. He knows what he's about to say is true, but it sounds like a lie. "She had a hernia and needed to head back to Boston. Part of a glandular issue, she said."

"How . . . unfortunate."

It is unfortunate. She could have been the perfect solution, or at least part of it.

Jack can't stop staring at the journal. Vivien smiles. She'll enjoy watching him wriggle at the end of her hook.

"Do you like my journal?" she asks sweetly, before turning sour. "Tom and I have been having problems and I've been writing about it in here.

Jack's lip curls in confusion. *What is she doing?* He knows it's Tom's journal. He's memorized each crease in the leather. He's internalized the binding. It's not hers, so what is she doing?

"And we've had even more problems ever since the whole Bertrand debacle," Vivien continues. "Tom's been, well, gone . . . but I'm sure you're familiar with all that already."

Jack realizes she's baiting him. He doesn't understand what game she's playing yet, but he can't help but play along. He needs to know.

"What Bertrand thing?" he asks.

"Oh, Tom didn't tell you?" Vivien says insincerely, "Oh, well, Tom was responsible for that horrible situation."

Worm. Hook. "What situation?"

Vivien cocks her head to the side. "Well, Bertrand . . . you know how he is."

Jack does know, but he doesn't want to. "Yes. I do. I most certainly do."

More silence. *Where does the game go from here?* Jack realizes all Vivien has to do is reel him in, but he doesn't care.

"What happened?"

Vivien simpers, but quickly turns it into a whimper. "Well, Tom wanted to work out some physical problems we've been having. He insisted really. I'm sure you can imagine what I'm referring to."

"I can."

"And he was desperately looking for a solution . . . Tom wants me to be taken care of. So, I arranged a meeting with Bertrand, and—"

Jack cuts Vivien off, trying to draw his own conclusion. "And Bertrand was there at your most vulnerable moment. Typical Bertrand behavior. Not your fault at all."

Vivien gives Jack a dazed look. Jack, hoping it's because he's right, continues leading the witness. "So, you and Bertrand . . ."

Vivien perches her hand on the journal ever so softly. It's a small movement, but she draws Jack's eyes. Yes, that's right. She has the journal. She has the power.

"Well, no, that was only part of it," Vivien says as she leans back in her chair, trying to elicit some emotion, some hurt, but relishing the pain she's about to inflict. "I'm afraid that Bertrand was equally corrupt with both of us."

Jack inhales sharply, but it may as well have been a gasp. "Us? What do you mean by 'us'? You and Bertrand?"

"And Tom," Vivien says, putting her hand to her mouth, pretending to hide her face, but she's only hiding her smile.

"But you and Bertrand—"

"And Tom."

She's said it twice, but he still doesn't want it to be true. "You mean Tom . . . ?"

"I'm afraid so," Vivien says sensitively, but only to line up her next attack. "Disgusting, really. Don't you agree?"

Jack realizes what she's getting at. He finally understands what game she's playing. *How could she be so crass? How could she be so vindictive?* She's hurt him, but it pales compared to the hurt Tom's inflicted. *How could he be so crass? How could he be so vindictive?* He slept with Bertrand? *How could he?* If Tom wanted help with his marriage in that way, why wouldn't he come to Jack? *Why wouldn't he ask me for help?* Jack could be the third. He wouldn't want to do it, but he'd rather do it himself than have Tom find his solution elsewhere. Sometimes two people can share a monsieur, but three is absurd.

"Yes, it's disgusting," Jack says with much more vigor than Vivien was expecting. He seems to find the idea as repulsive as she does. Did she misjudge their relationship? *No, I have the journal to prove it*, she concludes.

"Thank you for bringing this to my attention," Jack says as he stands to leave.

Should she ask him to pay for his tea? No, she shouldn't overplay her hand. "You're welcome," Vivien says as Jack walks out the door, although he doesn't hear her.

Jack is lost. No, he knows where he is. He's in the park. No, he's pacing in the park. Racing around a bench in the park. He can't sit. If he sits down his mind will start speeding even faster than it already is. Betrayal. All he can focus on is Tom's betrayal. Jack has waited too long. He thought love could overcome. He tried to be strong, but Tom wore him down like rain upon a stone. And now he's all alone. Jack thought eventually, they'd be okay. Tom has his demons, yes, but Jack thought he could be happy with him, anyway. Tom assumes that Jack will stay. There's no need to cater to any of Jack's wants. Any of his desires. Tom can relax, and ruin his life while he's at it. No, Tom. Jack has waited too long. Jack thought Tom would grow and change. He tried to support him. He knew their relationship would be strange. He waited patiently, nervously, like a rabbit trembling, hoping to hide. But now he can't wait any longer. He has to say goodbye. Jack hopes Tom will eventually realize that love can't be contained. It can't be moralized. Jack needs to be strong. He needs to head out on his own.

He's already waited too long.

31

W*here is it? Where is it? Where is it?* He left it in the drawer. He's sure he did. Tom searches frantically for his lost journal.

Click. Key in door. Vivien enters, still wearing her British Union of Fascists ensemble, holding a shopping bag and Tom's journal.

She sees Tom's eyes go to it. He knows. And what's better, he knows that she knows.

She has every right to be angry, every right to yell. But Vivien doesn't yell.

She turns her back to Tom as she shuts the door, drops his journal in her shopping bag and sets it down, but not before retrieving a new journal from it, one almost identical to Tom's.

She spins around with a smile on her face to conceal her sleight of hand and saunters over to the kitchen table.

"It wasn't me. It's been you all this time."

Tom swallows. "Vivien . . . give me my journal."

"How long?"

Tom tries to take it from her, but Vivien plays keep-away. Tom's been in this situation before. He tries for it . . . the other person takes it away. He realizes it might be futile, but he has to give it a go.

"Vivien. Give it to me!"

But she won't. "A long time, judging by this," she says as she waves it at him.

"You don't understand," Tom says apologetically.

And it's true. She doesn't, but she doesn't need to. "I understand as much as I want to."

Tom sits down at his desk, defeated.

"You lied to me," Vivien says hoarsely. "It's been nothing but lies since the beginning."

It has. It's all been a lie. And like a true liar, Tom can't face the fact. As long as he's here, he'll see that lie every time he looks at Vivien.

Tom stands up, throws some clothes into a valise. Normally, he'd fold them carefully, but doing things carefully takes time. He doesn't have time. He has to run from his crime. But what is he doing? Does he think he can run from this? He can't keep running from Vivien. Where would he run to? Who would he run to?

Vivien launches the journal at him. "You married *me*, you bastard. Not him!"

Tom scoops it up, flips through the pages. White. All the pages are white, new.

"What did you do?"

"I got you a new one. Thought it was time for a fresh start, don't you agree?"

Tom hurls the journal back at her, Vivien blocking it from knocking her in the face.

They stare at each other, foment a moment. Did he really just do that?

"Want to know what I did with it? I destroyed it! That's what."

Tom glances at the journal lying on the floor. It's empty. He feels empty.

Full. He needs to fill the valise. He tosses in everything within arm's reach.

His face is stoic, focused on his exit. He won't engage with Vivien's emotions.

And Vivien has emotions in spades. She pours her heart out,

hoping that something, anything, will connect with Tom, regardless of the tack she's taking.

"You're nothing! A fraud! I'll destroy you! Destroy you. Do you hear me? Don't assume I won't."

But Tom is already destroyed. *What more could she do?* "Do what you must," he says as he opens the door, stomps away.

"Destroy you!" she screams.

Vivien lays her heart down on the table. He's gone, but she's still speaking to him.

"Destroy you . . . destroy . . ."

She sobs. "Oh, God, please come back."

But her sobs won't make him return. Perhaps her words can. She runs to the door. "Come back! Don't leave me!"

She wants to run after Tom, but her legs can't support her weight. Her knees crumple as she slides down to the floor, whispers into the tiny crevices between the boards. "You bastard . . . please come back . . . you bastard . . ."

Slowly, she sits up in the doorway.

The shopping bag sits across from her on full display.

Yes, she's going to make that bastard pay.

Because bastards always run away.

Mark Twain knew that. Even if Huck Finn's parents were married, that boy was still a bastard.

Once upon a time, Tom ran away. He was a child. Like every good Missouri boy, he thought he'd live his life riding up and down the Mississippi like Tom Sawyer or Huck Finn. Tom Sawyer if he was lucky. Huck Finn if he was desperate. And right now, he's Huck Finn. He didn't have much time to pack. He doesn't even remember what he put in the valise, but he'll figure that out later. *There's so much to figure out.*

Tom sits on a bench across from the Pansy Club, his valise at his side. Perhaps he shouldn't have come here. Tom watches club patrons come and go. A small group gathers, talking, smoking, drinking, and laughing right out in front. He can hear short snippets of the music inside when the door opens, but then the door closes and the music stops.

Tom shudders when he sees Jack approach the entrance. His feet bob up and down. They want to run to him, even if Tom wants them to appear more restrained. But there's nothing restrained about Tom's gait as he sprints up to Jack, catching him right before he heads inside, right before the music envelops him.

"Jack!" Tom yells, but then calms down. "I've been waiting hours for you."

"Hello, Mr. Eliot," Jack says formally.

It's not the greeting Tom had hoped for, but nothing he hoped for seems to turn out how he thought, and he plows forward anyway.

"I went to your flat, but they said you moved."

Jack darts his eyes to the club, then down the street, anywhere but at Tom.

"Fresh start, all of that sort of thing."

"We need to talk," Tom implores. "I've got so much I want to say to you."

Jack crosses his arms, takes a quick step back. *What game is Tom playing?* Whatever it is, Jack wants no part of it, even though he says, "All right. I'm listening."

But Tom doesn't know what to say. He wants to talk to Jack. He wants to tell Jack everything, but how can he start? Even though he's fully clothed, and carrying a valise stuffed with his wardrobe, he feels naked. He's exposed, standing right outside the club. *Who might come by?* Who might see him, standing there?

"I don't want to say right here. Let's go somewhere more discreet. Maybe your new place?"

Jack turns away in disgust, heads inside the club. Tom is torn. Should he follow? He needs to talk to Jack, but he's been standing in front of the door for quite a while. Who might see him enter?

Tom puts his hand to his head. What should he do? A loud, piercing whistle penetrates his brain. But the sound isn't coming from inside, it's coming from down the street. Dozens of policemen descend upon the Pansy Club. Clubs bash. Skulls smash. The police detest these men. So, they arrest these men. But first, they beat them.

A man catches a club across his brow. Another raises his hands in the air to block, but that only increases the number of times he's hit. The police treat them like shit.

Tom uses his valise as a shield until they knock it out of his hands. The copper's clubs pelt down upon him. He collapses into a ball. It's a hailstorm, and they're chipping away at him.

When the storm passes, Tom looks up, but then realizes it hasn't moved on. He's only in the eye of it. The policemen are attacking other targets. They use their sticks like swords, slashing and stabbing everything around them. They carry patrons out of the club in handcuffs. Some men are undressed. Whether their clothes were ripped off in passion or violence is anyone's guess, but from the looks of it, violence is the safer bet.

One of them is Jack. He's naked. Tom usually likes to see Jack naked. But not now. Usually, when he sees Jack's natural form, it's a moment of pure exhilaration. But the only people who seem exhilarated are the policemen. And perhaps the onlookers.

Eyes peer. Lips sneer. A crowd of onlookers watches the proceeding. A crowd of onlookers watches the bleeding.

Jack has a big gash across his forehead. Blood drips down his face, mixes with his tears. It looks like oil paint, but Tom knows this is no dream. This is real. This is happening.

Click. Click. Tom's hands are cuffed.

Two policemen take Tom in their arms. *Are they the same policemen from his dream?* No, this isn't a dream. He won't wake up from this. But it's eerily similar.

The policemen howl with demonic laughter as they load Tom, Jack, and the other men in a paddy wagon. Flashbulbs explode as Tom's world implodes, lighting up the interior.

"Is that Robert Frost?" One of the reporters could have sworn he saw a poet. They scribble down notes as the men's blood dribbles. The tale of their demise will be out by sunrise.

Tom lies prone on the floor as the paddy wagon pulls away. He's bruised and bloodied. He deserves it. *I do deserve it. All of us deserve it.* It's finally happening . . . it's finally happening exactly how he thought it would. He'll die in jail like Oscar Wilde, but without achieving anywhere near the same level of success. No one will remember Tom. And if they do, it will only be as a warning.

There were so many warnings.

Jesus died for Tom's sins, and so did Oscar Wilde. And now Tom's ending up just like him. Defiled. Reviled. Exiled.

Are they going to torture Tom in prison? Tom hopes they will. That might be the only way to kill his current incarnation and make sure the new one is risen.

Coppers throw Tom in a cell, the first circle in his trip to hell.

If he's going to be tortured, manacles should be dangling from these walls. Where are the whips? Where are the pokers? The cages? *I should be tortured.* It wouldn't need to be much of an Inquisition. Tom is ready to admit to everything.

But this is no traditional torture chamber. No, they've devised an even more ingenious solution for him. They've left Tom alone in a prison cell with his thoughts.

Tom fingers his crucifix furiously.

Ah, yes. This is what a torture chamber should look like.

The prison melts away, melds with his vision of the Pansy Club, now a haunting wreck of its former glory. Broken chairs litter the floor. Furniture is overturned. The walls are crumbling, and they're covered with manacles. Everything that was previously designed to elicit pleasure has now been repurposed for pain, although its former occupants may get off on using it for both. The zeppelin is on fire, but don't worry, it's being used to heat pokers. The golden orb is black, covered with spikes. The spotlight can burn skin. And who will be Tom's torturers?

Mr. Prufrock is flanked by Madame Sosostris, Reverend Hammond, and Sweeney, an overweight Irishman. It seems they've added someone new to their roster. Apparently, there's more work than they can handle on their own.

"My God, what happened here?" Tom asks them.

"You've ruined everything," Mr. Prufrock points out. "Everything is ruined. Demolished. Collateral damage, I suppose you could say."

Why did he even ask? Tom knew that was the answer. "I didn't mean for any of this to happen," he says.

The torturers fan out, surround Tom as Mr. Prufrock portends, "Law and order, societal norms, moral integrity . . . without these, we're animals."

"What'll happen to me?" Tom asks, ready to accept whatever the punishment is.

"You'll be charged, convicted, and punished, I expect."

Again, all answers that Tom already knew, but there's something oddly satisfying about hearing someone else say it.

"Charged with what?" Tom asks. It's a question he doesn't know the answer to. He's always understood that what he was doing was illegal, that who he is was illegal, but he's never been comfortable enough to ask what crimes he was committing. Sometimes it's easier not to ask than to be confronted with the answer.

"The Buggery Act, of course," Mr. Prufrock states.

"I'll lose my job," Tom says severely.

"And you'll be deported."

"Deported?" Tom asks.

"But you don't need to worry about that," Mr. Prufrock says, sucking his teeth. "The sentence is up to life in prison. So, you may not need to leave England after all."

The full weight of this probability sits on Tom's chest. "Life in prison . . ."

"Yes, sad really. The death penalty was abolished fifty years ago."

"Death penalty?" Tom asks, his voice ascending as high as the zeppelin used to fly. "That can't be right."

"Oh, I assure you it is," Mr. Prufrock says. "Four hundred men have been sentenced to death." Mr. Prufrock consoles Tom's shoulder. "It's a pity. It should have been more."

Tom flinches. *More? It should have been more?* He's aghast. *That's impossible, isn't it?* The death penalty. *It's cruel beyond belief.* Yes, he should be punished, but society would never tolerate such cruelty, would it? Civilization would never lack this much civility . . . would it?

But has Tom not heard of The Wasteland? Has he not heard of the Great War? Has he forgotten it? Has Tom been so busy with his personal problems he hasn't realized the world is crumbling around him?

Mr. Prufrock, Madame Sosostris, Reverend Hammond, and Sweeney all laugh. *Why are they laughing?* Can they read his mind?

"Think about it for a minute," Mr. Prufrock says, answering Tom's question. "Death by hanging is a momentary inconvenience. But God condemns homosexuals to an eternity in the fires of hell. All we're doing is speeding up the process."

Tom's torturers circle him. *What are they doing? Are they about to attack?* Tom tries to spin along with them, waiting to see what they'll do.

"How unpleasant to meet Mr. Eliot," Mr. Prufrock pouts. "With his features of clerical cut. And his brow so grim. And his mouth so prim. And his conversations so nicely . . . restricted to what precisely?"

The torturers change directions, causing Tom to spin even faster.

"And if . . . and perhaps . . . and but . . ." Mr. Prufrock stammers, taunting him. "How unpleasant to meet Mr. Eliot!"

Now it's time for Reverend Hammond's turn. "How unpleasant to meet Mr. Eliot! With his thoughts of sinning and lust. With his thoughts of men . . . let me hear, 'Amen!' With his nightly diversions . . . and considerable perversions . . . that fill decent men with disgust. How unpleasant to meet Mr. Eliot!"

Madame Sosostris slithers, hisses into Tom's ear. "You had a blank card, Thomasss. You wasssted it."

She coils herself around him. "How unpleasssant to meet Mr. Eliot! Living in fear with hisss cautiousss life . . . and hisss sssafety wife. With hisss waxxxen and exxxpresssionlesss face . . . that alwaysss ssseemsss out of placcce . . . till he graccces a man with a sssneer. Isssn't that right, Sssweeney, dear?"

Sweeney strolls over with the arrogance of someone who's consumed too much liquor. But he doesn't immediately start insulting Tom, as the others have. No, Sweeney offers Tom a drink. He holds out his flask, but Tom shakes his head. It's not the time for celebration, although it does seem the time to dull one's senses.

"How unpleasant to meet Mr. Eliot!" Sweeney screams. "With his fear of sinning and fun. With his fear and shame . . . as if he's to blame . . . he's perfected . . . and erected and built . . . a constant and powerful guilt. A guilt that cannot be tamed."

The torturers join hands as they circle him and chant. "How unpleasant to meet Mr. Eliot! How unpleasant to meet Mr. Eliot! How unpleasant to meet Mr. Eliot!"

Tom's eyes bulge. His body trembles. They don't even have to touch him and he's already reeling from their blows. His breath is raspy as if his own throat were choking him.

"You're all wrong!" Tom says, even though he realizes they're right. "Go away! Go away!" he pleads. But they don't. They circle and taunt him. "How unpleasant to be Mr. Eliot! How unpleasant to be Mr. Eliot!"

Mr. Eliot. *Mr. Eliot?* Why do they insist on calling him Mr. Eliot?

"I command you to go away! I command you to go away!" Tom screeches as he stamps his feet. It's something children do to get attention. It's something children do when they feel powerless. They try to shake the very earth beneath them with only their feet and emotions.

Tom's torturers stop, stare at him. *What are they doing?* Tom stares back, unsure what they'll do next.

First it was the stick. Then it was the carrot. Then back to the stick. What will they do with Mr. Eliot? Whatever it is, they'll have to decide quick.

32

Bang. Bang. Ezra arrives, escorted by a guard clanging a cup across the bars.

"Bugger. Bugger. Bum Plugger. Prick tugger," the guard mumbles as he walks away, leaving Ezra standing outside Tom's cell.

Tom rushes over to the bars between them, but his feet are faster than his words. What will he say? Will Ezra ask him what happened? *Does he already know?*

"I bring good news," Ezra reassures Tom.

Good. Good news is good. "What is it?"

"I persuaded them to drop all charges. We can walk out of here like it never happened."

Never happened . . . it never happened. Tom was never here. Ezra never has to ask him why he's here. *That sounds nice.* That sounds good.

"Really?" Tom gulps. "Oh, my God. Thank you! That's amazing. That's . . . fantastic!"

It really is fantastic. Perhaps too good to believe.

"You only have to sign one thing, and we're out of here," Ezra says with a restrained tone.

But there's nothing restrained about Tom's response. "Yes. Of course! Let's sign me out of here!"

Tom is excited. *Why isn't Ezra?* Ezra grips a bar with his left hand. "The catch is . . ."

"Catch?" Tom interjects.

Ezra taps the bar with his index finger. Tap. Tap. Tap. His fingernail produces a small clink.

"You need to sign an affidavit that Jack took you there on false pretenses . . . and then attempted to have sex with you."

Ezra removes his hand, takes a step back, giving Tom room to react.

But Tom doesn't react. Tom is stoic. He doesn't display any emotion because he has none. He has no emotion because he has no thoughts. His brain isn't racing. It's still. Stuck on the moment. Stuck on the question. *Should I sign the affidavit?*

But Tom doesn't seem capable of answering it. He doesn't seem capable of anything in his current state. If Tom were a clock, he would need to be wound. Then he could come alive and keep working. Is that what Ezra is doing right now? Is Ezra winding him up? Because Tom is not a clock.

But then Tom blinks. And Tom thinks, perhaps more out of instinct. "I could never do that."

"I know. I know," Ezra intones, "but they've made the same offer to him. And it's only valid for one of you. If Jack signs first, then I'm afraid there's nothing I can do."

Ezra's eyes implore Tom. "Please. Sign it."

But Tom doesn't seem in the mood to sign anything. Tom doesn't seem in the mood to do anything. He stands there, looking blankly forward.

Ezra's eyes glance at the entrance. His feet shuffle back and forth. What will Tom do? The clock is ticking.

Ezra paces back and forth. Tick. Tock. Tick. Tock. "You know," Ezra says frantically, "I'd like to give you a speech about how much I like you. About how much I want to save you. About how much you need to sign this to save yourself. But if I'm honest . . . I don't like you nearly as much as I like your work."

Ezra sneaks a peek at Tom, but then continues on. "And I think you agree with me. Not just that you hate yourself. No. But that you believe the work is more important than any of us. You . . . me . . . Jack . . . none of us matter. Only the art matters."

Ezra searches Tom's eyes but comes up empty-handed. Will Tom allow his work to be locked up?

Ezra swallows his disappointment, takes a step back. Tom's inaction is signing his work's death warrant, and Ezra doesn't want to stay around for the execution. He shakes his head, walks away.

"Bugger. Bugger. Bum plugger. Prick tugger."

Did Ezra mumble the same words as the guard when he walked away, or is Tom only remembering them?

How long have I been standing here?

How long has it been since Ezra left?

Did he just walk out, or has Tom's mind been wandering?

His thoughts have been coming slower ever since Ezra told him about the catch, but how slow, he doesn't know.

All Tom can focus on is the question before him.

What will I do?

Tom will walk out of jail a free man. That's what.

He'll move forward with his life. *It didn't happen.* He wasn't in jail. And therefore he didn't have to do anything to get out of jail. He didn't need to sign anything. He didn't need to sign anything because nothing happened.

Was Ezra with him when he left? *It doesn't matter.* It doesn't matter because Ezra wasn't there because Tom was never there. *It didn't happen.* He didn't do anything. *I didn't sign anything.* And that's the way he'll remember it.

When one door closes, another opens—this one, a taxi door, sits wide for Tom.

Ezra's waiting inside. He's offering escape, but his presence taunts Tom's recollection of events.

Tom leans into the promise of escape as he enters the cab. Anything to get away from here.

"It was the right thing to do," Ezra says as the car peels away.

"No, it wasn't," Tom mumbles under his breath.

Ezra taps his finger on the door handle. Tap. Tap. Tap. "It was necessary. It was—"

"I don't want to talk about it anymore!"

"For the sake of—"

"Ever," Tom corrects. "I don't want to talk about it ever."

"All right." Ezra nods.

Rubber against stone. The only sounds between the men are the sounds of the tires upon the pavement. The city screeches by. *Where are we going?* Tom can't tell. Maybe he hasn't been to this part of the city before. Or maybe it's because of the tears in his eyes. No, it's definitely the former. Because he's not crying. Why would he be crying? Nothing happened, so he can't be crying.

But then Tom sees where they are.

"Are we going to the British Poetry Society?"

"We aren't, but I am," Ezra says curtly. "Or at least you aren't yet. They want to meet with you, but now isn't the time to put you in front of them. I'll say you were taken ill, or that you're speeding through some spurt of creativity. They'd like that, probably."

"You told me everything was resolved," Tom accuses him. "You said no one would find out."

"It's not about that . . . I don't think. They know nothing of your . . . recent troubles."

"What else would it be about?"

"Your nomination to the society. They want to hear the finished version of that second poem you read for them."

"The second . . . I only read fragments."

"And now they want the final version."

"But it's not done."

"Well, it needs to be by tomorrow. I can only stall them until then. And Horace is getting a bit anxious as well. So it's for the best all around."

Ezra taps his finger on the door handle. Tap. Tap. Tap. "What have you been working on all this time?"

"I haven't been. I . . . I lost my journal."

But Ezra can see through the lie. "Did you lose it or did your wife take it away from you?"

Tom's mouth falls open. "How did you find out about that?"

Tap. Tap. Tap. "I thought it was a joke, but apparently she's been going around asking people if they want to read it."

Tom freezes. "What do you . . . she said she destroyed it."

"And you believed her?"

Tom sweats as they pull up to the opulent English Baroque facade of the British Poetry Society. "We need to find it. We have to find her and get it!"

"You need to finish the poem," Ezra reiterates. "I'll find the journal."

Ezra opens the door, but doesn't get out. "And you need to handle this whole . . . Vivien thing. If she's going around trying to—"

"I understand," Tom says, giving Ezra a knowing nod.

Tom has his orders. He has to finish his poem. He doesn't need to worry about the journal since Ezra will take care of it. But it's all he can think about, especially since he has to handle this "whole Vivien thing" and she has the journal and if she gives someone the journal and they read it . . . *no, don't think about that.* He won't consider that possibility.

"Where to?"

Ezra is long gone. Tom sits alone in the back seat, considering the driver's question. Where to? He needs to write. His writing desk is at home.

"Take me home," Tom says.

"And how would I know where that is?"

"Sorry. Right across from the Bank of London."

Rubber against stone. The driver takes Tom home.

But then Tom realizes: He can't go home. That's where Vivien is. *Where can I go?* Home is across from the Bank of London. Tom works in the bank. He has a desk there. *Don't I?* Does Tom still work there?

When was the last time he showed up for work? He can't remember. Surely, he's been fired by now. If not formally, then practically. No, he can't go there.

He needs to find somewhere to work. Somewhere to do his real work.

"Sorry, take me to . . . a hotel," Tom says hesitantly.

They have desks there, don't they? Yes, they do. And he can stay up all night if he needs to. You can't do that in a library.

Tom lies down in the back seat. It's probably the last bit of rest he'll give himself until he's done, so he should savor it. But Tom's not restful. His finger raps the back window. Tap. Tap. Tap.

Nelson's Column. Trafalgar Square. Admiral Horatio Nelson flies past, high in the air.

The taxi pulls up in front of the Metropole Hotel, a stone's throw away from the River Thames. Tom hadn't specified which hotel, so the driver chose for him. No matter. Any hotel will do.

Tom walks up to the front desk.

"I'd like a room, please. All your rooms have writing desks, don't they?"

"Yes, sir, they do," the clerk says quizzically before opening the ledger. "What name would you like the room under, sir?"

"T.S. Eliot."

The clerk peers at Tom over his glasses. *Does he recognize me? Does he recognize my name?* His "Prufrock" has been popular. *Is this man a fan?* Should Tom have given a nom de guerre instead of his nom de plume? He doesn't have time to deal with any accolades.

"We have a message for you, sir."

How can they have a message for him? He didn't even know he was coming here.

The clerk darts behind the desk, returns with a card.

"She had me write it down like this exactly," the clerk says and then reads, "Will T.S. Eliot please return to his home, which he abandoned."

The clerk sets the card down, cups his hands in front of him.

"She didn't give me her name, but said she doesn't know where you're staying so she's leaving messages all over town."

I have to stop her. Vivien can't be running around bandying about his name with no consequences.

What's the matter with her? But more importantly, what will Tom do about it?

"I'll take a room," Tom says stoically. "And I'll be right back."

Crazy. Tom feels crazy. He should be locked in an asylum. That's what you do with crazy people, isn't it? He just wants to run away, but Vivien has been leaving messages for him all over town. He can't escape her. He can't escape her cycle. He can't escape her Samsara. Perhaps an asylum would grant him that escape.

It was easy to get there. The same driver was still sitting outside the hotel, and he already knew how to deal with him. He drove Tom where he wanted to go and didn't ask too many questions. Tom was already trying to answer enough questions. And as long as he kept paying the fare, the driver was more than happy to take Tom wherever he wanted to go.

The angel of Admiral Horatio Nelson soars overhead as the driver deposits Tom back at the Metropole Hotel.

Wasn't I just here? The same cycle keeps repeating over and over again. Tom feels crazy, but Vivien is the crazy one. She said she would destroy him, but now Tom's done something to destroy her, to destroy her credibility, something to make sure no one will ever listen to her. *Don't think about that.* He won't reflect on it because it's much too difficult. The actual act had been easy, though. It was surprisingly easy, barely an inconvenience.

Tom walks into his hotel room a free man.

He didn't go anywhere. He didn't do anything. And therefore, he doesn't have to remember what he did.

Tom sits down to write.

But there's no window, no sunset, nothing to inspire him. *It'll have to do.* He doesn't have time to find somewhere else. And he doesn't need somewhere with windows, anyway. He need not look outward. He'll look inward.

Or at least as much as he can.

Vivien said she'd destroy him, and she has his journal. It's the worst possible situation. *The absolute worst.* But Ezra says he's handling it. *Don't think about that.*

His mind spins. There are so many things he doesn't need to think about. So many things he won't think about. But they're the only things running through his mind as he sits down and puts hotel pen to hotel paper.

33

Vivien lights the candles, sets the table, and sits down for a romantic dinner for two, except she's the only one in the flat.

Her eyes check the kitchen, but she's focused on the door. There's a shepherd's pie in the stove, waiting to be reheated whenever Tom comes home. If he wants the shepherd, she'll gladly be his sheep. If the candles burn down, she'll replace them with new ones. She'll wait here all night if she has to.

She adjusts the cloth napkins, adjusts the tablecloth.

She checks the time. All the clocks read two minutes past ten. The clocks are no Ben, but they keep time just the same. She's made sure of it. She's been winding Tom's clocks. *Not like he would notice.* He doesn't seem to care about anything she does for him.

Tom's clocks chime. *It's time,* Vivien reassures herself. Time for Tom to come home. *But how did it get to be eleven?* It must be the ether. The ether does such a good job of making the time pass.

Vivien's eyes dart over to the window, over to her sorrow, out in the limbo, out where Tom is, but she stops herself, plops more ether in her wineglass. *Yes, the ether will stop silly little thoughts like that.* The ether will be here for her until Tom is.

But then she knocks over her wineglass, causing red liquid to stain the white tablecloth.

In a fury, Vivien slams her vial of ether onto the ground, but then immediately regrets it.

No ether. No Tom. *What have I done?*

Not nearly as much as she's about to. Vivien flips over the dining table, sends the setting soaring. Dishes scatter and shatter. A napkin bursts into flames as a candle falls on it, illuminating Vivien on her path of destruction.

She shatters the colorful glass lamp on the floor. She rips the red runner off the mantle, stomps the white edelweiss candleholders. She tears the tapestry, rips the long curtains from the window. She never wanted those things, anyway. She only bought them for him, but he never wanted her.

She can feel her family staring down from their pictures on the wall, trying to discern what she'll do next, judging her. Vivien never wanted to disappoint them. She wanted them to be proud, but life is a never-ending onslaught of disappointing people. She senses their mortification in her bones. She doesn't want their judgment in her body, but she doesn't have any ether to expel it.

Elephants never forget, but Vivien wants to. Perhaps the elephants would forget if she let them free. No one likes to be caged, so Vivien throws the elephant pillows out the window.

She needs to get rid of everything, everything that reminds her of him. Everything that reminds her of their life together, but she can't throw it all out in the street. No, that would arouse too much suspicion. So, she balls up the curtains and throws them down the garbage chute in the hall.

Ezra arrives as Vivien tosses in her second load, almost plowing into him before he can knock on the door. He sees her emptying the flat, but not paying any attention to the fire engulfing her.

Ezra springs into action, using the tapestry to flatten the flames. They've moved on from the napkins and tablecloth to a nearby cabinet, but luckily not much farther. Ezra does what he does best, and contains the damage. The tapestry smothers the blaze. Ezra jumps up and down on top of it, stamping out the embers. Then he shuttles pitchers of water back and forth from the sink.

Vivien only notices Ezra's arrival after the fire is out, but her eyes aren't. They're still ablaze with passion as she brings them close to Ezra's face.

"What are you doing here?" Vivien questions him.

Ezra tries to break her gaze, tries to avoid her blaze, but her head follows his. Ezra returns the question. "What were you doing?"

Vivien takes a step back. Is she about to lunge at him? Her whole body is tense. Ezra waits in suspense.

But she doesn't attack. And she doesn't answer.

"What were you doing?" Ezra asks again. Although Vivien is only an arm's length from him, her fixed, vacant stare suggests she's somewhere much further away. He sees that he won't get anywhere with his line of questioning, so he switches to a different one.

"Where is Tom's journal?"

But Vivien still doesn't respond. She doesn't move.

Ezra gently touches Vivien's shoulder. She flinches, but then places her hand on top of his.

"Tom?" Vivien asks, not looking at Ezra, but through him. "Is that really you, Tom?"

Now it's Ezra's turn not to say anything. What could he say?

Vivien smiles and embraces Ezra. "I'm so glad you're home."

Ezra cautiously caresses Vivien's back, his body instinctively hugging her even though he can't figure out what to do. She's out of control. When he came in she was hysterical. And that's normal. Women often devolve into hysterics, at least in Ezra's opinion. But now, this is something more. Vivien has entered some form of psychosis. How will he find Tom's journal if she's in this condition?

Ezra blinks rapidly. His hands are clammy. He pulls Vivien away from him, looks into the eyes he tried to avoid.

Vivien smiles wide. Her face is relaxed, but her mouth seems like it's trying to reach the farthest corners of her face.

"I love you, Tom," she says emphatically.

"I love you, too," Ezra says quickly, but then slows down for what he says next. "Where's my journal?"

She gapes at Ezra blankly.

"Where's my journal, Vivien?" he asks again.

Vivien laughs. At first, it's a guffaw, but then it builds into an outright cackle, getting louder and louder. Is she laughing at him, or screaming? But before Ezra can figure out which, Vivien has transitioned to crying. Sniffles turn into sobs.

"You want your journal?" she asks Ezra.

"Yes, where is it?"

"You want your journal, don't you!" Vivien yells. It's no longer a question, but an accusation.

Ezra grabs ahold of her, shakes her. That's what you do with women who are being hysterical, isn't it?

"Where's my journal, Vivien?"

Vivien breaks free of Ezra's grip, throws up her hands.

"I gave it to someone who wants to read it!"

"You did what? Who did you give it to?

But Vivien seems to have questions of her own. She narrows her eyes at Ezra.

"Tom?" But then she realizes Ezra's not him and panics. "Where's Tom? Where's Tom!"

"Where's the journal?"

Vivien spins around. "Tom? Are you here, Tom?" But when she sees that he's not there, she sprints past Ezra, out into the hallway. "Tom! Where are you?"

Ezra tries to catch up, but by the time he's made it to the hall, she's already made it down a flight of stairs, screaming, "Where are you, Tom?" By the time Ezra has made it down one landing, Vivien's already exited the building.

She's too fast for him, but he didn't come here for her.

Ezra returns to the carnage. He stands in the doorway, scans the scene. This must be what the Belgians felt like after the Germans bombed Liège from a zeppelin. No one person could have done all this destruction. It must have come from above. Ezra makes quick work of sifting through the rubble, trying to find Tom's journal, hoping Vivien hadn't given it away like she said she had, hoping that was only part of her psychosis.

But Ezra isn't a doctor. He can't make that diagnosis. Perhaps it's not psychosis. Maybe it's sarcoidosis, cirrhosis, or a lack of symbiosis.

Whatever it is, it compels Vivien out into the black of night. Vivien dodges a streetlight, peers around corners, sneers at anyone who isn't Tom. No one is who they appear to be in The Wasteland. She walks down street after street until her feet bleed. Why didn't she put on shoes? *No matter now*. The pain helps keep her awake, helps keep her focused on what's at stake.

She comes across a man with a sandwich board advertising "D. H. Lawrence at the Queen's Theatre! One night only!"

The man is of the sad sort who sleeps on the street, not having anywhere to go at night. He's a man who can be paid to be a pole, but now the man is using the sandwich board as an impromptu shelter, fast asleep underneath it.

Signs can be good to get the word out about certain things. Vivien has been using her voice, but it's become hoarse. She wants to make sure she has a little bit left when she finds Tom. She wants to tell him how much she loves him.

Vivien is not one to take someone's house away, but since her home has been taken away from her, this seems morally equitable, if only slightly. The loss the man will experience is nothing compared to hers. She's used to better.

Vivien slides the sandwich board off him. She finds a piece of chalk tucked into a crevice, wipes the slate clean before writing her own message.

She writes:

Come home, Tom. All is forgiven. Love, Vivienne

But then she scratches out the NE at the end. She could wipe it off, but something about crossing off the NE and leaving it on the board feels right. It's the compromise she made with Tom about her name, and marriage is all about compromise.

Her face is pale. She looks cold.

She looks like she's about to wail, and she won't be able to withhold.

The sun rises, emphasizes her mourning in its morning light. Has she been walking around all night?

Then she sees Bertrand seated at an outdoor cafe, having a bite.

She rushes up to him, still clutching the sandwich board tight.

"Tell me, Bertie. Is it true? Has Tom been beheaded?"

Bertrand nearly spits out his morning tea. "No, of course not! What would make you imagine something as truly heinous as that?"

He spots the sandwich board. "And what are you doing with that sign?"

"Isn't it obvious? I'm bringing Tom back."

Then he notices Vivien's bloody feet, sees that there's more afoot.

"You look positively . . . exhausted," Bertrand says before trying to console her. "But ravishing in your exhaustion." Only his tone comes across as joking. Bertrand has a problem with sincerity and Vivien has a problem with being teased.

"Why do you say that?" Vivien interrogates. "What do you mean by that?"

"I'm just kidding. Only kidding," Bertrand begs. "Here, sit down, unburden yourself of that sign for a minute."

He helps her remove the sandwich board from around her neck and stands it next to the table.

Vivien sits on the edge of her chair, her body cantilevered over the side. She looks around nervously, catching the eye of everyone looking at the odd sight she's creating.

"Let's get you something to eat," he says. "Have some tea."

Bertrand takes an empty cup from a nearby table, fills it.

Vivien mimes adding something to the tea like she used to do with the ether, but there's nothing in her hand.

The color comes back into her cheeks as the tea enters her stomach.

Now that he's brought some life back into her, Bertrand attempts a quid pro quo, trying to get information out of her.

"Now, tell me, what in the world are you doing with that sign?"

Vivien looks at Bertrand deathly seriously. "Like I said. I'm bringing Tom back."

"It's a serious matter to bring someone back from the dead," Bertrand says, trying to bring levity to the situation.

But Vivien swats down that notion. "Ah, but we die to each other daily."

She takes another swallow of tea. Bertrand takes one of air. "Whatever do you mean?"

"What we know of other people is only our memory of the moments during which we knew them," Vivien says matter-of-factly. "But they have changed since then. We pretend that they are the same, but every meeting is a meeting of strangers."

Bertrand leers at Vivien. *How very strange*. He's spent so much time toying with her, but now that she's broken, and is obviously not to be played with, he's never been more interested in her, her thoughts, her emotions. Like Venice, her decay is beautiful.

Bertrand offers her his breakfast, asks gingerly, "Here, would you like some cakes with your tea?"

But Vivien takes his offer as an agitation. "What's that? What do you mean? Why did you say that?"

She slips out of her chair and falls, but then bounces off the ground and is up on her feet before Bertrand can offer to help.

"Oh, never mind!" Vivien says, exhaling loudly. "I must go. I can't be here a moment longer. I must find Mr. Eliot. I need him, even if he doesn't need me anymore."

Vivien dashes down the street, but then dashes back for her sign. She knocks a table over on her way out of the cafe, but doesn't notice.

It looked like she was in a hurry, but she doesn't go far. Bertrand beholds her as she circles the street, talking to anyone willing to lend an ear, if only for a moment.

Vivien mumbles. "Please, can you help me? I can't seem to find . . ."

But no one stops. They're all unkind.

Then she repeats the same three sentences over and over again, drawing a crowd, cawing loud, "I've lost Mr. Eliot. I need Mr. Eliot. Even if he never needs me. I've lost Mr. Eliot. I need Mr. Eliot. Even if he never needs me. I've lost Mr. Eliot. I need Mr. Eliot. Even if he never needs me."

But the onlookers just stare at her. What is she? Out of her mind? She must be confined.

"Can I take you home?" Bertrand asks, trying to break her out of her trance.

And it seems to have done the trick. Vivien looks at him, suddenly clear-eyed, but still serious.

"I've done something," she says solemnly. "I've done something to destroy him, but I only want him to be happy. Even if I can't make him happy."

She lost Mr. Eliot because she crossed Mr. Eliot.

"I know, I know," Bertrand intones as if he understands.

He tries to sling an arm around her, lead her home, but she shuffles free of him.

"I need you to do something for me. I need you to promise," Vivien says desperately. "Will you promise me you'll do it?"

Bertrand nods. He's a man who makes many promises, but something tells him he'll keep this one, whatever the task.

"Anything. I'll do anything you ask."

34

There's a baker's dozen, but these men aren't bakers. That doesn't stop them from applying heat, though. They all sit in the same direction on the same side of a long table, all dressed in the same formal fashions, all stern and foreboding, all unsmiling to the point of goading.

Tom shuffles in, sits across from them, any semblance of his confidence eroding.

He takes a seat next to Ezra. "Did you find it?"

"Well, the good news is it's not lost anymore," Ezra evades.

"Shall we get started?" Lord William asks, but it's not a question.

Lord William, Sir Richard, and Viscount Jameson sit in the center of the mass of men. They're still the ruling triumvirate even if this might look more like a centumvirate. There are so many suits, but these three are the only ones with any real power. That is, besides the smattering of reporters behind them, ready to scribe any sensational news about to come out of this meeting between the British Poetry Society and the bright, rising star of T.S. Eliot. Is his star about to burn out? That's the story they want, the one their pens want to churn out.

"You do understand, Mr. Eliot, that this is not a formal proceeding?" Lord William asks, but his clothes, these men, and the reporters might dispute that fact. "Your presence here is strictly voluntary."

"I understand," Tom says softly.

"The purpose of this meeting is to resolve some questions, some allegations, some . . ." And with that, Lord William is suddenly at a loss for words, or perhaps he doesn't want these particular ones in his mouth.

"Some alleged aspects of your decorum that might have an impact on your admission to this prestigious society," Sir Richard states stridently.

"Yes. That," Lord William recovers.

"I understand," Tom says. If there's anything he understands about what's happening, it's that.

"Mr. Eliot, I'd like to begin by saying that none of us questions your skill, your potential as a poet," Lord William says. "While its lack of rhyme is problematic to my old ears, even I recognize the . . . power of your verse."

Is it happening? *Is that a compliment?* Could all this turn out much differently from what Tom expected?

"Thank you." Tom beams.

But then Lord William removes Tom's journal from a small case. He sets it on the table with a small thud. In Tom's ears, though, it's thunderous.

"I regret to inform you that a major concern has been brought before the committee," Lord William says with no real regret in his voice. "Your wife brought your journal to my attention, and I have shared its contents with the committee."

Tom panics. *They know. They all know.*

"Lord William says she was in such a state when she came to him," Viscount Jameson says.

"I am more than capable of speaking for myself," Lord William rebukes.

"Well, then, please proceed," Viscount Jameson counters.

"She was in quite the state," Lord William says. "She . . ." But again, he doesn't want the words in his mouth.

And Tom doesn't want to hear them. "I apologize for my wife," he blurts out. "She's been taken ill, but she's getting the help she needs."

He had the answer ready. He had many things ready. *And she will get the help she needs,* Tom thinks. But he doesn't need to think that. He knows. Or at least he hopes.

At the same time he says these words, at the same time he thinks these thoughts, other men are taking action. You don't need to bring someone to an asylum if the asylum can come to you. Tom paid attendants at the madhouse to collect Vivien so he wouldn't have to deposit her there himself.

Collect. Deposit. Tom is reminded of his days at the Bank of London. The well-heeled men would often send subordinates to do their bidding. Does that mean Tom is becoming a well-heeled man, too?

Vivien claws at the attendants, so they strap her in a straitjacket, manhandle her into an ambulance.

"My poor wife has suffered a mental breakdown," Tom tells the tribunal. He's tense, but his tone is relaxed, as if he's said these words before. "I'm afraid I must commit her. Unavoidable, really. For her own good."

Tom looks at the men with hope in his eyes. He hopes that will put this matter to bed, hopes that they won't care with whom he goes to bed.

"But that does not resolve the matter of the content of your journal, Mr. Eliot," Lord William says.

If Tom were a balloon, Lord William would be a pin.

"Our objection is somewhat more sensitive," Lord Williams starts, but has trouble finishing. "I'm . . . I'm not sure how to put it delicately."

"Lord William, will you permit me?" Viscount Jameson asks.

"Please."

"We have received information that you may have a repugnant moral flaw of a most serious nature. Specifically, homosexuality," Viscount Jameson spits out, along with a few droplets on the table. "At first, we thought this was impossible given your marital status."

He waves Tom's journal around as if it were a Bible. "But this journal seems to contain material that would be supportive of those charges."

"Charges?" Ezra asks. "I thought this was an informal proceeding."

Viscount Jameson uses the journal as an extension of his hand, dismisses the discrepancy. "Regardless, we have arranged for a witness who will substantiate the charges."

"Maître d'! You can bring out the witness!" Lord William bellows, but the man who brings in the witness is not the maître d', but a copper. And the witness is not a witness, or at least Tom could never imagine him as one, he's so much more than that.

It's Jack.

Jack stands before Tom, before God, before all these men. He stands before them knowing the truth, but will he tell it?

Crack. Viscount Jameson slams Tom's journal on the table. This time, it really was thunderous, but to Tom, it only felt like a thud. *This must be what Vivien feels like on ether.* This must be the exhilaration of suppressing emotions you want to hide.

"Mr. Eliot, are you, in fact, a homosexual?" Viscount Jameson asks incredulously.

In fact . . . in fact . . . he asks that question with no tact.

Tom shares a glance with Jack, but would like to share so much more with him. He hasn't only burned his bridge with Jack, though, he's bombed it, like so many other bridges in The Wasteland.

Jack will be a good witness. He's seen everything. *He was there.* He's credible.

Tom realizes he must confess. He understands his crime. "Honored members—"

"They're mine."

Jack steps forward, cutting Tom off.

"I beg your pardon?"

Lord William is the one who found the words first, but the question could have come from almost anyone in the room.

Eyes peer. Necks crane. Everyone wants to see the queer. Everyone wants to see the profane.

"The poem is mine, not his," Jack continues.

"We have on good faith that this is Mr. Eliot's. His wife delivered it to Lord William personally," Sir Richard states.

Tom hangs his head. "It's my journal."

He lets the words slide out of his mouth. There's no use lying. There's no use fighting it.

But don't tell Jack that.

"It may be your journal, but that poem is mine," Jack reiterates. "At least the one I'm sure they're talking about. The one they think makes you out to be a homosexual."

When was the last time Jack spoke to Tom? A brief rush passes through his body before he turns his attention to the other men.

"I wrote it to tease him. Look at the handwriting. It's completely different from his."

Lord William lifts one eyebrow. Men of Jack's sort don't deserve both, and they don't deserve his belief.

"Let's see, shall we."

Lord William examines the journal, but only for a moment. He's seen all he wants to and slides it over to Sir Richard and Viscount Jameson. The two men look at the handwriting carefully, soaking in the pages, trying to discern the truth.

But Lord William stares right at Tom. He already knows the truth. And it disappoints him.

"The handwriting doesn't match," Lord William monotones.

Murmurs emanate from the men flanking the triumvirate.

Jack shifts his stance. "As I said, he's not a homosexual. God knows I tried to seduce him, but he's as heterosexual as all of you. Whoever told you he was a faggot is lying . . ."

Jack looks at the journal on the table.

"Or crazy."

Crazy. Yes, you'd have to be crazy to think that. And we all remember what happens to crazy.

The murmuring men turn to each other. That seems to explain that.

Sir Richard and Viscount Jameson look relieved.

"Well, this just goes to show that we've made the right decision by allowing your consideration into the society," Sir Richard says.

Viscount Jameson agrees. "We don't consort with men of that sort."

"Take the prisoner away," Lord William orders.

The bobby leads Jack away, out the door, down the street, back to jail, back to his penitentiary suite.

It's for the best.

Out of sight, out of mind. Or, if you can see the blight, better make yourself blind.

Ezra leans in. "Now that that's settled, can we get down to the real business at hand here?"

Lord William glares at Ezra. He doesn't enjoy being rushed, especially since he didn't imagine they'd reach this moment. He turns to Tom. "So, we asked you to show us you're a serious man with serious poetry. What will you be reading for us?"

Reading? Tom didn't plan on reading his poem. He stayed up all night writing it. And then spent the morning making copies. He didn't practice performing it aloud.

Ezra places his hand on Tom's shoulder.

Tom flinches, but then realizes it's only Ezra trying to reassure him. If only it was Jack.

"I . . . I'd prefer you read it for yourself . . . if . . . if you don't mind," Tom stutters.

He passes out copies.

"I'm sorry there's not enough for each of you. Some of you will have to share. I didn't realize there would be so many people here."

"We expect members to follow our rules," Lord William says. "And the rules clearly state that a prospective member must read their poem to the selection committee. We will, of course, analyze the poem on our own time, but the purpose of bringing all these esteemed gentlemen together is to see how you might handle an audience. How well you would represent the Society."

Tom's pupils dilate. Suddenly the men seem much farther away. He can see the whole room before him. He feels like a bug about to be squashed.

"I'm sorry. I didn't write it to read it. I mean . . . I didn't write it to be read aloud. I want the words to speak for themselves, if you know what I mean."

"Perhaps you should have had the words say *that* then," Sir Richard shoots back.

"Please?" Ezra begs. "Just read it. You owe him that after putting him through this charade."

Ezra's slap on the wrist seems to have landed on their faces. These men aren't used to being spoken to in that way.

Sir Richard shakes his head, whispers in Lord William's ear. Lord William purses his lips. He must not be agreeing with whatever Sir Richard is saying.

"We'll read the poem first," Lord William acquiesces. "But then I'll decide whether to bend the rules and allow a vote without Mr. Eliot's oratory."

Tom swallows, nods his head as the members of the selection committee lower their heads and start reading.

It's funny. Tom hasn't noticed until now, but when someone is reading, their heads are bowed, giving reverence to whatever is in front of them. And that's precisely how he'd like them to interact with this text. Poetry can be beauty incarnate when read aloud, but the work he's handed them is one that should be read in its own time. They should be allowed to read lines over again, stop, consider whether they recognize something in the words, an emotion, or something that refers to another text. When performed, the poem might wash over you too easily, and Tom wants them to see the dirt.

How long will it take them to read it? How long has it been already?

Tom would love to have some of Vivien's ether to make the time pass more quickly. She probably wishes she had some ether with her right now, too. *No. Don't think about that.* He can't think about her. *It's too painful.* It's too painful to contemplate her pain.

Tom closes his eyes, prays that Vivien and God will forgive him for what he's done.

The selection committee sits in reverent silence. *Is their silence a good thing or a bad thing?* Tom can't tell and won't interrupt their reading to ask Ezra.

Tom tries not to ruminate on Vivien. He tries not to remember Jack. He tries not to focus on all the things he's put into his poem.

Lord William raises his head, leers at Tom for a long moment. His face doesn't seem as severe as it did before, but it's still far from inviting. Sir Richard and Viscount Jameson catch him out of the corners of their eyes, take their cue to finish.

Twenty-six eyes stare back at Tom. Each one is a spotlight, tearing into his soul.

After a few moments, Lord William ends the silence.

"I'm sorry. I insist that you read this aloud."

Tom is dizzy, shaky. He tries to keep still, tries to keep his dread inside, but he drags his palms down his pant legs.

"But not here," Lord William continues. "No. This demands a much bigger audience."

35

Wild men and women clamor to have their voices heard. But they're not trying to get just anyone's attention, they're trying to attract one man in particular.

Tom takes the stage in the Queen's Theatre. His admirers' feet hardly touch the ground as they bounce up and down with excitement.

The theater is so opulent it seems oppressive, but Tom looks like he fits in, he looks impressive. He's wearing a top hat and tails and is sporting a cane with a carved wooden handle in the shape of a parrot's head.

The footlights glare. The audience blares. The packed room greets Tom with deafening applause, and he can hear each and every one of them.

All his friends are there. Ezra . . . Hemingway . . . Bertrand . . . Lord William, Sir Richard, and Viscount Jameson from the British Poetry Society . . . and . . . and . . . that's the end of the list. *There's no one else who should be on it.*

Tom takes off his top hat and uses it to tamp down the applause.

The room quiets down. He hangs his hat on the corner of the lectern.

Tom seems happy, at home in front of the audience.

Where did he get all this confidence? It's hard to discern.

"Thank you, thank you, all," Tom says, arranging some pages in front of him. "I thought I'd begin with some extracts from my notes for *The Waste Land*."

More applause. More tamping.

Tom clears his throat, tries to clear his mind, tries to focus on the performance he's about to unwind, a performance he's come near to perfecting.

"April is the cruelest month, breeding . . ."

But then his mind wanders to Jack in the basement of the bank, a lilac in his vase. Then he remembers standing in front of Pierre's, wilted lilacs in his hand.

"Lilacs out of the dead land, mixing
Memory and desire, stirring
Dull roots with spring rain."

It's been a while since he thought about Vivien and Jack, but as soon as he starts reading, all of those memories flood back.

"I was neither living nor dead, and I knew nothing."

Jack lies in bed, laughing.

"Looking into the heart of light, the silence."

Madame Sosostris's shop is abandoned, newspapers taped to the windows.

"Madame Sosostris, famous clairvoyante,
Here, said she,
Is your card, the drowned Phoenician Sailor,
(Those are pearls that were his eyes. Look!)"

Vivien smiles as she hands him a cup of tea at George's.

"You know nothing? Do you see nothing? Do you remember
'Nothing'?"

Tom is back in the bank, a few minutes until six. Violet light bounces in through a doorway.

"At the violet hour, when the eyes and back
Turn upward from the desk, when the human engine waits
Like a taxi throbbing waiting,

throbbing between two lives,
the profit and loss."

He remembers his first reading at the cafe, how Vivien helped him, but then he sees her circle a bleak room with dozens of other patients.

"I see crowds of people, walking round in a ring.
And the dead tree gives no shelter, the cricket no relief,
And the dry stone no sound of water.
I will show you fear in a handful of dust."

Tom doesn't want to imagine Vivien in this state. So, he imagines her listening to the radio. She has a live feed to the Queen's Theatre. He hopes she's heard his words. He hopes she can hear the apology in his voice, even though he has nothing he needs to apologize for.

Vivien doesn't do what he wants.

She grips the bars on a window, tries to tear them off. But two attendants drag her away, past other patients listening to the broadcast as the radio announces, "And that was T.S. Eliot, live from London."

Tom emerges from the Queen's Theatre looking fresh-faced, like a newborn from the womb, or Christ from His tomb.

He exits the theater with a crowd surrounding him. Ezra's arm straddles his shoulder, basking in the vicarious glory.

Flashbulbs light up the night.

"Mr. Eliot! Mr. Eliot!"

"Can you sign my book?"

"Over here! Can I get an autograph?"

Tom signs them all, one after the other, making sure his fans get the time with him they deserve.

But he can't help notice a fan across the street on a bench reading a book.

Tom extricates himself from the crowd, saying, "I'll be back in a moment." And then walks over.

He was right. This man is a fan, or at least he hopes he still is.

Tom sits down next to Jack. They have a lot to say to one another, but they sit quietly for a moment before Jack begins.

"It wasn't your fault."

"Which part?" Tom wonders.

Jack closes the book, a copy of *The Waste Land.*

"None of it," Jack exhales.

But that's not true, Tom recollects. "I should have—"

"It wouldn't have made any difference."

Jack didn't know what Tom was about to say, but he didn't want to hear it. Whatever it was, it can't change the past.

Tom's mind spins. He can't figure out what to say in response. He feels wound up. Jack clocks his spiraling, changes the subject.

"Bertrand put up my bail."

"I should have done that," Tom replies.

"You did . . . in a way," Jack says consolingly. "Bertrand said Vivien put him up to it."

Rain falls from the sky. A drop hits Tom's left cheek. Tom wipes it away and looks up to see if they need to seek shelter, but he can't see any clouds, only blue sky. *That's odd.* But it's even odder when another drop hits Tom's right cheek. He wipes that one off, but then notices that the rain isn't coming from the sky. It's coming from his eyes. And it's not rain, but . . . well you know what it is. Tom didn't, though. It had been so long since he felt any real emotion that he almost forgot what it felt like.

Chime. Chime. Chime. Big Ben chimes in the distance. Tom clocks his pocket watch. It's nine o'clock at night, but it's not night yet. The sun sets so late in London during the summer. Big Ben is about a twenty-minute walk away, and Tom could probably get there in time. The sun sets on so many things, but in London, it will set on Big Ben last, and Tom wants to see it. He wants to see if Jack wants to go with him. It might be fitting. But he can't ask him that.

"So, now what?" Tom wonders.

"I'm moving to Paris," Jack says. "Fleeing the scene of the crime, so to speak."

Tom's face falls. *He can't go*. "Won't they come after you?"

"They'll just be glad I'm gone."

But Tom won't be.

Jack looks up at the top of the Queen's Theatre. The sun wears the top of the theater like a crown.

"Bertrand will lose his bail money," Jack continues, "but I'll pay him back. Eventually."

"And when will that be?" Tom asks, but he's not concerned about the money. "You won't be able to come back here. Ever."

Jack's hand tries to scrub away the pained expression on his face. He doesn't regret anything yet, but if he doesn't say it now, he will. *But what can I say to Tom that will make him hear me?* He's such a narcissist, but that just means they both love the same thing. Perhaps the best way to get through to him is with his own words.

Jack opens Tom's book and takes his opportunity while the sun is still shining.

He reads:

His vanity requires no response,
And makes a welcome of indifference.
(And I Tiresias have foresuffered all
Enacted on this same divan or bed;
I who have sat by Thebes below the wall
And walked among the lowest of the dead.)
Bestows one final patronising kiss,
And gropes his way, finding the stairs unlit . . .

The sky seems to fall upon Jack's cheeks, but unlike Tom, he knows they're tears. Jack flips a page, continues:

She turns and looks a moment in the glass,
Hardly aware of her departed lover;
Her brain allows one half-formed thought to pass:
"Well now that's done: and I'm glad it's over."
When lovely woman stoops to folly and
Paces about her room again, alone,
She smoothes her hair with automatic hand,
And puts a record on the gramophone.

Another page, another tear. The cycle continues:

"My feet are at Moorgate, and my heart
Under my feet. After the event
He wept. He promised a 'new start.'
I made no comment. What should I resent?"

Tom brushes away a few of Jack's tears, but Jack doesn't acknowledge him. He just turns the page:

My friend, blood shaking my heart
The awful daring of a moment's surrender
Which an age of prudence can never retract
By this, and this only, we have existed
Which is not to be found in our obituaries
Or in memories draped by the beneficent spider
Or under seals broken by the lean solicitor

In our empty rooms

DA

Dayadhvam: I have heard the key

Turn in the door once and turn once only

We think of the key, each in his prison

Thinking of the key, each confirms a prison

Only at nightfall, aethereal rumours

Jack puts down the book, unable to continue. He shuts his eyes, slowing but not stopping the floodgates. His chest shudders and heaves.

He bereaves.

"Those are my favorite parts," Jack says through sobs.

Tom hangs his head. They're his favorite parts, too. Jack has good taste.

Tom looks at Jack tenderly. Jack leans in. Perhaps they'll kiss?

"Come with me. Please. To Paris," Jack pleads.

But Jack doesn't have good sense.

"I wish I could."

Jack tries to take Tom's hand, but Tom glances back at the theater instead, back to his adoring crowd. Tom moves to the other side of the bench.

Jack's heart shrinks to the size Tom's must be.

"Life doesn't need to be unhappy," Jack says. "Dante's 'Divine Comedy' didn't include only *Inferno*. There was *Paradiso*, too."

Jack stands. His face is golden, not just in the fading sunlight, but gleaming with passion.

"And you don't need to live in Inferno, or even Purgatorio. You could live in Paradiso. We . . . we could live in Paradiso . . . together."

Tom meets Jack on his feet, but his face isn't shining.

"I love you, Jack."

He lets the words hang in the air for a moment.

"You're a wonderful man, everything I could want . . . if what I wanted was a wonderful man, or a wonderful woman for that matter. I . . . my poetry is . . . it's impossible. I don't have any choice, you see?"

Jack clenches his fist. "You do. You do have a choice. And he's standing right in front of you."

"You're right. I do have a choice. The choice between sin and what is right. Between love for you and sleeping sound. Between days of love and nights of fright, a life that leaves me drowned."

"You love me and I love you. It doesn't have to be this hard."

Tom shakes his head. "Are you listening to me? Life is hell without you, Jack . . . but it's hell with you, too. And our actions on earth aren't something we can undo. There's no choice."

Jack relaxes his fist, but his voice retains his anger. "Life is full of choices, but there's only one that matters. You can choose love or fear. Don't let your life be ruled by someone up above, just keep your loved ones near."

Tom clutches the crucifix around his neck.

Tick. Tock. Tick. Tock. Tom wants this to be true. *It is true.* But then why is his heart beating so fast?

He needs to breathe, and steps away for a moment.

It's an eternity, but it's only the start of their time apart.

Tom keeps putting eternities between them, until he's back at the theater. But then he remembers. He left something across the street. His heart.

EPILOGUE

A small cot. A small dresser. A small lamp. Everything in Mr. Eliot's flat is small, except for the large crucifix. He's gotten rid of everything that reminds him of Vivien. The room has the austerity of a monk's cell again.

He hangs up his tuxedo, changes into his nightclothes.

Mr. Eliot kneels beside his bed and prays aloud. "Lord Jesus, for too long I've kept you out of my life. I know that I am a sinner and that I cannot save myself. No longer will I close the door when I hear you knocking. No longer will I enter doors I should not when I hear them calling. By faith, I gratefully receive your gift of salvation. I am ready to trust you as my Lord and Savior. Your mercy flows to me in spite of my faults and failures. I understand that even though I feel scared, my emotions don't have to control my actions. Father, may your sweet words saturate my mind and direct my thoughts. Help me release the hurt and begin to love as Jesus loves. Thank you, Lord Jesus, for coming to earth. I believe you are the Son of God who died on the cross for my sins and rose from the dead on the third day. Thank you for bearing my sins and giving me the gift of eternal life. I believe your words are true. I believe my words are true . . . please come into my heart, Lord Jesus, and be my Savior. Amen."

He climbs into his cot, but leaves the light on.

Mr. Eliot lies there, haunted, eyes wide open.

He lies awake in his own private Wasteland.

"It's *The Waste Land*," Mr. Eliot corrects. "Waste Land is two words, not one."

An onlooker might assume Mr. Eliot is still praying, but we know better.

If only Mr. Eliot knew better. The Wasteland is a much better title; he should have gone with that.

"I'm Tom."

No, you're Mr. Eliot.

"I know who I am."

Are you sure about that?

"I'm Tom, and this is my story to tell. You're not even doing it well. You're getting everything . . . wrong."

Wrong? What did I get wrong?

"There are so many things. Big and small. Do you want me to list them all?"

It doesn't matter what I got wrong. The only thing that matters is what I got right.

"You'll justify anything, won't you? The Rolls-Royce Phantom you described in the beginning . . . that car didn't exist yet. I worked at Lloyd's Bank, not the Bank of London. I never saw Gladys Bentley perform. The British Union of Fascists was formed a decade after *The Waste Land*. I published my first collection of poetry myself . . . and I had another book between these two."

But it didn't have as big an impact, did it? You hated that.

"It had 'Gerontion' in it. It was hailed."

Only two and a half pages. Hardly anything of real merit. And it only got any recognition because the narrator is an older version of me. You're welcome. And it's just a preface to The Wasteland anyway.

"Waste Land. Get it right."

How about we compromise and call it The Wasteland. That's how compromise works, right? You do what I tell you? That's how you compromised with Vivien.

"I didn't . . . you . . . you don't know anything about us. I married Vivien much earlier than you said . . . and I didn't . . . I haven't institutionalized her yet . . . I . . . even when it happens, I'm not as involved as you think."

Not as involved as I think? The last time you saw her . . . you avoided her for years . . . the poor thing finally tracks you down at a book signing and all you say to her is, "I cannot talk right now . . ." And then you leave. She never sees you again. You make sure of that.

"That's not how it happens! This isn't how any of this happens! It's not how it happens with Vivien. It's not how it happens with Jack . . . and that's because there is no Jack!"

Wasn't there?

"No. There wasn't."

Or is it just that you don't want to remember? I can do the remembering for both of us.

"No. You can't. There never was a Jack."

That's right. There were many Jacks, weren't there? And maybe a few Jacques?

"I don't want to talk about them . . . and there were more poems that had . . . things like . . . you know, there were more of those poems than just the one you mentioned."

Whose case are you trying to make?

"You're telling the story wrong, Alfred."

Seems fitting that you'd start attacking yourself.

"I'm not attacking myself. I'm attacking you."

But, Mr. Eliot. I am you.

"No, you're not. Alfred . . . please. I need you to leave me alone."

You can't get rid of me. I will always be a part of you.

"People don't want to read about my private sexual misery."

You're right about that, Mr. Eliot.

"It's Tom. How many times do I have to tell you that? I don't need you anymore."

It doesn't matter if you need me. I'm—

"I need to tell my own story, not the perverted one you're peddling."

Perverted? I'm not—

"I hate you and everything you make me remember . . . I don't need you and I don't want you . . . I can handle this on my own."

I don't think you can.

Mr. Eliot lies there, resolute.

But, okay, Tom . . .

Let's see what you can do.

"I can never be real, never be true—not even to myself."

—T.S. Eliot

"To her, the marriage brought no happiness.

To me, it brought the state of mind out of which came *The Waste Land*."

—T.S. Eliot

Harper Jameson Collection

(Historical Fiction)

ISBN: 978-1-64630-010-5

When a handyman discovers a mint condition Satchel Paige baseball card worth over $100,000, he is transported back to 1947 when Paige, the biggest baseball star in the Negro Leagues, is passed over for the younger Jackie Robinson to break the color line.

ISBN: 978-1-64630-008-2

During the Great Depression, a woman gets swept up by the fervor for Catholic radio priest Father Coughlin, until his pro-Fascist, anti-Jewish message becomes too much for her (and the US government) to take. Inspired by true events.

ISBN: 978-1-64630-006-8

Based on a true story: Helen Duncan, a British spiritualist, accurately describes the highly classified sinking of a Navy ship during WWII and becomes the last person found guilty of being a witch.

ISBN: 978-1-64630-014-3

When Germany invades France during WWII, a world-famous nightclub performer uses her celebrity to secretly help the French Resistance pave the way for the Normandy Invasion. A thrilling tale of espionage based on the true story of American expat Josephine Baker.

ISBN: 978-1-64630-012-9

As Germany occupies Belgium during WWI, a British nurse finds the courage to heal enemy and ally alike in the face of impossible odds—and to create an underground railroad for Allied soldiers caught behind enemy lines. Based on the life of Edith Cavell.